LION & LAMB

James Patterson is one of the best-known and biggest-selling writers of all time. Among his creations are some of the world's most popular series, including Alex Cross, the Women's Murder Club, Michael Bennett and the Private novels. He has written many other number one bestsellers including collaborations with President Bill Clinton and Dolly Parton, stand-alone thrillers and non-fiction. James has donated millions in grants to independent bookshops and has been the most borrowed adult author in UK libraries for the past fourteen years in a row. He lives in Florida with his family.

Duane Swierczynski is the two-time Edgar-nominated author of ten novels – including *Revolver* and *Canary* as well as the graphic novel *Breakneck* – many of which are in development for film or TV. Most recently, Duane co-scripted James Patterson's *The Guilty*, an Audible Original starring John Lithgow and Bryce Dallas Howard. He lives in Southern California with his family.

A list of titles by James Patterson appears
at the back of this book

JAMES PATTERSON

& DUANE SWIERCZYNSKI

LION & LAMB

PENGUIN BOOKS

PENGUIN BOOKS

UK | USA | Canada | Ireland | Australia
India | New Zealand | South Africa

Penguin Books is part of the Penguin Random House group of companies
whose addresses can be found at global.penguinrandomhouse.com

Penguin
Random House
UK

First published in the UK by Century in 2023
Published in Penguin Books 2024
001

Printed and bound in Great Britain by Clays Ltd, Elcograf S.p.A.

The authorised representative in the EEA is Penguin Random House Ireland,
Morrison Chambers, 32 Nassau Street, Dublin D02 YH68

A CIP catalogue record for this book is available from the British Library

ISBN: 978–1–529–15978–3

www.greenpenguin.co.uk

Penguin Random House is committed to a
sustainable future for our business, our readers
and our planet. This book is made from Forest
Stewardship Council® certified paper.

For Parker and Evie
— D.S.

PROLOGUE
SUNDAY, JANUARY 23

ONE

12:20 a.m.

THE NIGHT Philadelphia lost its mind, police officer Deborah Parks was patrolling the Ninth with her rookie, Rob Sheplavy.

He was a nice enough kid, maybe a little overeager. They'd been together since just after New Year's Day, when the red-and-gold holiday decorations were quickly replaced by Eagles-green banners to celebrate the team clawing its way to the NFC playoffs.

Now it was just after midnight on a freezing Sunday in late January, when Philly was at its darkest and coldest. The Birds were facing off against the Giants, and aside from a few rowdy drunks with their faces painted green, the residents of the city had apparently decided to take a collective breather before tonight's kickoff.

As they went around the Museum of Art toward Eakins Oval, Sheplavy's face lit up. "Check out that sweet Maserati."

Parks followed his sight line to the sports car, which had been detailed with a laser-blue holographic wrap. The thing literally glowed in the street, where it appeared to have paused at a stoplight at the far end of the traffic circle. Only problem: The traffic circle had no light. But still, the Maserati had come to a dead stop, nose slightly out of its lane.

"What is up with this guy?" Parks said. "Look, we're going to pull up a little closer and I'll check it out. You stay here."

"Wait—can't I come with you?"

"I need you to hang back. And don't touch the radio!"

Parks hated being rough with the new kid. But he had a tendency to go rogue, and she knew something was off about this even before she climbed out of the car.

As Parks moved closer, she could see someone slumped behind the wheel of the glowing vehicle. Was the driver passed out drunk?

No. The body language was all wrong—his head was tilted at an unnatural angle, his shoulders were completely still, and there was no sign of breathing.

Parks glanced back to make sure the rookie was where he should be. "Stay in the car, Sheplavy!"

If the rookie heard, he didn't respond.

Steeling herself, Parks moved to the driver's side, hand near her service weapon just in case this guy turned out to be (a) alive and (b) drunk and pissed. But she knew that would be the best-case scenario.

Parks called out to him, trying to wake him up. The driver didn't stir. She reached in and touched the side of his neck with two fingers. The man's skin was ice cold, and there was no pulse.

Parks had forgotten to put on gloves, and when she lifted her fingers away from the driver's neck, she was surprised to find them tacky. She looked down at her hands and realized that the city's new LED streetlights had made the body look as if it were covered in shadows.

But it was blood. *So much blood...*

TWO

Audio transcript of police officer Deborah Parks's body-cam footage

OFFICER DEBORAH PARKS: What are you doing with that radio in your hand?

OFFICER ROB SHEPLAVY: I called in the plate number. Figured I'd save us some time.

PARKS: Damn it, Shep, what'd I tell you about shutting up and staying off the radio?

SHEPLAVY: Why are you freaking out? We're supposed to call this in, right?

PARKS: I told you to wait, and that's all you needed to know. Now get out of the car and get the crime scene tape out of the trunk.

SHEPLAVY: What happened over there? Is that guy all right?

PARKS: No, he's pretty much the *opposite* of all right. Which is why I need you to go in the trunk and dig out some flares and crime scene tape.

SHEPLAVY: (*Grumbles*) Jesus...

PARKS: You got a problem, rookie?

SHEPLAVY: Whatever's in that car, I can handle it. I'm not a toddler.

PARKS: Look, I'm sorry for snapping. But you just put out the license plate of a potential murder victim's car over the radio. You know who listens to the police band? TV reporters. Not to mention people bored or twisted enough to come check out a crime scene.

SHEPLAVY: I'm sorry, I didn't—

PARKS: Everybody's excited about the first dead body until they actually see it.

SHEPLAVY: Oh, Christ. Look, I said I'm sorry . . .

PARKS: It's fine. Just remember rule number one: Do not touch *anything*. You got me?

SHEPLAVY: I know. I promise, Parks, I'm good.

(*The officers approach the Maserati. The vic is partially obscured by the wheel and the door of the Maserati. Sheplavy crouches down for a better look.*)

SHEPLAVY: You've gotta be kidding me.

PARKS: What is it?

SHEPLAVY: It couldn't be . . . I mean, tonight of all nights?

PARKS: Sheplavy, *what*? Hey, you okay? Take a deep breath. We need to secure the scene. I'm thinking this is a carjacking gone wrong, that's all.

SHEPLAVY: I can't believe . . .

PARKS: Look, we're going to see this kind of thing from time to time. Are you . . . Sheplavy, are you *crying*?

SHEPLAVY: I can't believe it's actually *him*.

PARKS: Can't believe it's who?

SHEPLAVY: Look at his face!

THREE

AS THE rookie was sobbing, a tall man in a dirty gray hoodie cut across Eakins Oval.

When he spied the two cops, he stopped in his tracks. He pulled his phone from his pocket and snapped a photo. Then he inched closer, a stunned expression on his face.

"Hey, back off!" Parks shouted. "Crime scene!"

Too late. The hoodie guy snapped another photo and ran away, thumbing something into his phone as he went.

"Hey! Stop!"

A photo of the vic was going to be online in a matter of seconds. Shit! But what was she supposed to do, chase after him and— what? Confiscate his phone? While leaving a rookie alone at his first murder scene?

It turned out that Parks had been right to worry; when the two images of the blood-covered man in the Maserati hit social media, it was over. The news traveled worldwide at breakneck speed. People enlarged the grainy photos until the victim's face was pixelated but identifiable. The reaction everywhere: utter astonishment.

Some claimed the photos were photoshopped or deep-faked. But most who saw the images believed they were real. The powder-blue Maserati alone was confirmation of the victim's identity.

Online there was collective grief and an instantaneous out-pouring of tributes. There were also macabre jokes, as always. And even though it was well after midnight, locals began to gather at the scene, arriving from Center City and Spring Garden and Fairmount and West Philly. As the crowds got bigger, more images from the crime scene spread online. Some people took awkward selfies in an attempt to place themselves in this historic moment. Some simply stared in shock. Some wept inconsolably, held by their friends.

Fortunately Parks and Sheplavy had been joined by half a dozen other officers from the Ninth, and they'd established a wide perimeter around the car, so between that and the wall of bodies, the victim's face was largely blocked from view.

Unless you were in a helicopter.

Parks had been right about local TV news always keeping an ear on police radio. An overnight staffer chained to the assignment desk at the local NBC affiliate heard the word *Maserati* and had a cop friend run the license plate on a whim—maybe some local CEO or sports figure had been involved in an embarrassing traffic accident.

But when the Maserati's owner's name popped up, the staffer knocked over his Diet Coke in his scramble to get to the assignment editor.

That station's news chopper was kept at Penn's Landing, which was thirty minutes from any location in the city. The art museum was so close, however, that the chopper was circling overhead within five minutes. A minute after it arrived, the station was interrupting the local broadcast to go live with footage from the air.

Until they had official word from the Philly police brass—that meant a captain or higher—the station couldn't confirm exactly who was in the powder-blue Maserati.

But the word was already out, and distraught fans on the street knew the truth.

Philadelphia would never be the same.

FOUR

HOMICIDE DETECTIVE Mickey Bernstein, forty-three, was the son of a Philly PD homicide legend, Arnold "Arnie" Bernstein.

Dad was famous for working the city's most violent cases and resolving them with lightning speed, usually thanks to his hunches and gut feelings. He nailed gangsters (the guys who blew up Leo "Chicken Man" Caranchi) and serial killers (coed slayer Herman "the Guru" Bludhorn). Every administration since the early 1960s loved Arnie—he got results. Nobody questioned him. Ever.

Arnie's only son operated in much the same way—except Mickey had a degree from UPenn under his belt and extensive forensic training to back up his hunches, so he got even more respect than his famous father.

What was not to love? He was a street-smart cop with an Ivy League degree who knew how to talk to TV and print journalists. *Philadelphia* magazine had run a fawning profile on him a few years back, and the cover still hung in his parents' retirement home in Margate, Florida.

If you were doing a true-crime doc about something that happened in Philly and you *didn't* check in with Mickey Bernstein, you were just not doing your job.

So when Mickey climbed out of his glossy black Audi A3,

murmurs rippled through the crowd, and TV reporters started fighting their way to him. Mickey pushed past them and made a beeline for the crime scene.

The detective was easily identifiable—six foot three with the kind of handsome, chiseled face that you see on coins. The looks, people assumed, came from his mother, a statuesque Atlantic City showgirl back in the day. (Arnie was many things, but attractive wasn't one of them.) In a city starved for celebrities, Mickey Bernstein would probably have been a star even if he weren't police royalty.

Parks saw the detective approaching and hurried over to meet him. The sooner she could put this scene in Bernstein's hands, the better.

"Well, this isn't how I imagined spending my Sunday morning," Bernstein said with a sly smile. "Are you the one who caught this?"

"Yeah, me and Sheplavy. He's my partner."

Bernstein assessed him in about two seconds. "Rookie?"

"Uh-huh."

"You made the ID?"

"My partner recognized him right away."

Bernstein raised an eyebrow. "And you didn't?"

"Not really a sports fan."

"Heresy, Officer Parks!" Bernstein exclaimed with fake outrage, clutching his chest. "How can you call yourself a Philadelphian?"

Ordinarily this kind of comment out of a detective's mouth would have rubbed Parks the wrong way. And throughout the brief conversation, most of his attention was on the scene. But something about Bernstein's delivery—that boyish smile and deadpan sarcasm—made it okay.

The detective crouched down by the corpse as if he were about to have a little chat with him. *So what happened here, buddy? Looks like somebody punched your ticket real good.* "Something's missing, Parks."

"What's that, Detective?"

"Anyone else come near this crime scene after you arrived?" Only now did Mickey Bernstein give Parks his full attention. He studied her face for tells. His eyes were ice blue and didn't miss a thing.

Parks felt guilty even though she'd done everything by the book. Damn, this guy was good. "No, Detective," she assured him. "We kept everyone away."

"How about the rookie?"

"No, he's fine."

Bernstein went back to examining the scene, a sour look on his face.

"What's missing, Detective?" said Parks. "If you don't mind me asking."

"A certain piece of jewelry."

"All due respect, how could you possibly know that?"

"Do me a favor, Parks. Can you push those crowds back a bit more? I want to take a look in relative peace and quiet."

"Of course."

"And, oh—the missing piece of jewelry? It's a Super Bowl ring."

FIVE

FOR DECADES, the City of Philadelphia had been promising its hardworking police officers two things: sparkly new headquarters and a state-of-the-art computer system.

Neither had appeared yet. Mickey Bernstein was sitting in the same building, the concrete Roundhouse on Race Street, that his father had worked in years ago. Dad had used an electric type-writer to hunt-and-peck his murder reports, but Mickey didn't have it much better. He was forced to use a nearly comatose PC with an operating system twenty years out of date.

Eh, screw the things you can't change, Mickey thought. That was one of many twisted pieces of wisdom from Dad. Mickey cracked his knuckles and got to work.

Philadelphia Police Department / Homicide Division
Case No. 22-9-3275
Investigating Detective: Michael Bernstein

2445 Captain called with a report of a Black male found dead inside sports car in front of art museum.

2450 Notified my partner, Detective T. Mason, #4977, of the murder. She was at least thirty minutes out so I headed to the scene alone. I was already in Center City, just a few minutes away.

0100 Arrived at scene. Briefed by Officer Parks, #6332, who was
   first at scene. Partner: Officer Sheplavy, #8841. Parks reported
   a man in a gray hoodie in area at the time of her arrival. Witness took photos with a phone and fled scene. Parks did not
   pursue. See statement, attached.
0130 Coroner investigator V. Waters arrived at scene. Rolled prints
   of victim identified as Archie Hughes, DOB 12/27/89. Crime
   lab tech Wolfinger completed photographs. Victim suffered
   GSW. No shell casings found at scene.
0200 Requested all surveillance video in immediate vicinity.
0241 Coroner took possession of body. Cleared scene.
0437 Made death notification to Hughes's wife, Francine Hughes,
   10▮▮▮ Country Club Drive, Radnor, PA.

Which brought Bernstein up to the present, 5:00 in the morning. This was going to be a crazy day, with zero chance of sleep in
the foreseeable future. He hit the PRINT key and prayed it worked;
Bernstein didn't want to have to wait for some guy in IT to show up
so he could begin the murder book that would define his career.

Small miracle—the pages printed without a hitch.

Bernstein saved the file and got up to find a gallon of coffee.
Then he stopped. Sat back down. Cracked his knuckles again.

Better to pave the road now and save himself some grief later.

SIX

Madam Commissioner:

The Archie Hughes case is a guaranteed clusterf███, even if every-thing goes right. However, I have some thoughts on how we might minimize the damage.

The Eagles quarterback is arguably the most talented pair of hands ever to touch the pigskin. If he's not the greatest of all time, he's a serious contender for the title. Archie Hughes's family, friends, and fans all over the world will demand swift justice. We must give it to them.

I was next up on the wheel for this case, as the captain will confirm. But I understand that this may not sit well with the rank and file, who might assume it was handed to me on a silver platter. Also, full disclosure: I am on friendly terms with Eagles ownership, though I did not know Mr. Hughes personally. Nonetheless, I know I am the best detective for this case, despite the optics.

My suggestion, Madam Commissioner, is that we create a task force. Let the city know we have all hands on deck.

Not only will we have the eyes of the entire city on us, but there will be massive national and international media attention. It's vital that we have a unified voice giving simple, direct updates on the status of the investigation. I volunteer my services for this role.

As you know, I have excellent relations with the local news outlets and have appeared on national news multiple times over the past ten years.

The truth is, this case will most likely be solved with surveillance cameras, which is how we solve ninety percent of homicides. I'll be working closely with my colleagues in the Special Investigations Unit to review the footage and we will have answers soon. As my dad liked to say, "We don't sleep until the killer is tucked neatly into bed."

Thank you in advance, Madam Commissioner. I hope we can bring this case to a rapid and satisfactory conclusion.

Yours,
Det. Michael Bernstein

SEVEN

11:50 a.m.

WINTER LANDSCAPING on Philadelphia's Main Line was mostly about preventive care. Which was why Mauricio Lopez, fifty-three, had winterized the sprinkler system way back in October and wrapped the young trees to protect them from frost. He'd also fertilized in advance of the first hard freeze. And he made sure to replenish the mulch as needed.

Mauricio insisted on using the leaves he raked up in the fall as mulch in the dead of winter, despite his employer's wife telling him not to bother, that they could afford to buy a fresh supply. Mauricio told her it was not about the money; it was about the health of the roots beneath the freezing soil. The mulch acted as an insulating blanket. Nature supplied it for free. Why not use it?

Much of that work had been done, so Mauricio had little to do aside from occasionally pruning dead branches and brushing road salt away from the front-facing bushes. Otherwise, daily maintenance of the vast grounds was simply a matter of looking around for anything out of place.

And Mauricio saw something *very* out of place late Sunday morning.

Any foreign object on the ground almost always turned out to be an errant golf ball from the nearby country club. Sometimes the children in the neighborhood left a baseball or toy. Once Mauricio even found a hobbyist's drone that had crash-landed near a birdbath. And occasionally, there were dead animals—birds, mostly. When Mauricio found them, he quickly disposed of the corpses. If the kids were around, they'd want to hold a funeral. Which was sweet, but it ate up a lot of his workday.

This morning, he noticed a foreign object that was mostly buried in a flower bed. The only reason Mauricio saw it was that the low winter sun glimmered off its surface.

A car, Mauricio thought. The older child had had an obsession with Matchbox sports cars last summer; this had to be one of them.

Mauricio knelt down, hearing his knee joints pop, and brushed away some of the frost and mulch covering the toy. But it wasn't a little sports car buried in the flower bed.

Mauricio Lopez lived his life largely unplugged. He had a landline so Mrs. Hughes could reach him as needed, but he avoided "smart" devices. He did not own a computer, TV, or radio. He enjoyed reading books about ancient history. He liked to garden.

So when Mauricio arrived for work that morning, he had not heard the news about his employer. For all Mauricio knew, Mr. Hughes was preparing for this evening's game. In fact, despite his closeness to the family, Mauricio Lopez might very well have been the only person in the tristate area who didn't know Archie Hughes had been shot and killed in front of the art museum the night before.

But still, the sight of a gun caused him to tremble violently.

MONDAY, JANUARY 24

CHAPTER 1

7:32 a.m.

AFTER EXECUTING the most perfect display of parallel parking ever seen in the city of Philadelphia, Cooper Lamb realized not a single soul had witnessed it.

Not his ex. Not his children. Not a random passerby. Not even a meter maid, who normally would be on him like a heat-seeking missile. If no one saw this private eye's incredible display of automotive prowess, did it actually happen? It was another bummer in a long string of them.

Lamb fished his phone out of his jacket pocket, hit the memo app his assistant, Victor, had loaded for him, and began to speak. He always felt better when he was talking out loud.

COOPER LAMB / VOICE MEMO #0124-735

Victor, I regret to inform you this is the end of the world.

Maybe not your world. But my world, for sure. I am currently sitting in my car trying to process it all. Trying to figure out what I'm going to tell my kids. Damn . . . what *am* I going to tell my kids?

Don't transcribe that last part, Victor. Yes, I know you're not personally transcribing these words, that the computer program you designed is doing all of this automatically. But humor me. I can't stand the idea of talking to a machine.

So let's review the facts at hand while I await the arrival of my lovely and brilliant offspring, whom I adore completely.

Fact number one: Eagles starting quarterback and national treasure Archie Hughes was shot to death last night. The entire city is in a state of shock and mourning. We woke up to a different world today, Victor.

Fact number two: The NFC championship game has been postponed for some unknown amount of time. Which means nobody will know what to do with themselves until it's rescheduled.

Fact number three: I was not in possession of tickets to the game, but maybe this is an opportunity. Victor, can you see if there are tickets available? Possibly something in a box? Maybe some fans won't be able to make it, they'll be so heartbroken over the loss of the amazing Mr. Hughes. A guy can dream, right?

Fact number four: On Saturday I placed a fairly siz-able bet—on the Eagles, of course—with my army buddy Red Doyle down in Atlantic City. I was already sick to my stomach knowing I'd have to wait twenty-four hours to see how it turned out, and, more important, if I'd be ducking my landlord for the next two months or not. Now I get to enjoy a full week of anguish and torment. Victor, next time I mention making a bet, talk me out of it.

Fact number five: Speaking of disappointed, at this very moment my kids are running out of their mother's house and...oh, it doesn't look good. Seems as if the awful news has reached my children's impressionable ears. To be continued.

CHAPTER 2

THE REAR passenger doors of Cooper Lamb's car were wrenched open and his children climbed into the back of his vehicle with the force of a small hurricane.

"Dad!" his son exclaimed. "Did you hear what happened to Archie Hughes?"

His daughter was already annoyed. "*Of course* Dad heard. But what I want to know is, who would do something like this the night before the game?"

"Are you going to find Archie's killer?"

"Are they going to cancel the Super Bowl?"

"Do you already know who killed Archie, Dad?"

Lamb clutched the steering wheel tight to avoid being sucked under and drowning in all that raw emotion.

His wonderful, amazing, and, at times, exasperating children—Ariel, ten, and Cooper Jr., eight—lived with their mother in a three-bedroom townhome in trendy Queen Village. Funny how you blink and things become "trendy." This used to be a solid immigrant neighborhood; Lamb's own ancestors had toiled at the factory that received sugarcane from the Caribbean and processed it to satisfy America's never-ending sweet tooth. For years Lamb's great-grandfather wouldn't even *look* at sugar, let alone eat dessert.

Happily, that particular family trait went to the grave with the old man. Lamb was starving, and he was sure his kids were too.

"How about a quick before-school breakfast at the Down Home Diner? I could practically inhale a stack of buckwheat pancakes right now."

"*Dad!*" Ariel cried. "Are you even listening to us?"

"Just don't let me drink from the maple syrup container again. Last time I did that, I was up all night."

"Dad!"

"I was up all night peeing. Very, *very* slowly . . ."

"Ewww!" Cooper Jr. said.

"Jesus, Dad."

Lame dad humor? Guilty as charged. But had Cooper also managed to change the conversation and stanch the flow of tears from his children's weary eyeballs? Yes, Your Honor. No further questions.

"I will explain all that I know over breakfast at Reading Terminal Market. I don't care to discuss homicide while driving through Center City. It makes me . . . twitchy. Until then, strap in and start contemplating the menu. I know you two have it memorized by now."

"Father," Ariel said solemnly. "You're trying to distract us with food, but we're serious. We want to know what's going on."

"Daughter, I hear your question, but right now your mother is approaching and she doesn't look entirely pleased."

Sure enough, Lamb's ex, the former—and possibly future?— love of his life, was approaching the passenger side. Ariel helpfully pushed the button to lower the window.

She had never been Lori Lamb; Lori Avallone thought she wouldn't be taken seriously at the museum with an alliterative name. Lamb had considered offering to take *her* name, but Cooper Avallone sounded like a country-and-western lounge singer, so that was out.

"Don't worry, I'm taking the kids to breakfast," Lamb said.

"They already ate," Lori replied. "It's almost eight, and they have to be at Friends Select in twenty minutes. For future reference, the school frowns on the kids cutting first period to eat waffles."

"We do it all the time!" Cooper Jr. said.

"When we're with Daddy, we do," Ariel confirmed.

"You were supposed to be here an hour ago," Lori said.

"I was . . . wrapping up a case."

"Does this 'case' have a name?"

"*The People versus Cooper Lamb*. Because people are *always* getting on my case."

Cooper Jr. knew he shouldn't laugh at that, but a giggle escaped his lips anyway.

"Thank you, son," his father said, turning and lifting his hand for a high five. The look on his ex's face, however, revealed exactly zero amusement. Both Cooper Sr. and Cooper Jr. put their hands down.

"I'm sorry, Lori. I'll do better." Lamb searched her eyes for a reaction but failed to find the one he'd hoped for. "I *mean* it."

Thing was, Lamb actually *did* mean it. If this was the end of the world, and it was sure looking that way, he'd better start getting his act together.

But first, pancakes thick and fluffy enough to choke a horse. Book learning could wait.

CHAPTER 3

11:02 a.m.

"JUST SIT back and relax."

"I am perfectly relaxed."

"Oh, and you can take your sunglasses off."

"I know I can. I prefer not to."

"Um, is it too early for a nice glass of wine? We have red and white."

"Red *and* white, huh. Tempting, but I don't like to drink while I'm working."

The girl in the disposable face mask and nitrile gloves smiled. Or at least, her eyes smiled. "But are you working right now?"

"I don't know. Are *you*?"

Veena Lion knew that was probably too much, but the young nail tech had lost all credibility with the wine thing. *Red or white?* Then again, maybe she was expecting too much from a random Korean nail joint on this end of Chestnut Street.

Veena liked to change things up, rarely visiting the same salon twice in a season. Mostly because she resisted the idea of having a regular place where people could easily find her. That ruined the indulgence of having her nails done in the middle of the morning.

Said indulgence lasted for another seventy-five seconds before Veena Lion's phone alerted her to an incoming call. She lifted a hand from the manicurist's table and tapped the bud in her ear twice.

A haughty voice spoke. "This is the district attorney's office. Is this Veena Lion?"

"What is this concerning?"

"You'll have to speak with the district attorney about that."

Veena sighed. "Why don't you spare me the suspense."

"As I said," the voice continued, barely containing the speaker's annoyance, "you'll have to talk to the dis—"

Veena tapped the earbud, ending the call. She exhaled slowly, letting the tension leave her body. The girl in the mask raised her eyebrows. Veena held up her index finger: *Wait for it.* Her phone buzzed again.

"Apologies, Ms. Lion—please don't hang up!"

"Who is this?"

"It's the district attorney's office! This is about Archie Hughes. Might you have a moment or two to speak with Mr. Mostel?"

"Let Mr. Mostel know that I'll stop by his office at my earliest convenience."

"Couldn't you spare a moment now?"

"Right now," Veena said, "is not convenient."

Veena ended the call. Waited. The phone did not buzz a third time. The girl in the mask raised her eyebrows again. Veena shrugged. The girl in the mask resumed her work. "You know what? I believe I will have some wine."

"Red or white?"

"Consider what you know about me, then follow your instincts."

The nail girl's mask twisted up, barely hiding the wry smile beneath. "I thought you didn't drink while you were working."

"Sometimes it's absolutely necessary. And *sometimes* happens to be right now."

While Veena waited for her beverage, she tapped her earbud three times.

CHAPTER 4

Transcript of encrypted message exchange between private investigator Veena Lion and her executive assistant, Janie Hall

VEENA LION: Looks like we're getting the Archie Hughes case from that dirtbag Mostel. I hate the creep, but how can we resist something like this?

JANIE HALL: Hang on. You sure about this, boss? Do you remember the document you signed swearing you'd never, ever work for the DA again?

LION: This is different.

HALL: You had me notarize that document.

LION: Ha, that's right. I did, didn't I?

HALL: Not only that, but you had me become a notary just so I could notarize that document. There was a course, a written exam, a background check, not to mention the fees—

LION: Thereby giving you a lucrative side hustle. You're welcome.

HALL: My point is, you were pretty sure about never working with DA Mostel again.

LION: Point taken, but this is the Archie Hughes case. There is no other case right now. This is the Beale and Adderall of murder cases.

HALL: Are you speaking your texts again? Did you mean the *be-all and end-all*?

LION: My fingers are occupied at the moment.

HALL: Ah, nice. Which color did you pick?

LION: You'll see in about twenty minutes when I'm back at the office. In the meantime—

HALL: In the meantime you would like me to compile every possible scrap of coverage and footage from the past thirty-six hours as well as the usual deep-background dossier on Mr. Hughes and all of his known business associates.

LION: And everything the police have. Did you get that last part, Janie?

HALL: Oh, I see Detective Mickey Bernstein is on the case.

LION: Easy there, lady.

HALL: Yum.

LION: Archie Hughes files first, flirt with the handsome detective later.

HALL: Yes, boss. Anything else?

LION: A triple draft latte from La Colombe, please.

HALL: Cold espresso? You know it's like two degrees outside, right?

LION: I have to swallow an ingestible recorder capsule and it goes down easier with something cold.

HALL: Is that a good idea, Veena?

LION: The latte or the hidden recording device?

HALL: Either. But especially the device.

LION: It will dissolve in a few hours, you know that. Just make sure the file has uploaded to the server and have a transcription prepared.

HALL: What I mean is, if Mostel finds out—

LION: I'm after the truth, no matter what state privacy laws say. Also, that pompous windbag won't suspect a thing.

CHAPTER 5

Transcript of conversation between Veena Lion and Philadelphia district attorney Eliott K. Mostel

ELIOTT K. MOSTEL: So, to be clear, you're prepared to swear on a Holy Bible that you don't have a tape recorder on you? Like, anywhere?

VEENA LION: Do you see a recording device anywhere, Eliott?

MOSTEL: I'm not falling for that again, Veena. You tape *everything*. I found out the hard way, if you recall. I'm thinking of the Gillespie case specifically.

LION: I recall the Gillespie case. Specifically. And I never used the tape in court.

MOSTEL: I just want to make it clear that if you *do* have such a device and this conversation is being recorded right now, it's a felony. Pennsylvania takes privacy law seriously.

LION: Do you want to send me to jail or do you have a job for me?

MOSTEL: At times I find you needlessly infuriating, Veena. Do you know that?

LION: How about we skip the flattery and get down to it.

MOSTEL: Can you at least take off the sunglasses? I'd like to see your eyes as you insult me.

LION: No.

MOSTEL: You drive me [unintelligible].

LION: That makes two of us, Mr. District Attorney. Please continue.

MOSTEL: As you know, we're going to have to eventually prosecute the son of a bitch who killed Archie Hughes. I want an airtight case, and I'd like your help.

LION: I'll do it on one condition. Just a simple question, but I want the truth.

MOSTEL: Ask away.

LION: Was I your first call or was Cooper Lamb?

MOSTEL: Veena, how long have we worked together? You know you are my first and only choice when it comes to these kinds of cases.

LION: Eliott, there's never been a case like this. And I want to know where your head is at. If Lamb turned you down and I'm merely your backup—

MOSTEL: I swear to Jesus, you were my first call.

LION: You're Jewish.

MOSTEL: Can we please focus on the murder of one of our most beloved and high-profile citizens?

LION: Fine. I'll take the assignment. I'm going to need a direct line to your office, someone on call twenty-four/seven, preferably one of your top ADAs. Real-time updates, with my executive assistant blind-copied on every piece of correspondence.

MOSTEL: Done, done, and done. And naturally you'll have access to everything the police know in real time.

LION: I'm more interested in what the police *don't* know.

MOSTEL: What a coincidence. That's what interests me the most too.

LION: Afraid I'm not following you, Eliott.

MOSTEL: (*Pause*) I'm going to be frank with you. Mickey Bernstein pushed his way onto this case and I don't like that. Frankly, I don't like him.

LION: Sounds a little personal.

MOSTEL: No, what I mean is, I don't trust him. He's dirty, just like his old man. Everything he touches is tainted. He and his family are symbols of how corrupt this city used to be. We don't live in that city anymore.

LION: So prosecute him.

MOSTEL: Yeah, *you* try getting past the big blue wall. Especially when it's led by Her Majesty the commissioner, who is too focused on her path to the mayor's office to care about the carnage on the streets.

LION: You don't think the commissioner is keeping her eye on the ball?

MOSTEL: Look, forget I said anything—and see, this is why I'm paranoid about you taping every single conversation. Let's keep this about Archie Hughes.

LION: Agreed. (*Pause*) Oh, and Janie, you can stop the transcription here.

MOSTEL: What? Who are you talking to? You said you weren't recording this!

LION: Just a little joke, Eliott. Tell me what you have.

CHAPTER 6

12:05 p.m.

ELIOTT K. MOSTEL kept an incredibly close eye on the mayor's office.

Veena knew this to be quite literal. The district attorney's office occupied several floors in a high-rise that sat catty-corner from the mammoth pile of Philadelphia City Hall. If you ran a rope from one building to the other, you could zip-line from Mostel's private office down to the mayor's reception room.

If only it were that easy. Mostel desperately wanted that job for himself and considered the police commissioner his fiercest rival.

None of this political maneuvering mattered to Veena. But whatever came out of Mostel's mouth had to be viewed through this filter.

"Archie's wallet, watch, and Super Bowl ring are missing," Mostel said. "So it's theft on top of murder."

"Not unexpected."

"Well, how about this for unexpected—they've already found the murder weapon."

Veena adjusted her sunglasses. "Where?"

"In a flower bed behind the Hughes mansion, out on the Main Line."

This was a bombshell. Veena tried hard not to show any reaction. "Ballistics are solid?"

"I have no reason to doubt the technicians or the report. But wait until you hear whose prints they found on the barrel."

"The prints of his wife, Francine Pearl Hughes."

"How did you know?"

"About a third of all homicides are perpetrated by someone close to the victim."

Mostel nodded solemnly and let the fact hang in the air for a moment. "This is completely confidential, by the way. Nobody else knows except at the highest levels. And it's going to stay that way until further notice."

"Understandable." Veena maintained her poker face, but her mind was whirling with possibilities. Either Francine Pearl Hughes—who'd been Philly's sweetheart since she was just a kid—had murdered her superstar athlete husband in cold blood or she was innocent but certain forces were determined to have the world think otherwise.

Francine Pearl Hughes was arguably more famous than her husband. She'd rocketed to fame as the lead singer of a preteen R and B trio from West Philly. Multiple Grammy Awards later, she embarked on a solo career, and each album she released broke new ground and shattered sales records. And only last year, her film debut in a wildly popular indie feature (*The Guilty*, Veena noted with no small amount of irony) resulted in an Academy Award nomination for best supporting actress.

Now imagine telling the world that this same brilliant woman had pumped a bullet into her superstar husband's chest the night before one of the biggest games of his career.

No wonder Mostel was bringing in the big guns (namely, Veena). Screw this up in public and you might as well point a gun at your own career.

"I want you to put together your own murder book," Mostel said. "Do your thing, work your magic, but keep it a completely clandestine and independent investigation."

"No matter what I find," Veena said.

"No matter what you find."

"And you'll give me everything I've asked for—I have your word on that?"

"Yes, you do. And you can record me saying that if you'd like."

"No need, Mr. District Attorney," Veena replied.

CHAPTER 7

12:07 p.m.

"YOU GUYS must be losing your minds."

"We are very concerned for our client."

"I'd be concerned too," Cooper Lamb said, easing his tall, lean body back into the lawyer's two-thousand-dollar leather sofa. "Because it's obvious she did it."

"I'm sorry...what did you just say?"

"Can you hold that thought for a sec, Lisa?"

Cooper fished inside his jacket, retrieved a small fabric pouch, and pulled out a tiny morsel of dried salmon. His associate Lupe, a year-old Rhodesian ridgeback, snapped to full attention. Cooper said, "Gentle," then held out his hand, treat nestled in his palm. The noble Lupe quickly and carefully made it disappear.

The defense attorney, Lisa Marchese, was momentarily distracted by this utterly adorable display. Then her brain patiently reminded her of the last thing Cooper had said.

"Lamb, did you say my client is guilty?"

"I said *she did it*," Cooper repeated, and he hated repeating himself. "No idea how she feels about it."

"Let me get this straight. Francine Pearl Hughes, the bereaved wife—you honestly believe she killed her husband?"

Cooper looked around the spacious office for an imaginary judge. "Your Honor, Counsel is badgering her guest."

"For Christ's sake, Lamb. How can you possibly say such a thing about Francine?"

Cooper rubbed Lupe's head and murmured something about not paying attention to the mean lawyer lady and her profanities.

Both private investigator and pooch were sitting in the posh 1818 Market Street offices of Kaplan, DePaulo, and Marchese LLP, the city's top criminal-defense firm. Senior partner Lisa Marchese had asked to meet with Cooper at nine a.m., but he told her he had other plans. (He did; morning walks with Lupe were sacred.) He ignored calls from the DA's office—Cooper hated that guy—and finally agreed to a noon meeting with Marchese. "I'm bringing my associate," Cooper had warned her, not letting her know that the associate happened to be canine. But everybody loved Lupe. He instantly improved the vibe of any room.

"I'll tell you exactly how," Cooper told Lisa. He gave Lupe another dried salmon treat for being a good boy, then continued. "You just told me that her prints were found on the murder weapon, which ballistics has definitively matched to Archie's murder. The weapon was hastily buried in a frozen flower bed on the Hughes estate. My guess is, sooner or later there will be surveillance footage connecting her to the crime. There are dozens of cameras on the parkway; I'm sure there will be multiple angles of your client pumping a few slugs into her husband's heavily muscled torso, then hurrying away from the scene of the crime."

Lisa Marchese stared at him in horror. "You don't really believe that, do you?"

"No, but I'll bet you're terrified that a jury might believe it. That or whatever compelling version the DA's office is putting together as we speak."

Marchese exhaled. "You scared me there for a moment. I was

afraid the legendary Cooper Lamb, ex–army intelligence and the best PI in the city, had lost his mind."

"Flatterer."

"We'd like you to clear Francine's name. And, if possible, find out who really killed Archie."

"Of course."

"The police will have their own ideas, but we want the truth."

"Who doesn't?"

"So, can we count on you to join the team?"

"Hell no."

CHAPTER 8

Transcript of private conversation between Cooper Lamb and Lisa Marchese, senior partner at Kaplan, DePaulo, and Marchese, captured using an ambient recording app on Lamb's smartwatch

LISA MARCHESE: You're seriously going to walk away from the biggest murder case in Philadelphia history?

COOPER LAMB: Why don't you try Veena Lion? She's the best. Well, second best, if I may be so immodest.

MARCHESE: Maybe we already called Veena.

LAMB: Nah, she'd never work for you guys. She hates big law firms even more than she hates authority figures.

MARCHESE: You've had no problem cashing our checks in the past.

LAMB: And in the past, the checks have been generous. But when it comes to ... what did you say? "The biggest murder case in Philadelphia history"?

MARCHESE: Ah. I see. You're negotiating.

LAMB: Of course I am. I wouldn't want you to lowball me simply because I'd kill for this job. I loved Archie and I pretty much bleed Eagles green. I bet on them every week, even during their not-so-stellar seasons. And I've had a massive crush on

Francine Pearl ever since that music video where she's wearing that…ah, never mind. But yeah. I'm all in. Wait, what are you writing there?

MARCHESE: How's this for a retainer?

LAMB: That is…impressive. Lupe, my faithful friend, I think that will keep you in dried salmon treats for months to come.

MARCHESE: So we have an agreement?

LAMB: Just one thing. Two things, actually.

MARCHESE: Go on.

LAMB: I'll need full access to the team. And the owners.

MARCHESE: You don't honestly believe one of Archie's own teammates murdered him, do you? Or the Sables?

LAMB: Maybe I'm a huge fan *and* milking this situation for all it's worth.

MARCHESE: I'm sorry, what?

LAMB: Maybe I promised my kids some autographs.

MARCHESE: But—

LAMB: Or maybe I'm really good at my job, and you should trust my instincts.

MARCHESE: (*Sighs*) Fine. What's the other thing?

LAMB: If you hire me, I'm not going to stop until I find the truth.

MARCHESE: That's what we want.

LAMB: Even if the truth is very bad for your client?

MARCHESE: (*Slight hesitation*) That's what we want, Lamb.

LAMB: You've got yourself a private eye, Marchese.

CHAPTER 9

1:12 p.m.

COOPER LAMB fork-and-knifed his way into a hot pork sandwich at the DiNic's counter at Reading Terminal. Sitting one stool away was Victor Suarez, his unflappable assistant, nursing a mug of black coffee.

"So what do you want?" Victor asked.

Cooper shook his head, then pointed a forkful of broccoli rabe and pork at his assistant. "No, my friend. Question is, what do *you* want?"

Victor sighed. Or perhaps it was just him exhaling—the differences were subtle, and even a trained ear like Cooper's had a difficult time telling them apart.

"I mean," Cooper continued, "you can't just sit at this counter and torture yourself with that sad, lukewarm cup of alleged coffee. The roast pork here is the best in the world."

"I assume you've got a list for me, boss?" Victor asked.

"Of course I have a list." And with that, Cooper began to reel off the items. He was confident Victor could find him the information he wanted because Victor Suarez could find out *anything*. Seriously. No matter the organization—the local police, the Feds, freakin' Facebook—Victor knew how to slip through the digital back door. He'd take a discreet look at the most highly protected files and go—no one ever knew he had been there, and it wasn't as if Victor himself went around bragging about it. Sometimes Cooper wondered if his longtime inside guy had seen so much brain-melting top secret intel that he no longer reacted to any news, no matter how shocking.

"I need everything on Archie Hughes—"

"Already compiled and on this flash drive." Victor slid a slender metal fob across the counter toward his boss.

"No so fast. I'm also gonna need everything Mickey Bernstein has."

"On this same flash drive."

"Yeah? Well, how about everything Mickey Bernstein is think-ing now and will be thinking soon, including what he'll order for breakfast tomorrow? And while you're busy hacking into the detective's brain, also get me a full background on the lovely Mrs. Hughes—one Francine, née Pearl."

"It's on the same—"

"Flash drive, got it." Cooper slid the flash drive off the counter with his finger, palmed it, and made it disappear with a flourish. If Victor was impressed by this semiprofessional demonstration of close-up sleight of hand, he didn't let on.

Hiring someone with the hacking prowess of Victor Suarez might have given other investigators pause. But the way Cooper saw it, Victor must have dug deeply into Cooper's past, and since he'd still agreed to work with him, Cooper couldn't be in better hands.

"That it?"

"No," Cooper said. "Have some pork, put it on the company tab."

"I'm good."

"Yes, you are. But this isn't a cold case. Things are going to evolve very rapidly."

"As things happen, I'll have them for you."

"You sound pretty sure of yourself there, Victor."

"That's because I *am* sure of myself."

Cooper tried to see beyond his assistant's stony expression, catch a glimpse of the man's inner life. But such a thing was impossible. Cooper shrugged. "All right, go do your nerd thing. I have two very important phone calls to make, and the sound of your furious illegal hacking distracts me."

"Whatever, man."

CHAPTER 10

Transcript of Cooper Lamb's phone call to Red's Bar and Grill, Atlantic City

COOPER LAMB: Lemme talk to Red.

BARTENDER: Red's busy.

LAMB: Yeah, yeah, he's not too busy for me. Put the old buzzard on.

BARTENDER: Telling you, he's not here.

LAMB: Which is it, he's busy or he's not there? Tell him it's Cooper Lamb.

BARTENDER: Who am I going to tell? The thin air? It's the middle of the day, there isn't nobody in this place, it's freakin' dead.

LAMB: That's *Cooper Lamb*. Go on. Say my name out loud.

BARTENDER: What kinda name is that?

LAMB: Just say it.

BARTENDER: I ain't sayin' nothing.

LAMB: Sayyy it...

BARTENDER: You're a goddamn pain in the ass, you know that, Lamb? Here you go.

RED DOYLE: Hey, kid, what's up?

LAMB: Nice employee you got there.

DOYLE: Trained him well, didn't I? He's better than a German shepherd in the front yard.

LAMB: I'll bring Lupe in sometime to meet him. They can talk dog to dog.

DOYLE: Okay, enough chitchat. You're calling about Archie Hughes, right?

LAMB: You sit at the dark nexus of the criminal underworld, Red. Tell me what you know.

DOYLE: Next of what? I don't know anything. Not this time, Lamb.

LAMB: Red, don't do me like that.

DOYLE: No, I'm serious. I'm not playing around here. You know how many people are calling me about their bets? This is costing me boo-coo bucks.

LAMB: Speaking of . . .

DOYLE: Oh no, don't you freaking start with me too!

LAMB: It's just that, without Archie on the team, I'm not feeling as bullish about the Birds, if you know what I mean.

DOYLE: If I hear anything about the murder, I'll let you know. But in the meantime, your bet stays the same, capisce?

LAMB: You are an international man of mystery, Red. I'm counting on you.

DOYLE: Yeah, yeah, I'll keep my ear to the ground.

LAMB: Right next to your mind in the gutter.

CHAPTER 11

Transcript of phone call placed by Cooper Lamb to a private number

COOPER LAMB: This is the Federal Bureau of Homework Management. May I speak to Ariel Lamb, please?

ARIEL LAMB: *Dad,* I know it's you.

LAMB: I'm sorry, I think you have mistaken me for some other odious authority figure. I am calling to let you know that . . . well, hold on a moment. Can you put your brother on the line as well? I do not care to repeat myself.

ARIEL: This isn't 1995, Dad. There are no other *lines*.

LAMB: This is super-serious and of deadly importance, Ms. Lamb. And your brother needs to hear this as well.

ARIEL: Don't you have work to do or something?

LAMB: That's exactly why you need to put your brother on the phone. He's going to lose his tiny little mind.

ARIEL: (*Shouting*) Coop! Dad's on the phone! (*Pause*) He said he's coming.

LAMB: How's Mom doing, by the way?

ARIEL: I'm not a double agent. Instead of this sneaky way of checking on Mom, why don't you just ask her?

LAMB: I am *not* being sneaky.

ARIEL: Are *too*.

LAMB: Am *not* to infinity!

ARIEL: (*Sighs*) Coop's here.

LAMB: Goody. Can you both hear me? Am I on speaker? Excellent. Tomorrow I am headed into the mouth of madness that is the locker room of the Philadelphia Eagles. Yes, your father, the man who provided quite a bit of your DNA, will be interviewing the possible NFC champions tomorrow. I'd like you to give me your autograph requests in order of preference..

COOPER LAMB JR.: Cool!

ARIEL: Isn't that highly unethical? To use your privileged access for personal gain?

COOPER JR.: Will you shut up, Airy?

LAMB: No, Coop, my boy, your sister makes an excellent point. And you know what? I'm scared straight. See this leaf? It's turning over. Thanks for setting me straight, daughter.

ARIEL: Uh-huh.

LAMB: (*Whispering*) Coop, text me who you want. Don't tell the killjoy.

CHAPTER 12

FOR IMMEDIATE RELEASE
MONDAY, JANUARY 24
STATEMENT FROM COMMISSIONER MAHONEY
REGARDING THE INVESTIGATION INTO THE DEATH OF
ARCHIE HUGHES

As the city of Philadelphia—and, indeed, the world—continues to mourn the loss of "Greatest of All Time" Eagles quarterback and beloved father and husband Archibald "Archie" Hughes, I want to assure my fellow citizens that justice will be sure and swift.

We have created a special task force composed of dozens of highly trained detectives, forensic analysts, and scientists.

Detective Michael Bernstein is leading the task force investigating this brutal crime, and he assures me they have made tremendous progress in the past thirty-six hours. There are already several persons of interest.

Our hearts and prayers are with Archie's friends and family, especially Francine Pearl Hughes and their wonderful children, Maddie and Archie Jr., in this extremely difficult time. I urge the citizens of this city to treat the family with the greatest respect and understanding and refrain from any ugly public displays. Such behavior will not be tolerated.

If you have any information regarding the case, you may contact the department safely and anonymously on our tip line.

CHAPTER 13

"HENDRICK'S MARTINI, up, with Noilly Prat vermouth, just a splash, and three blue-cheese-stuffed olives."

Veena Lion gave her order without looking up from the menu. The bar was dim, but her eyes remained hidden behind her sunglasses.

"And I'll have the Citywide Special," Cooper Lamb said. "Thanks, sweetie."

Veena raised an eyebrow. "You know we're not at Dirty Frank's, right?"

"The Citywide Special, as the name implies, is honored all over the city," Cooper said. He looked up at the server. "Is this not true?"

The server smiled shyly. "I'll see what I can do." Cooper watched her leave, then turned to see that Veena had been watching him watching the server leave. "What?"

Veena shrugged. "She's going to bring you the Rittenhouse Hotel version of the Citywide, you know."

"A thimble's worth of WhistlePig and a jewel-encrusted goblet of Duvel?"

"My point is, it's going to be more than five bucks."

"Good thing you're picking up the tab."

"Oh, am I?"

"Of course you are—you've got that big DA paycheck coming."

Only now did Veena remove her sunglasses. She placed them on the table between them. Cooper knew her secret. She didn't wear shades to be mysterious. It was the intensity of her jade-green eyes. When Veena Lion looked at you, you felt as if she were gazing into the secret chambers of your soul. This made most people supremely uncomfortable.

But it worked the other way around too. Veena's eyes often betrayed what she was really thinking. "You're working for Francine Hughes," she said, pure delight in her eyes.

"Technically, her *lawyers* hired me."

"No need to get technical with me, Cooper."

"Oh, I know. I just didn't want you getting all jealous, imagining a scene that never happened."

"You mean the scene where the hot grieving superstar heaves her bosom in your direction and plies you with alcohol until you swear to her that you'll find her husband's killer?"

"Eh, something like that."

"Speaking of…"

Their drinks arrived. Veena coldly noted the presence of *four* blue-cheese-stuffed olives. While she no doubt preferred overkill to the alternative, Veena liked her directions to be followed to the letter. The server was trying too hard, and the slight hint of disapproval in Veena's eyes made Cooper smile.

"And for you, handsome, a Citywide Special," the server told Cooper as she set an oversize tumbler and a pint glass in front of him.

"Which here at the Rittenhouse is defined as…"

"If you can guess what's in that glass," the server said, "the drink's on me."

"You know," Veena said, "it's not technically a double entendre if your meaning is painfully obvious."

"I'm sorry? I—"

Cooper interrupted. "Challenge accepted! But if I get it right, I'm still paying five bucks. Otherwise, it's just not a Citywide Special."

"You've got a deal."

Veena rolled her eyes.

Cooper sipped at the shot like a hummingbird sampling the nectar of a daylily, paused to consider, then unceremoniously knocked the rest of the shot back.

"The fluid in that glass," Cooper said, "was definitely alcohol."

The server laughed, maybe a little too much, and left Cooper and Veena to their libations. Cooper raised his pint glass and turned to Veena. "Shall we toast?"

"To what?"

"To working another case together."

"We're not working this case together," Veena said. "In fact, we're working for opposing sides. You remember, don't you? Prosecution on one side, defense on the other?"

"Ah, but we're still on the same side."

"And what side is that?"

"The side of truth, no matter what."

CHAPTER 14

10:01 p.m.

"TRUTH IS, this case is a flaming garbage fire," Veena said, then downed half the martini. It was cold and bracing and exactly what she needed.

"Please," Cooper said. "Not with us working together as a team."

"Cooper, the only thing worse than being on a team *with* you is being on a team opposite you. Which is why I wanted to meet."

"And here I thought you just wanted to tie one on. Speaking of..." Cooper looked around for their server, who had departed only a few moments ago.

"We're friends and all, but I want to establish some ground rules," Veena said.

"Perfect. This calls for a drink."

"Rules first, drinks after."

"Okay, fine," Cooper said with a slight pout in his voice.

"We share everything. I mean every last shred of intelligence."

"Done."

Veena blinked. "Really? That was too easy."

"Not at all. It's the smart move. I mean, my man Victor can grab anything he likes from your files—"

"Just like my number two, Janie, can from yours."

"See? So we're saving valuable snooping time. Anything else?"

"Yes. We need to agree that we won't trust anything that comes from Mickey Bernstein."

"Done," Cooper said. "I hate that tall handsome prick. He's nothing but a haircut, a Penn degree, and a last name. What else?"

"No bullshit, now—who do you think killed Archie Hughes?"

"My gut take right now, based on the available facts?" Cooper asked. "Some of which came from Bernstein's initial report?"

Veena made a sweeping *The floor is yours* gesture with her freshly manicured hands.

Cooper nodded. "It was a random carjacker. He saw the fancy Maserati, not the guy behind the wheel. Once he realized who he'd killed, he took the Super Bowl ring to pawn it for some getaway money, but then figured out it would be like tattooing *Guilty* on his forehead."

"Interesting theory. So this random carjacker is also a master criminal who can evade dozens of surveillance cameras in the area and knows how to elude the cops in a citywide manhunt?"

"Eh, beginner's luck," Cooper said. "This is probably the guy's first time, which is why Mickey B. and his goons are having so much trouble finding him. And until they do, the entire city will continue to lose its collective mind. So that's my take. Who do you like for this?"

"Oh, the wife killed him," Veena said. "Absolutely."

"Really."

"No doubt about it."

Cooper made a *Give it to me* motion with four fingers.

"Let's put aside for the moment *why* Francine Pearl Hughes definitely murdered her husband," Veena said. "Instead, let's discuss why they'll never arrest her."

"I don't know. Could it be because . . . she absolutely didn't do it?"

"No. It's because this city loved her long before any of us had even heard of Archie Hughes."

"True. Francine is Philadelphia's sweetheart. What was that cringey soul trio she used to front?"

"You're pretending like you don't remember the Puritones, but I know you do."

Cooper smiled like a boy caught in a fib. He was completely unaware that their server was approaching as he broke into a horribly off-key rendition of the Puritones' hit "Cross My Broken Heart." Veena considered Cooper a highly talented investigator who had many skills across a variety of disciplines. Singing wasn't one of them.

"*I'll swear it to the ennnnnnd,*" Cooper crooned, "*cross my broken heaaaaaaarrt!*"

"So glad Lupe isn't here to see this," Veena said.

"Can I, uh, get you anything else?" the server asked.

"Only my dignity," Cooper said, his cheeks slightly red. "As well as another round."

"Not for me," Veena said. She downed the second half of her martini.

"Come on, one more," Cooper pleaded. "Cross my broken heart?"

"Nope." Veena left cash, including an incredibly generous tip for the server. "By the way," Veena told her, "don't go home with him. He's a gifted orator and can probably talk you into it, but do yourself a favor and pass."

"I'm mortally wounded," Cooper said, clutching his chest.

"What business is it of yours?" the server asked. "Are you his ex or something?"

"Maybe someday," Veena said.

TUESDAY, JANUARY 25

CHAPTER 15

THE WINTER gust skimming across the surface of the icy Delaware River was cold enough to cut through cloth, skin, and bone. Cooper Lamb and Lupe were standing at Penn's Landing looking across the river toward Camden, New Jersey.

They'd been partners for almost a year now. Lupe—Cooper Jr. called him "Loopy"—had entered Cooper's life just one week after his wife had left it. Friends joked that poor Lupe would soon grow tired of Cooper's bullshit and file for emancipation. Cooper didn't doubt it. Sooner or later, everyone had enough of him.

Cooper didn't have to turn around to know that Victor Suarez was approaching. He could hear Lupe's happy little yelps. The dog adored Victor.

"Damn, it's cold—who decided to meet out here?" Cooper demanded, shivering.

"That would be you, boss. To make it easy for you to head down I-95 straight to the Linc, remember?"

"Poor Lupe here peed icicles a few minutes ago."

"So here's what I've got. This won't be announced officially for another hour, but the Eagles-Giants game has been rescheduled for this Sunday."

"They're not going to try to push back the Super Bowl?"

"Turns out, you can't move a thing like the Super Bowl."

"Only a week between games. That's rough."

"Just keep it in mind as you talk to everybody this morning. The tensions are running a little high at the Linc, from what I hear."

"What else you been hearing?"

"I picked up some interesting details from the players' chatter on their various private social media accounts."

"Private accounts?"

"Separate from their public accounts, which are run by their management teams. This is what they use to hit on women and generally act stupid. Anyway, if the chatter is to be believed, you're going to have a long suspect list. Not many people on the team—or on the staff, for that matter—liked Archie Hughes very much."

"Reallllly."

"Quite a few players seriously *hated* the guy, as a matter of fact."

"Professional jealousy or something else?"

"Yeah, there was a bit of *something else*. Some of them are convinced that Archie was cheating on Francine."

"How could any mere mortal step out on a woman like Francine Pearl?"

"Don't know yet. But from reading their messages, I got the idea that some of the players would be more than happy to comfort Francine in her time of need."

"Those dirty dogs," Cooper muttered. "Sorry, Lupe. It's just an expression. Anyway, good work, Victor. Do you have a list of the players who seemed the most hostile or angry?"

"Texted it to you a few minutes ago."

"How about the ones who have taken a fancy to the Widow Hughes?"

"That would be the entire team," Victor said. "But I also texted you a list of the players who were especially vocal about it."

"Among themselves." Cooper pondered this for a moment.

"Think two of them teamed up to take out their quarterback and move in on his hot wife?"

"You don't pay me to make those kinds of guesses."

"I don't, but I'm asking you anyway. You're the one listening to this chatter."

"Pretty sure two people plotting to kill a coworker wouldn't do it on social media. Not even in direct messages. These guys sounded like they were just venting to each other, maybe even joking around a little. Or just being horndogs."

"Thanks, Victor. Lupe here speaks their language. I'll see if he can get one of them to confess."

"One more thing, boss. I'm coming along for the ride."

CHAPTER 16

Transcript of phone call placed by Cooper Lamb to a private number

COOPER LAMB: Good news, not-yet-fully-grown humans. I've
decided to ignore professional ethics and totally hook you up
with some Eagles autographs. Don't worry, I'll get those first,
because I've got some tough questions to ask, and I'm probably
going to have to be put in traction when I leave this stadium. If
you don't know what *traction* means, look it up. Preferably
using Google Images, because it will freak you out.

ARIEL LAMB: Sir, this is a Wendy's.

LAMB: Nice one, daughter! Now quit blabbering so I can get to
work.

ARIEL: Do you have Lupe with you?

LAMB: Please. Would I *ever* leave home without my secret
weapon?

Excerpt from Cooper Lamb's interview with Eagles receiver Lee McCoy

LEE McCOY: Cute dog, man. They just let you bring him back
here? What the heck is he, anyway?

COOPER LAMB: Lupe here is a Rhodesian ridgeback. But never mind him for the moment. I'm here to talk about Archie.

McCOY: My brother!

LAMB: So you two were close?

McCOY: Dude. C'mon. Are you serious? Were we *close*? How can you ask me that? I would die for that man.

LAMB: Looks like he beat you to it.

McCOY: I'm sorry?

LAMB: Nothing. Did Archie ever talk about threats against him or his family? You know, overeager fans stalking him, anything like that?

McCOY: We get that all the time. I mean, when you're a public figure, it comes with the job. I don't expect you to understand, but it's a real pain in the ass.

LAMB: I'm sure. Have *you* received threats?

McCOY: Well...no. I don't think anybody is crazy enough to come at me, you know what I mean?

LAMB: Yeah, I know what you mean.

McCOY: Can I, uh, give your dog a treat?

LAMB: Depends. Can I have an autograph for my kid?

[Cooper Lamb's handwritten annotation: *McCoy—a lot of bluster, but not much to back it up. All bark, no bite.*]

Excerpt from Cooper Lamb's interview with Eagles center Bobby Devaux

COOPER LAMB: You played center at Notre Dame, right? I was a huge fan.

BOBBY DEVAUX: Wait up. Who do you work for again?

LAMB: I'm just doing a little routine background work for Francine's lawyers.

DEVAUX: Yeah, you can drop all that *routine* stuff with me. Not a damn thing routine about this case and you know it. This city is losing its damn mind.

LAMB: Then help me out here. Who should I be talking to? Did Archie have any stalkers, any enemies? What are the police missing?

DEVAUX: I'd be curious to hear what you've found so far. You're working for Frannie's lawyers, so I guess you want to take some of the attention away from her.

LAMB: You think she deserves the attention?

DEVAUX: Of course not. I love Frannie. I just don't know what you want from me.

LAMB: Look, I'm just starting out here, and I was hoping you could help.

DEVAUX: Don't detectives always try to figure out who'd benefit the most from someone's death? Also, people might take you more seriously if you didn't bring your [expletive] dog.

LAMB: I suppose an autograph is out of the question.

[Cooper Lamb's handwritten annotation: *Devaux—guarded. Probably a cat lover. Also kind of a dick.*]

Excerpt from Cooper Lamb's interview with backup quarterback Terry Mortelite

COOPER LAMB: I'll bet you wish this was all happening under different circumstances.

TERRY MORTELITE: Well, sure, but don't worry. We're gonna win this thing for Archie!

LAMB: I mean, you must have dreamed about this day—being the starting quarterback! That has to be a career high, right?

MORTELITE: Look, I'm just gonna give everything I have for Archie and Frannie.

LAMB: Were you two close?

MORTELITE: No, but I'd like to be. I mean, especially now. She must be lonely. I haven't reached out to her yet, but it's a weird time and—

LAMB: I meant you and Archie, but sure, let's keep going down this road. If Francine were here right now, what would you tell her?

MORTELITE: I just want to make her proud. If you talk to her, will you tell her that for me?

[Cooper Lamb's handwritten annotation: *Mortelite—had the most to gain, clearly has the hots for Francine. Too obvious.*]

Excerpt from Cooper Lamb's interview with tight end Jimmy Tua

COOPER LAMB: I'm really sorry for your loss. Everybody is telling me how close you were to Archie. To the entire Hughes family, for that matter.

JIMMY TUA: Yeah, thanks. I still can't believe it's real. Feel like I'm walking around in a dream these days. The world's worst dream.

LAMB: Since you were all so tight, I wanted to talk to you about the gossip flying around about Francine.

TUA: (*Angry*) What gossip?

LAMB: Everyone always points a finger at the spouse.

TUA: Someone points a finger at that beautiful woman and I'll snap it off and make 'im *eat it*, you feel me?

LAMB: Easy, my friend. I'm on her side!

[Cooper Lamb's handwritten annotation: *Tua—big guy. Built like a side of beef. AVOID BEING PUNCHED BY THIS MAN. Unlike the other players, Tua seems truly close with the Hughes family. Especially Francine.*]

CHAPTER 17

1:14 p.m.

"HOW'D IT go with the team?"

"It was just like a football game," Cooper said. "Lots of waiting, and I feel like I've taken a series of blows to the head. Did you get what you need from the front office?"

Victor was scrubbing his hands with a disinfectant wipe. His motions were thorough and meticulous, as if he were prepping for surgery. Cooper's assistant was borderline OCD when it came to leaving zero physical traces behind.

"Yeah, I had plenty of time before the Sables came back. Speaking of—that's them over there."

Across the broad green field, a lean, tall man was huddled with two obese men who looked like unmade beds. The latter were Harold and Glenn Sable, the father-and-son owners of the Philadelphia Eagles. They carried themselves like a pair of feudal lords watching over their knights, vassals, and peasants as they made furious preparations for war.

The tall man approached. Cooper knew him by sight, the handsome bastard. Enter homicide royalty, Detective Mickey Bernstein.

"The Sables seem awful chummy with the homicide dick," Cooper said to Victor.

"What do you mean?"

"Look at them all," Cooper said with disgust. "Laughing and backslapping. Does Detective Mickey look like a man hell-bent on finding the killer of the greatest quarterback ever?"

"I don't know, Cooper. You're the one who's good at reading people. All I know is, whatever their deal, we'll know a lot more by the end of the day."

Cooper turned to face Victor and clutched at nonexistent pearls in mock horror. "My God, Victor! Please tell me you didn't do something...*illegal*?"

"I've got their offices and reception areas fully wired for sound. Oh, I wired up their matching convertible Rolls-Royce Dawns, too. Even if these guys had someone doing routine security sweeps— and by the way, I checked their financial records, and they don't—"

"Nobody will be able to spot your bugs," Cooper finished. "Excellent work, as always."

Victor shrugged, which was about as close as the man came to accepting a compliment.

"Now, let's see if I can rattle these big boys a little," Cooper said. "I'll let you know."

CHAPTER 18

Transcript of Cooper Lamb's interview with longtime Philadelphia Eagles owners Harold Sable (age seventy-one) and Glenn Sable (age forty-eight)

COOPER LAMB: First of all, let me tell you both how sorry I am for your loss.

GLENN SABLE: (*Muttering under breath*) *Loss*—yeah, that's the word for it.

HAROLD SABLE: (*Annoyed*) Glenn...

GLENN: What?

HAROLD: How can we help, Mr. Lamb?

LAMB: You two knew Archie better than almost anybody. Can you tell me if anything seemed, you know, *off* in the weeks leading up to the playoffs?

HAROLD: See, here's the thing. It's interesting you're asking *us* this question. Your client could tell you a lot more than we ever could.

LAMB: My client?

HAROLD: You're working for Kaplan, DePaulo, which means you're working for Francine. I mean, why else would you be here?

LAMB: Look, I want the same thing you guys do—to find Archie's killer. Which is why I'm asking you, again, if anything seemed strange in the past week or so. Maybe somebody you didn't recognize hanging around? Any of the players have a beef with him?

HAROLD: You gotta be crazy if you think one of my boys did something like this to a fellow player!

LAMB: Of course not. But sometimes tempers flare, somebody speaks out of turn, and the next thing you know…

GLENN: You're not going to find anything like that in this franchise. It's been one hundred percent hustle. I mean, it's the freakin' Super Bowl on the line! Going all the way would mean everything to us.

HAROLD: And the city of Philadelphia. You have to admit, Mr. Lamb, this city could desperately use a win. On so many levels.

GLENN: And every single member of this franchise is focused like a laser on that goal. There's no time for beefs or rivalries or whatever the hell you said. Who you should be looking at is the family.

LAMB: I'm pretty sure his children didn't leave him for dead in front of the art museum.

HAROLD: (*Shocked*) Mr. Lamb, my son didn't mean—

GLENN: Pop, don't do that. I'm perfectly capable of saying what I mean. But seriously, I don't know why you're wasting your time here when you should be grilling the nanny.

LAMB: The nanny… (*Checks notes*) You're talking about Maya Rain?

GLENN: Just giving you a friendly heads-up. You should seriously talk to her. If there's trouble in that household, look no further. She's pretty hot. For a hillbilly from West Virginia.

LAMB: Trucker's tan, blond from a bottle, couple of missing teeth… does that kind of thing float your boat, Glenn?

GLENN: What did you just say to me?

HAROLD: Glenn, I'm sure Mr. Lamb is just teasing.

LAMB: No, Mr. Lamb is just trying to do his job. Francine Hughes deserves better than cheap cracks and innuendo.

HAROLD: We have nothing but love and compassion for Mrs. Hughes. She is truly a legend. But so was her husband, and he meant the world to us. I'm talking personally—I'll forever be in his debt. So please do us a favor and find out who did this. No idea what kind of retainer you've got from Kaplan, DePaulo, but I promise you, the Philadelphia Eagles will handsomely reward you.

LAMB: I'm not in this for the money.

GLENN: Not in it for the money? What kind of bull▮▮▮ is that?

CHAPTER 19

COOPER LAMB drove north on I-95 toward Center City with Victor slumped comfortably in the passenger seat, right knee propped up on the dash.

As a rule, Victor refused to drive. When he was barely a teen, Victor had hacked his way into an insurance company's servers, read a bunch of mortality tables, and vowed never to sit behind the wheel of a motor vehicle. When told that he was taking the same risk by being a passenger, Victor merely shrugged and said that it was up to God.

This would seem like a complication, but Victor was very skilled at using public transportation—without paying—to reach every corner of the city. Victor almost always beat Lamb to any given destination.

"I presume you were listening to my chat with the Sables. Did I rattle them?"

Victor shrugged. "The hillbilly crack was kind of cheap."

"I was dealing with vulgar men."

Again, Victor shrugged. It was his favorite form of personal communication, which drove Cooper a little nuts. He liked to joke that if Victor ever wrote a tell-all memoir, it would be about three pages long.

"Anyway, you promised me a surprise," Cooper said.

Victor reached between them and handed his boss a thick black binder bursting with pages. "Here's my report."

Cooper grabbed it, weighed its heft. "How did you find time to do all of this?"

"The business office has a good laser printer. And, yeah, I might have raided their supply closet a little."

"Nobody questioned you?"

"I'm a Latino dude in khakis and an off-white polo shirt futzing around with office equipment. No one batted an eye."

"God bless the bigots." Cooper placed the binder in his lap and used his right hand to awkwardly thumb through. It contained a dizzying array of invoices, e-mails, and tax documents.

"Keep your eyes on the road," Victor warned.

"It's going to take me all day to read this."

"The first five pages are a summary."

Cooper thumbed backward. "So they are."

"But let me just tell you what's in there. Basically, the team is a mess from the top down."

"Tell me about the top."

"Business operations are a joke. There's, like, no oversight. The Sables are tax evaders, gamblers, extortionists, and con artists. They try to screw anything that moves, and I mean that literally. It's amazing the business side of this team hasn't already imploded."

"Yeah, they don't seem to be guys who bother with the little things," Cooper said. "Business ethics, sound accounting practices, personal hygiene..."

"Boss, you don't know the half of it. You'll find the rest in the report."

"What about the players?"

"There are summaries of dozens of quashed lawsuits and NDAs in the files. But to sum it up: These guys are spoiled brats. Most of them, anyway. Nobody's telling them no, and when they get into trouble, the team's lawyers keep everything quiet. They employ *very good* lawyers. And lots of them."

Lamb continued to flip through the binder until he reached a short transcript at the very end. "What's this part?"

"I'd seriously appreciate it if you focused on the wheel, boss."

"This looks like a transcript of—"

"Your interview with the Sables, yeah."

"Transcribed in real time and printed a minute later? You're incredible, Victor."

"If I'm so incredible, maybe keep your eyes on the road so I don't die."

"For you, my friend, anything."

CHAPTER 20

12:23 p.m.

VEENA LION was sitting on a Paoli/Thorndale train headed to Ardmore holding a legal pad on which she wrote names, drew arrows, crossed names off, and added them again, ranking all the people who had a reason to kill Archie Hughes.

A dull gong from her phone interrupted her brainstorming. The gong meant a text from Janie, but when Veena flicked open the message, there was no text, only a camera icon. *Okay, it's story time.* Veena tapped the image and listened over her earbuds.

On-screen was Janie, who had positioned her own smartphone to capture her desk with the computer's display cocked at a precise angle to avoid glare or distortion. Always thoughtful, that Janie. "Apologies for all of the . . . awkward," Janie said, waving her hands around as if to illustrate *the awkward*. "I received a small tsunami of files and footage from the DA's office. I was going to cc you on all of it, but since it required a bit of explanation, I thought it would be easier to walk you through it. I mean, I can show you the whole thing when you get back to the office, but . . . okay, I'll stop talking and just show you."

Veena couldn't help but note that right next to Janie's keyboard was a half-demolished hoagie from Cosmi's in South Philly. Specifically, the Godfather: prosciutto, soppressata, and enough roasted peppers and sun-dried tomatoes to stock a salad bar.

On the monitor, black-and-white surveillance footage from a section of the Ben Franklin Parkway.

"Okay, here's the Museum of Art on the night of the Archie Hughes shooting. The interesting thing is that Archie's car is parked just out of view." Janie paused to take a bite of her hoagie, then continued to narrate through the prosciutto. "Sorry. I'm starving. Anyway, you can sort of make out a bumper."

Janie tapped a few keys. The image zoomed into that bumper, then back out again.

"The weird thing is, Archie managed to stop his Maserati inside a perfect dead zone between two surveillance cameras."

That can't be a coincidence, Veena thought.

"I know what you're thinking," Janie said. "That can't be a co-incidence, right? I went back and checked on where those cameras *should* have been aimed. Looks like both of them were angled approximately twenty-three degrees away from where they were supposed to be pointed, creating that dead zone."

This was a setup, then. Either Archie Hughes was lured to that exact spot or someone had dumped him and his car there, which implied he had been shot and killed elsewhere. *Please tell me you went back and checked when those cameras were moved,* Veena thought.

"Before you ask," Janie said, "I went back and checked both feeds. The cameras were moved six minutes and twenty-three seconds before the police discovered Archie Hughes's body."

There we go, Veena thought.

"But that's not the best part," Janie continued. "Watch this."

She tapped a few keys and took a bite of her Godfather as the computer jumped to another stream of surveillance footage. It took Veena a couple of seconds to identify the location: Spring Garden

Street, between Twenty-Third and Twenty-Fourth Streets, just a few blocks from the art museum. "Check out *this* guy."

On-screen, a white male hurried up the street, using his T-shirt as a mask to cover his nose and mouth; a gray hood covered most of his head.

"This was captured just minutes after a couple of patrol officers discovered Archie's body. Definitely looks like he's running for his life, doesn't it?"

"There was a reference to him in the police report," Veena said.

"Yes, but this is the first time he's popped up on surveillance. We now have a better physical description."

Could be an athlete, Veena thought. *Maybe even a football player.*

Transcript of encrypted message exchange between Veena Lion and Janie Hall

VEENA LION: Stellar work, Janie. Enjoy the rest of your God-
  father.
JANIE HALL: Sorry about that, V., but a girl's gotta eat. You headed
  to the Linc to figure out which member of the team had it in
  for Archie? Need me to prep some background files on the
  team?
LION: That would be fine, but no, I'm not headed to the stadium.
  I was just sitting here realizing that I need a window into the
  Hughes household.
HALL: Please don't tell me you're going to break into their
  mansion.
LION: Who am I, Cooper Lamb? I'm just going to follow your
  lead.
HALL: ???
LION: Can you send me the home address of their personal chef?
  The one the file said they'd just fired?

CHAPTER 21

1:07 p.m.

VEENA LION was horrified the moment she stepped into Chef Roy Nguyen's cramped kitchen.

Not by the kitchen itself, which was compact, clean, and tidy. So tidy, in fact, it looked as if Chef Nguyen rarely cooked a meal at home. No, Veena was horrified by the lunch Chef Nguyen was currently preparing: leftover spaghetti. At some point, the sauce-heavy pasta had been a take-out meal, and now the chef was frying it up in a high-end skillet over a medium flame. Sauce smoked and splattered as the chef pushed a wooden spoon around the edge now and again.

"Hungry?" Chef asked.

"I had a late breakfast," Veena lied. "So, I understand Ms. Hughes let you go fairly recently?"

"Let me go?" Chef asked. He made an annoyed huffing sound. "Let's get it straight. That snooty bitch *fired* me. Over, like, nothing."

"Have you found employment somewhere else?"

Chef Nguyen stared at the tangled strands of spaghetti as if they could tell his fortune. "It's not exactly easy to line up another gig like that one. You have no idea how hard I busted my balls trying to get her attention in the first...hey, you're not even listening to me!"

Chef had looked up in time to catch Veena furiously thumbing her phone.

"I am listening to every word. But I'm also texting a head-hunter friend of mine, who will be contacting you within the hour. She specializes in matching executive-level chefs with discerning families."

Chef's grimace disappeared. "Are you...are you serious?"

"Just pay attention to your phone over the next hour. Her name is April White."

"Why would you do this? You don't even know me."

"You're actually doing *me* a favor. April's clients will be falling all over themselves to retain your services. But help me understand something."

Chef turned his attention back to his sizzling pasta, which was on the verge of burning. "Sure. Yeah. Anything."

"Tell me about your time in the Hughes residence. Sounds like they were a very tight-knit family."

"Ha. Only three members of that family were truly tight."

"Mom and the kids?"

"Please. Parents are *supposed* to be tight with their kids. I'm talking about the threesome."

"You're going to have to tell me more."

"First I want you to try some of this."

"No, really, I'm fine. If my assistant, Janie, were here, she'd be all over your, uh, leftovers."

"I really just insist. I can see you give me those *Ew, gross* stares. You think I'm just heating up leftovers, but don't judge it until you put a forkful in your mouth."

With a flourish that finally revealed the man's skill, Nguyen spooned a small sample of the fried pasta into a glass bowl. He stabbed the pile with a tasting fork, then slid the bowl across the counter toward Veena.

"Go on," Chef said.

Veena knew the point wasn't negotiable. She twisted the fork around until she had a few thick strands of pasta in a tight little ball and put it in her mouth. She had to admit, the fried spaghetti was insanely flavorful, with a perfect blend of crispy bits and soft noodle bits. It was an entirely different approach to the household staple.

"You seriously need to make this for April," Veena said. "She'll lose her mind."

"Oh, this? This is nothing. Just lunch, you know?"

Veena made a series of mental notes (which she would commit to a yellow legal pad during the train ride home): *Chef Nguyen more than what he shows on the surface. He hides his massive ego behind a faux everyman exterior. He is the savory bite behind the fried pasta. What is he hiding?*

"So tell me about Archie, Francine, and Maya."

Chef Nguyen smiled and swirled himself a bite of spaghetti. "See, you figured it out for yourself. The threesome."

"But only *you* saw how they behaved."

"Oh, believe me, everybody saw. They were shameless. Everybody on the Main Line talked about them. And I should have known better. The moment I crossed that Maya Rain chick, my days were numbered."

"What did you do, ask her out?"

"Of course I asked her out. Have you *seen* her?"

Veena said nothing as she twirled more pasta around her fork. She hated herself for wishing there were more in her bowl.

"It's the whole nanny thing too. Sweet and shy on the outside, but once the kids are tucked away in bed..."

"You can stop painting the picture, Chef."

"What if I don't want to, Ms. Lion?" he said, chuckling.

CHAPTER 22

Transcript of phone call placed by Cooper Lamb to a private number

COOPER LAMB: Hey, it's your old man. Guess who I'm going to be meeting in two minutes.

ARIEL LAMB: Francine Pearl Hughes.

LAMB: Whoa! Nailed it on the first try.

ARIEL: C'mon on, Dad. You're working for her law firm, so one can only assume you'll be meeting with Francine at some point.

LAMB: You're good, kid. Unlike your dopey brother.

COOPER LAMB JR.: Hey! I'm standing right here.

LAMB: Relax, sparky. I knew you both were on speaker this whole time. I could hear your snuffles. By the way, are you taking your allergy medicine? And shouldn't you be getting back to basket-weaving class or whatever they teach at that expensive Quaker school?

ARIEL: Ignoring you. Say hello to Ms. Hughes for us! Tell her we're huge fans.

LAMB: I'll bet I'm a bigger fan than you guys.

ARIEL: Oh, really. Name one Francine Pearl song.

COOPER JR.: I hate that allergy medicine. It tastes like puke.

LAMB: If you could learn how to swallow a pill, you wouldn't have
    to drink the puke. As for your question, my dear doubting
    daughter: "The Star-Spangled Banner."
ARIEL: That's not a Francine Pearl song.
LAMB: I heard her sing it once. At a Super Bowl, in fact!

Cooper Lamb had been in more impressive homes than this.
But those homes were Monticello, the Hearst Castle, and 1600
Pennsylvania Avenue. And none of those homes had had Francine
Pearl Hughes living in them.

"Sit anywhere you like, Cooper," Francine said. "I'll be right
with you after I get the kids their snacks. Care for something
to drink?"

"Just some tap water for me and my dog, Lupe, if you don't mind."

"I think we can do a little better than that," she said, smiling.

Most people would be pondering the correct drink request.
Not Cooper. He was too busy strategizing the proper place to sit.
Sure, this was a friendly interview at his client's home. But make
no mistake, Francine's kitchen was also her battlefield. Especially
now that she had fired her general (Chef Roy Nguyen) and
assumed command of all the family meals. She might be dressed
in the casual manner of a Main Line mom, but she was still a
superstar.

"I have some updates for you," Cooper said, opting for a spot
directly across the kitchen island from Francine as she sliced
vegetables to accompany kid-size trays of pita and hummus.

"Really?"

Not really. This was one of Cooper's favorite techniques, espe-
cially with an interview subject who was theoretically on your side.
You didn't show up with a tape recorder and a list of questions.
No, you acted like a proper houseguest and came bearing a

gift—information. This made you collaborators, not detective and witness.

"The team is a mess," Cooper said. "The Sables are up to their ears in corrupt schemes, and the players are more or less kindergartners with millions in disposable income."

"That's not really an update, Cooper," Francine said. "That's been my reality for the past five seasons."

"Why didn't you encourage your husband to take his considerable talents elsewhere?"

"I presume you never had the chance to meet Archie in person. Nobody could ever *encourage* him to do anything he didn't want to. I'd better get these snacks to the kids—"

"One second, Francine. I really think there's something rotten with the team, and it may have something to do with your husband's death. I'm hoping you can point me in the right direction."

Francine's smile—her armor—faded a little. Only now did she look like a woman trying desperately to keep the oceans of grief at bay.

"Archie liked to say that he was *in* this world, but he was not *of* this world."

Cooper stared at her across the kitchen island. "You just tied a knot in my brain."

"What he meant was, he knew what he was getting into with the Sables. But he kept his nose clean and his head above the filth. The team had nothing to do with Archie's death. At some point, when the media calms down and cooler heads prevail, the police will find the truth."

"And what is that?"

"That Philadelphia is a violent city, and sometimes it takes even the best of us. Can I feed my kids now?"

"I'm sorry... just one more thing. Please."

Francine stared at him.

"Look, I *have* to ask this question," Cooper continued, "because it's going to come up sooner rather than later."

"Go ahead."

"Why were your prints on the gun found in the garden? The gun you said you didn't recognize?"

Francine nodded and smiled, as if she had been expecting this question. "I've just told you that Philly can be a violent place. If you grow up here, you're taught to protect yourself. All of this"—she waved a hand around her designer kitchen—"doesn't mean a thing if you can't take care of yourself."

"So you and your husband kept guns in the house, and you've handled them all at some point?"

"When I told the police I didn't recognize the gun, it was like saying I didn't recognize a particular hammer in a toolbox. Why would I? I never gave it much thought."

The explanation was delivered casually. But Francine locked eyes with Cooper with such intensity, she was clearly issuing an unspoken challenge: *Go ahead. Tell me I'm lying.*

Cooper stared right back. *Hey, it's not me you have to convince.*

Finally, Francine broke the tension. "I'd better get the kids fed, Mr. Lamb."

"I have a feeling they may have already feasted on my dog."

"Lupe? Are you kidding? They love him!"

"Everybody does," Cooper said. "He's the worst private-eye side-kick ever."

CHAPTER 23

"OH, AND this is Maya," Francine told Cooper.

Maya Rain—the "hillbilly from West Virginia," as Glenn Sable had called her—was sitting cross-legged on the floor with the Hughes children as they played with Lupe, who was relishing all of the attention.

"Traitor," Cooper told his pup.

"Quiet, kids. Mr. Lamb is a private eye," Maya said in mock fear. "His job is to listen to everything we say."

"I think Mr. Lamb is a sheep!" announced five-year-old Maddie Hughes, who was utterly adorable. *"Baaaaa,"* she said. This was followed by a giggle fit.

"I've been called worse," Cooper said. "And don't worry, Ms. Rain, I'm just here to retrieve my partner, Lupe, who is clearly falling down on the job. Unless he's managed to take statements from all of you between treats?"

Three people in the room—Francine, Maya Rain, and Maddie— smiled at the joke, but not twelve-year-old Archie Hughes Jr.

The boy sat on the floor too, legs crossed, but his attention was miles away. Cooper had seen that look before. Back when he was in the army, Cooper had spent countless days in Fallujah and Baghdad staring into the eyes of children who'd lost a parent and couldn't understand why everyone was acting like nothing was wrong. Cooper felt his heart implode.

Maya Rain caught Cooper looking at Archie Jr. and quickly stood up. "Let me show Mr. Lamb out while you kids have your snack."

"Thank you so much, Maya," said Francine.

"Children, I'll be right *baaaaaack,*" Maya said, which made Maddie giggle all over again. Maya looped her arm through Cooper's and gently guided him toward the servants' entrance.

The touch wasn't flirtatious—it was as if she knew he needed to touch another human being in that moment, which was even more startling.

Transcript of recorded conversation between Cooper Lamb and Maya Rain

COOPER LAMB: I'd love to speak with you too, if you have a minute.

MAYA RAIN: Not here. Not right now.

LAMB: Where and when?

RAIN: Hmm. That eager to see me again?

LAMB: I'm just doing my job, and your name has come up a lot.

RAIN: I'm sure it has. I'll be in touch.

LAMB: Where and when?

RAIN: I don't know. The kids keep me pretty busy most days. Cleaning up messes, that's what I do.

LAMB: Funny—looks like we're in the same business. But name the time and place. Seriously.

RAIN: I'll let Lupe know. And be careful on your way out, Cooper. Mr. Lopez is picky about the grounds.

* * *

COOPER LAMB: Hey, you're Mr. Lopez, right? My name is Cooper, and I'm working for Ms. Hughes's lawyers. Do you have a moment?

MAURICIO LOPEZ: That stupid dog is going to dig up my garden!

LAMB: That dog's name is Lupe and he will do no such thing. I wanted to ask you about the g—

LOPEZ: I can't speak right now. I'm sorry.

LAMB: It's just a simple question and nothing you haven't already told the police.

LOPEZ: What is that in your hand? No tape-recording!

LAMB: I promise I'm not recording. I have a nervous habit of holding my phone.

LOPEZ: Please, I'm very busy today.

LAMB: I promise this will just take a second. It's a matter of life and death.

LOPEZ: Fine. What is it?

LAMB: I can't seem to keep my hydrangeas alive from season to season. What am I doing wrong? You can be honest with me.

LOPEZ: (*Confused*) What?

LAMB: The winter months in Philly, they're brutal. Obviously you do a ton of work maintaining these grounds. I mean, that's how you saw the gun, right?

LOPEZ: I have to go now—

LAMB: But Ms. Hughes said it would be okay if we spoke.

LOPEZ: I believe she would be very angry if we spoke.

LAMB: No, she said it would be okay. Well, she *implied* it would be okay. I mean, we're all on the same team here! What have you got to lose?

LOPEZ: (*Sighs*) Everything, Mr. Lamb. I have *everything* to lose. My
    job. My status in this country. My freedom.

LAMB: Has someone threatened you, Mr. Lopez? Because if that's
    the case, we can protect you.

LOPEZ: Nobody has threatened me, Mr. Lamb. I live always under
    this threat. Now, please, take your dog and leave the grounds. I
    have much to do to repair the mess he's made.

(*After a gap in the dialogue of approximately one minute, a car door
    slams.*)

LAMB: You heard that, right, Victor? Mr. Lopez has a problem with
    Lupe, which clearly means he's evil. Kidding. But seriously, he
    may know something. I need to find out what. And Maya
    Rain... okay, I need to know *everything* about her.

CHAPTER 24

REPORT TO C. LAMB BY V. SUAREZ
TUESDAY, JANUARY 25

Finished my latest analysis of audio surveillance at the Hughes home and there is nothing unusual to note after you left.

You asked me to keep an ear out for the nanny, but she spends most of her time with the kids. She's good at keeping them distracted. Very inventive, lots of creative brain games. Stuff like having them look outside and tell her the makes, models, years, and colors of all the cars they see. (I found myself distracted by this too, to be honest.) The Hughes kids are quick. Who knows how they'll eventually turn out, but they might make great private investigators someday. Maya Rain is quite the teacher.

Francine Pearl Hughes spends a lot of time shopping online. I'm tracking all internet activity and I have a list of the high-end clothing and jewelry stores she's been visiting. The clothing appears to be purchased for herself, though I do not know the nanny's measurements. (Yes, I'm working on it. Ms. Rain's digital trail is either thin or carefully obscured.) The jewelry appears to be for a woman, presumably Ms. Hughes.

One other thing, boss—and this may be nothing, but I wanted to mention it anyway: Francine Pearl Hughes does a lot of singing around the house. Her own hits, but also older show tunes and stuff from the Great American Songbook. This is not surprising, of course, because Ms. Hughes is a singer, and I'm sure she's keeping her vocal cords in shape. Could be just habit. But is this the behavior of a woman in mourning for her husband?

More updates as I learn them. As I type these words, however, I hear there's a visitor to the Hughes home—your old friend Veena Lion is there to talk to the nanny.

CHAPTER 25

4:37 p.m.

"THANKS FOR agreeing to speak with me, Ms. Rain."

"Of course. Ms. Hughes thought I could help. I just have one request, and this is on the advice of the family lawyer. Please don't record this interview."

Veena Lion pretended to give it some thought. "Okay, I won't."

While Veena paused, she took a quick mental snapshot of Maya Rain, who did not appear to be your stereotypical home-wrecker. Her lithe body was clad in a tailored Banana Republic top and pants—rugged enough for someone who chased after children all day, classy enough for a member of the Hughes household's staff.

"Can you say that out loud?" Rain said, smiling.

"You want me to say that I'm not recording our conversation?"

"Thank you."

As a rule, Veena recorded all of her conversations. This was a matter of habit as well as personal protection. She was forever in pursuit of the truth, and while the truth could be twisted, tape never lied. But something told Veena it was best to relax that rule for the moment.

Veena matched Maya's warm smile with one of her own. "How did you come to work for the Hughes family?"

"Everybody in town has a salacious story about that," Maya said, blushing a little. "You know, rumors that Archie picked me up while I was waiting tables at Gullifty's or stripping at Delilah's or something along those lines."

"Is that where you were working before you came to take care of the kids?"

"Which one, the family restaurant or the high-end strip club?"

Veena could tell Maya was teasing her. "You tell me."

"The truth is much more boring than that, I'm afraid. I'm working toward my master's in psychology at Villanova, and my adviser recommended me for the job. There was a lot of competition from people in the department because, you know, the Eagles and all that. But I'm not even a football fan."

"Don't let anyone hear you say that in this town," Veena said.

"Tell me about it! It's better to admit you're a mass murderer or something."

"Did you grow up on the Main Line?"

"No. Pretty much the opposite of the Main Line—Buckhannon, West Virginia. Ever hear of it?"

"I'm afraid not," Veena lied. She recalled the 2006 mining disaster near Buckhannon that took a dozen lives, and she'd seen a documentary focusing on the town's opioid epidemic. And she could hear echoes of Appalachia in Maya's voice, which Maya took great pains to hide. She probably hadn't become "Maya Rain" until she'd crossed the state line into Pennsylvania.

"Then you're just like everyone else," Maya said, examining the tops of her shoes. "I'll admit, Buckhannon doesn't have a lot going for it. I spent years saving up my babysitting money so I could escape. And strangely enough, all of that work landed me here, taking care of the sweetest children in the world."

"Here's what bothers me," Veena said.

Maya's eyes narrowed. "What's that?"

"You're too good to be true."

"I've been told that," Maya said. She laughed. "But all I do is clean up messes. It's pretty simple, really."

"Seriously, though, do you enjoy your work with the Hughes family?"

"Are you kidding? Archie and Maddie are amazing. Even now—especially now, going through the shock and grief of losing Archie…" She seemed to search for words. "I hope that someday I'll be as strong as Mrs. Hughes and those kids. Want to meet them?"

CHAPTER 26

VEENA KNEW the kids were a deflection, but she went along with it; she'd wanted to meet them anyway. The boy was in sixth grade, and the girl—who was a miniature version of her famous mother—was a kindergartner. Both were absorbed in their hand-held devices and barely noticed Veena's entrance.

"This is Miss Veena Lion," Maya said. "She's a private investigator who is working with the district attorney."

"*Rowrr,*" Maddie said, then collapsed into giggles.

The son, Archie Jr., looked up. "You're helping the DA find out who did this."

"I'm trying my best, Archie," Veena replied. "What are you watching on your phone?"

"Just some stuff on YouTube."

"The hour before dinner is device time," Maya explained. "I don't want you thinking the worst of me."

"No judgments here. I live on my phone."

"The police asked us lots of questions already," Archie Jr. said. As he lowered his phone Veena stole a glance at the screen. Based on the graphics and framing, the boy was watching some sort of true-crime show.

"Yeah? What kinds of things did they ask you?"

Maya rubbed Archie Jr.'s shoulders. "You should probably wash up before dinner."

"Lions go *rowrr*," Maddie said, then giggled again.

"That's right, they do."

"Do all private eyes have animal names?" Archie Jr. asked.

Responding to Veena's puzzled expression, Maya said, "A colleague of yours was by earlier today."

"Ah, Mr. Cooper Lamb," Veena said, nodding.

"Lambs go *baaaaa* and lions go *rowrr*," Maddie announced. "Do you know his dog, Loopy? He's so cute!"

"I know Lupe, and he is indeed adorable," Veena said. "But watch out for Mr. Lamb. Sometimes big bad wolves like to hide in sheep's clothing."

This caught Maya's attention, just as Veena had intended it to.

CHAPTER 27

HIGHLY CONFIDENTAL
EYES OF THE POLICE COMMISSIONER ONLY

Dear Madam Commissioner:

A quick update on the Roy Nguyen situation.

I know speculation has run wild in the media. It's understand-able—first, someone murders Archie Hughes, then, barely two days later, his former personal chef is badly beaten and shot. (I'm keeping in constant touch with the hospital, by the way, and will let you know the moment his condition improves . . . or worsens.)

This is why I immediately drove to Ardmore to learn what I could from the Lower Merion PD. Cutting to the chase, this appears to have nothing whatsoever to do with the Archie Hughes murder.

From what I hear, Nguyen is big into sports gambling. And while it's true that he had a lot of money riding on the Birds this year, I understand he owes quite a bit all over town. It's messy, but it could explain why a well-known chef would have taken a high-paying gig in the Hughes home.

I spoke to the Lower Merion detectives and forensics team. They're still working on their report, but it's clear that the attack was about intimidation, and things rapidly escalated. There were signs of a pretty brutal struggle inside Nguyen's apartment (broken furniture, doors) that spilled over into the hallway, where the chef was shot in the chest twice, at close range.

If this were a professional hit, Nguyen wouldn't have heard him/them coming, much less had the opportunity to fight him/them off. (It's possible there were multiple attackers, but all signs point to a single perp.)

My unofficial take: A leg-breaker showed up to scare some money out of Nguyen. The chef fought back, which caught the leg-breaker by surprise. Things spiraled out of control. The leg-breaker pulled a gun, at which point Nguyen probably tried to take it away. Two shots to the chef's chest later, the leg-breaker hightailed it out of there. (Again, had this leg-breaker been a pro, he would have made sure Nguyen was dead.)

I want to assure you that I will follow every detail of this case as it develops to see if there are any solid connections with the Hughes murder. But at this point, my gut is telling me no.

And like my dad used to say: "When your gut is talking, listen to it. Then go eat something."

Yours,
Det. Michael Bernstein

CHAPTER 28

Transcript of conversation between Detective Michael Bernstein and Glenn Sable, co-owner of the Philadelphia Eagles

GLENN SABLE: Mickey, my man. What's up?

MICHAEL BERNSTEIN: I don't know yet. I'm calling you from Ardmore. Maybe that will tell you something.

SABLE: What the hell's in Ardmore?

BERNSTEIN: A personal chef who may have baked his last soufflé.

SABLE: Shit, the Asian guy? Is he gonna make it?

BERNSTEIN: It's kind of touch and go. He's young, though, and I've seen people pull through worse than this.

SABLE: How could it be worse? I heard he took two in the heart.

BERNSTEIN: Two in the chest. Bullets are funny things. They can follow all kinds of paths in a human body.

SABLE: You have the chance to, uh, talk to the chef?

BERNSTEIN: Glenn, the dude's unconscious.

SABLE: No, no, I mean before. Like, about the other thing.

BERNSTEIN: It wasn't on my to-do list. Listen, my friend, I have to ask, just to make sure . . .

SABLE: Ask what?

BERNSTEIN: How much was the chef into you for?

SABLE: Hold on a sec. You think *we* had someone do this?

BERNSTEIN: Look, I'm not judging, I'm just asking. I told you before, I need to know everything, no matter how minor.

SABLE: Far as I know, the chef was current. I didn't even know he was part of our thing until my dad told me.

BERNSTEIN: So you had nothing to do with . . .

SABLE: Screw you, of course we had nothing to do with this!

BERNSTEIN: Glenn, calm the hell down, okay? And don't get me wrong, this was not anything professional. But it does look an awful lot like someone paid the chef a visit to smack him around a little, and things went haywire. I just want to be sure I know all of the details before I, you know, massage things.

SABLE: You want a massage, *Mickey,* go to a rub-and-tug. Don't call me up and accuse me of this bullshit. What, did I offend your tender sensibilities?

BERNSTEIN: No, man, I'm just sitting here enjoying my afternoon.

SABLE: Look, I'm sorry. I know how hard you're working. Things are just tense around here. I've got private eyes up my ass—

BERNSTEIN: Who?

SABLE: You know. The sheep guy.

BERNSTEIN: (*Chuckling*) You mean Cooper Lamb?

SABLE: Yeah, him. He's working for Francine, so I gotta play nice, but there's a guy I'd like to put through a wall.

BERNSTEIN: A lot of people feel the same way.

SABLE: Then maybe somebody should do something about it.

BERNSTEIN: I'll look into it.

SABLE: Yeah, you do that.

CHAPTER 29

Transcript of encrypted message exchange between private Veena Lion and Janie Hall

JANIE HALL: Hey, V., you know that chef you interviewed earlier today?

VEENA LION: Oh, did April find him a job already?

HALL: What job? No. Veena, this is important: He's over at Lankenau. Someone beat the hell out of him and then shot him twice. You there? You've been typing a long time...

LION: Is Roy alive?

HALL: I'm waiting for a call back from one of the nurses. She's a friend from high school, a straight shooter, so she'll give me the real deal.

LION: Okay, I'm headed there now. Give me any updates as soon you hear.

HALL: Of course. But V., be careful out there.

LION: I appreciate that, but I'm not the person who was attacked.

HALL: Sure, but the person who did the attacking is still out there. And he might have been watching Chef Nguyen. More to the point, he might have watched you meeting with Chef Nguyen just a few hours ago.

CHAPTER 30

Transcript of Detective Michael Bernstein's recorded interview with Justin Sugarman, aka Shuggie, currently residing in a homeless camp on Lemon Hill

MICHAEL BERNSTEIN: Justin? Hey, man, you around? I'm looking for Justin Sugarman!

JUSTIN "SHUGGIE" SUGERMAN: Quiet down, yo, I'm tryin' to sleep.

BERNSTEIN: That you, Justin? It's your old pal Mickey Bernstein!

SHUGGIE: Man, stop that Justin shit. You know everyone calls me Shuggie.

BERNSTEIN: Ah, there you are. Come on out, let me see that pretty face. How's it going, Shuggie?

SHUGGIE: Living my best life, man. You know me. The usual ups and downs. Mostly downs, if I'm being honest. But I don't let that keep me down, if you know what mean.

BERNSTEIN: I don't understand half the shit you say, if *I'm* being honest. But I think you can help me out with something.

SHUGGIE: No way, man. I don't help the police. Y'all hear that? (*Shouts*) I don't help law enforcement, like, ever!

BERNSTEIN: Save the outrage, Shuggie. No one else is around right now. Who could handle all the raccoons and garbage?

SHUGGIE: No, that's cool, man. You always insult people whose help you desperately need?

BERNSTEIN: Often as I can. Did you happen to see Archie Hughes's Maserati a few nights ago?

SHUGGIE: Come on, man. Get out of my camp.

BERNSTEIN: This so-called camp belongs to the city. I could tell *you* to leave.

SHUGGIE: Yeah, that's just perfect. Price hardworkin' people out of every affordable living space so we're all forced to live in a dump like rats. And then you want to take away our dump! So what are the rats supposed to do, huh, Mr. Detective?

BERNSTEIN: I don't know, Shug. Maybe the rat should just answer my questions. Did you see the Maserati or not?

SHUGGIE: Screw you.

BERNSTEIN: You'll have to talk to the missus about that, but I don't think she's flexible.

SHUGGIE: I'm serious, man. I don't need this grief.

BERNSTEIN: In that case, Mr. Working-Class Rat, start packing your things because I'm gonna have a sanitation crew up here in twenty minutes, and you'll be spending the next few days fishing your crap out of the Schuylkill.

SHUGGIE: [unintelligible]

BERNSTEIN: What's that, Shuggie? Couldn't quite make that out.

SHUGGIE: I didn't see no Maserati.

BERNSTEIN: But . . .

SHUGGIE: But . . . I heard about a guy who's trying to fence a Super Bowl ring. That might be of some interest to your current investigation.

BERNSTEIN: See that, Shug? I knew you were the right man to talk to. Who's selling the ring?

SHUGGIE: You must be high if you think I'm giving you a name.

BERNSTEIN: Dude, you're as high as giraffe balls right now. And I
    know you're going to give me a name because you don't want
    me throwing your skinny little ass into the river with the rest
    of your junk.

SHUGGIE: Damn, man.

BERNSTEIN: Come on. Nobody's around—it's just you and me,
    brother. Tell me a name. I probably know the guy already.

SHUGGIE: Brother, my ass. You know the guy. It's Percy.

BERNSTEIN: Crazy Percy Marshall? From Kensington?

SHUGGIE: Told you.

BERNSTEIN: What's Crazy Percy doin' with a Super Bowl ring?

SHUGGIE: I'm just telling you what I heard.

BERNSTEIN: Okay, Shug.

SHUGGIE: He's killed people, you know.

BERNSTEIN: Is that a fact.

SHUGGIE: I'm serious. You'd better be careful out there.

BERNSTEIN: Always am.

SHUGGIE: No, man, don't you get it? The line? You know, from
    Hill Street Blues? Probably before your time ...

BERNSTEIN: Try that joke on my dad sometime. I'm sure he'd
    appreciate it.

SHUGGIE: Your daddy was a psycho fascist and everybody in the
    city knew it.

BERNSTEIN: Want to know a secret?

SHUGGIE: What's that?

BERNSTEIN: I'm worse.

CHAPTER 31

TWO SURPRISES awaited Veena Lion at Lankenau Medical Center.

One was the armada of TV reporters blocking the entrance to the emergency department. She'd known word would travel fast, and the media was starving for any crumbs they could link to the Archie Hughes murder. But it was rare for TV reporters to beat Janie Hall on a breaking development. This case was going to test all of them.

The second surprise was waiting just behind the security checkpoint, which Veena got past by telling the officer she was Roy Nguyen's personal attorney. "How many lawyers does this guy have?" asked the beleaguered Lower Merion cop. "Your colleague is over there, by the vending machines."

Cooper Lamb, who was no lawyer, was busy ripping open a plastic bag of turkey jerky. *"Rowrr."*

"Baaaaa," Veena replied.

"I didn't know you were close with the chef."

"Yeah. He makes incredible fried spaghetti."

"If that's an in-joke, I'm missing the gag."

"Life doesn't revolve entirely around you, Cooper. What's the latest?"

The latest was that Roy Nguyen was still in surgery, and the hospital was clearly not prepared for all of the attention or the constant inquiries from private investigators.

"So we might as well go for a cocktail," Cooper said. "Unless you want to get in on this jerky with me. We can even split a root beer."

"I need to talk to Roy the minute he wakes up."

"Get in line. The police are downplaying this, but did you know that Chef Roy was fired by the Hughes family just *two days* before the murder?"

"Yeah, I did."

"Do you know why?"

"Of course."

"See, I don't think you do. He probably told you that Francine Pearl was just a bitch or something. But no, the dude flat-out *stole stuff* from the house. Watches, jewelry, sports memorabilia. And he was caught on a *nanny cam*."

Veena frowned. "That doesn't sound right. Who's your source?"

"Nobody you'd know."

"Is it Red from Atlantic City? Your old army buddy?"

"Damn it. I wish I'd never told you about him. Look, Red knows his stuff. Including the fact that your boy Roy owed a lot of people in Atlantic City a lot of cheddar. Which would explain the not-so-petty larceny from the Hughes home."

Veena considered this and replayed some of their lunchtime conversation. She thought about her legal-pad list of suspects. She thought about Maya Rain. But mostly, she considered that the day had been a very long one.

"Throw that crap away," she said, "and let's have that cocktail."

CHAPTER 32

9:08 p.m.

EARLY IN his career, Mickey Bernstein had spent a few years undercover. He'd told his superior he just wanted more street experience. But his real motivations were more complex.

A lot of it was wanting to be out from under his dad's thumb. But it was also the secret thrill of letting himself disappear into the rougher sections of the city and enjoying some of the pleasures associated with those places. Being the son of Philly's most famous cop meant he'd grown up under constant scrutiny, both inside his home and out. It was nice to slip into another man's skin.

And he could still do that from time to time.

Like now, walking toward a dive bar near the infamous intersection of Kensington and Allegheny. They said this area was slowly gentrifying, just like nearby Fishtown, but Mickey knew better. Woe to the hipster moron who stepped off the El looking for avocado toast and a craft IPA. Mickey didn't want to look like that. Or, even worse, like a cop. So he'd pulled on workman's clothes, skipped his evening shave, and got into character.

Bernstein opened the door to Dmitri's and found an empty barstool. People gave him the usual once-over, but nobody seemed to make him. He ordered a shot of Jack, a Bud back, and a fifty-cent bag of greasy potato chips. In the corner was a long-defunct

Donkey Kong console that now doubled as an ashtray and a place to hang Christmas lights, which were apparently up all year.

Mickey's dad loved places like this. Real salt-of-the-earth joints in the old working-class nabes. For all he knew, his dad had dragged him and his mom here at some point. Young Mickey had probably pumped some quarters into that very Donkey Kong machine.

When Mickey was two rounds in, Crazy Percy walked through the front door. Nobody bothered to look up. According to Mickey's regular snitches, Crazy Percy was always in here this time of night. Mickey didn't even have to come up with a tactic for the approach; Crazy Percy slid his large frame into the empty stool to Mickey's left.

"Hey, Crazy. Want a beer?"

"Oh, shit, man." Percy's frame deflated a little. "Gimme a Jack instead. A double."

Mickey nodded his permission to the bartender, who didn't exactly measure as he poured the whiskey into a tumbler.

"You look like garbage," Percy told Mickey, which was quite a statement coming from a man nicknamed "Crazy." This was not a nickname Percy embraced, but for years he'd been the guy who was willing to do pretty much anything (steal cars, break legs, maybe even murder) for low, low prices, so the moniker was hard to shake. Percy was forever looking for a way to turn a fast buck, but he always undervalued himself. With a little ambition, Mickey thought, he could be a proper criminal.

"I couldn't be better," Mickey said. "In fact, I'm getting married."

"Thought you *were* married."

"I'm in the market for a ring, and here's the thing—my sweetheart is a huge Birds fan. I mean, she, like, lives for it. So I'm looking for something like . . . a Super Bowl ring."

Percy groaned, then downed his whiskey as if it might be taken away from him.

"Heard you had a line on one," Mickey continued. "Something really special that just came on the market."

"I wouldn't even know what a Super Bowl ring looks like. What, does it have little footballs or buffalo wings on it or something? I don't know what you're talking about."

"Percy, you're breaking my heart here."

"Look, okay, I know where you're going with this. I didn't have anything to do with Archie Hughes."

"But you saw his car."

Crazy Percy stared at his drink, knowing that this conversation could go one of two ways. He decided on the easy way. "Yeah, I did. There was another fancy car parked nearby too."

Mickey tried to hide his excitement. "You remember the make and model?"

"A Bentley. Red or maroon, something like that. The thing was gorgeous. Couldn't believe somebody had left it out there that time of night." The thought of boosting it had clearly crossed Percy's mind. But maybe he wasn't *that* crazy.

"Did you see anyone behind the wheel? A woman, maybe?"

"Nah, there was nobody in the car. Unless they were hiding in the back seat."

"You sure?"

"I didn't see a soul. Not until you cops rolled up, and then I got the hell out of there."

The car, though. That was enough.

Francine Hughes drove a red Bentley.

CHAPTER 33

9:32 p.m.

"WHAT'S THAT? Hang on, kiddos, let me find out. Excuse me, miss?"

The waitress at the Rittenhouse Hotel bar was the same one from the night before, but gone was any hint of flirtation. In its place was an icy veneer. Veena must have *really* rubbed her the wrong way. That's what Veena did for a living, but Cooper needed to make it right. He liked it here.

"Yes?" she said quietly.

"I'm on the phone with some old war buddies...okay, that's a lie." Cooper showed her his best smile. "My *kids* are on the phone, and they have a very important mixology query. What's the real difference between a Rob Roy and a Shirley Temple? I mean, is it the same thing only sexist?"

"Order your kid a Rob Roy," the waitress said, "and I could have you arrested."

"Come again?"

"You're thinking of a Roy Rogers, which has Coke in it. A Shirley Temple uses Sprite. That's the difference."

"You hear that, kiddos? This impossibly beautiful woman just saved me from prison." Cooper looked up at her and mouthed, *Thank you.*

But it was something else—probably the words *impossibly beautiful*—that melted the ice, and suddenly all was calm and good in the lounge at the Rittenhouse Hotel once again.

That is, until Veena Lion arrived, pulled out her chair with a teeth-shredding scrape, and barked out an order for a double martini with three blue-cheese-stuffed olives, easy on the vermouth. Cooper said good night to his kids, told them he loved them, and placed his phone on the table.

"Okay, what the hell is going on with this case?" Veena said.

"So are we finally past the whole ethics thing? Can we talk straight?"

"We shouldn't be talking at all, but I need to know the truth."

"Amen to that. And here come our libations."

They drank in silence for a while, recalibrating their nervous systems. Then Veena said, "Speaking of the nanny cam . . ."

"Ah," Cooper said. "So you've met the lovely Ms. Rain too."

"Eh. She's too good to be true."

"I like her."

"Based on?"

"Gut feeling. I know, I know, I'm keeping an open mind. But I'm going to be terribly disappointed if she had any part in Archie's murder."

Veena watched him carefully with her green eyes, analyzing every word, every micro-expression. "My God. How did you do it?" she asked.

"Do what?"

"Fall in love so quickly."

"It was easy. Happened the minute she slipped her arm through mine and escorted me into the garden."

Cooper's intention was to playfully jab back at Veena for that falling-in-love wisecrack. But she surprised him by leaning across the table and kissing him on the cheek.

"That almost hurt," Cooper whispered.

"Rowrr," Veena whispered back.

"Does this mean you want to come for a sleepover tonight?"

"No, it does not."

"Well, that hurt even more." Cooper was confused about where all of this was going. Was it the usual flirtatious banter? Or were they about to cross *all* the lines in their professional relationship?

He had just resolved to hang in there and find out when a harsh *buzz* on the table broke the spell, followed by a second *buzz* a moment later.

Both of their phones.

Lion and Lamb scooped up their devices quickly to read the incoming flurry of texts from Janie and Victor, respectively. The TV newscast droning in a corner of the lounge had the same breaking news one minute after that.

"Holy God, Chef Nguyen—" Cooper muttered.

"Didn't make it," Veena said.

WEDNESDAY, JANUARY 26

CHAPTER 34

3:13 a.m.

THE CELL phone on Cooper's nightstand vibrated. Lupe gave a short, muffled bark—more of a *woof*—to alert his master. But his master was already on full alert. "Shhh," he whispered. The pup immediately fell silent.

Cooper reached down and grabbed the shotgun he kept clipped to the underside of his bed. Cooper knew the easiest way to disorient a target in his home at night was to call him. While your target fumbles for the phone in the dark, you take your shot; it's over before he's even fully awake. Cooper refused to make that mistake.

Only with the Winchester SXP Defender pump-action shotgun in his hand did Cooper answer his cell.

"Honey," he said calmly, "I told you *never* to call me at work."

The person on the other end of the line hesitated. Cooper heard a confused muttering before the caller finally snarled: "Walk away. That's what Chef Boyardee should've done."

Cooper said, "Red—is this you?"

Click.

CHAPTER 35

EARLY MORNING was the best time to do a home search, in Detective Mickey Bernstein's professional opinion.

Surprise 'em while they're not fully awake and still in their pajamas. When you have a choice, serve that search warrant before the coffee machine drops its first drip.

In this case, however, Mickey *didn't* have a choice.

He'd left Dmitri's around ten o'clock and pulled an all-nighter that involved the commissioner (already on board), his homicide captain (a pushover), a federal judge (an elderly political hack), and his counterpart at the Radnor Police Department (a nobody). Even with the dice loaded, for a while there Mickey wondered if it would actually work. Testimony from a lowlife named Crazy Percy wasn't exactly the strongest piece of evidence. However, that piece was needed for all of the others—most important, the murder weapon in the Hugheses' flower bed—to click into place.

It helped that the judge was a longtime pal of his father's and was used to wild Bernstein hunches. The moment His Honor signed off on the search, Mickey mobilized his team but pretended that the Radnor PD was taking the lead.

They knocked at exactly 6:03 a.m.

Francine was up and looked almost as if she'd been expecting company. *Nobody rolls out of bed this put together,* Mickey thought, *not even a multiple Grammy winner.* She was breathtakingly gorgeous. She even smiled at him.

"Good morning, Detective."

"Sincere apologies for the early-morning call, Ms. Hughes. I hope you understand that an investigation like this follows its own timeline."

Mickey had rehearsed what he would say to Francine on the ride over; this was the best he could do on zero sleep and in his wrinkled clothes. She seemed to take it in stride.

"You've got quite a crew with you," Francine said, looking over his shoulder at the small army of uniformed officers waiting for the signal to proceed. "I'd better put on more coffee."

But even a super-gracious host like Francine couldn't keep up with the sheer number of investigators examining every inch of her house. Little Maddie Hughes tried to pitch in, bringing the uniformed officers homemade chocolate chip cookies ("Our friend Maya helped us bake them last night"), organic lemonade, and helpful pieces of advice such as "Remember to check the bottom of the hall closet!" and "Don't forget the safe room!"

Mickey floated around the house checking in with various teams who'd been assigned different parts of the sprawling mansion. "I'm sure the Oval Office is tucked away somewhere here," grumbled one of the uniforms, who probably lived with a wife and three kids in a cramped Northeast Philly twin. Mickey shot him a look that told him he agreed but *stow it right now.*

Whenever he could, Mickey put eyes on Francine Pearl Hughes. She was eerily calm for a woman watching more than a dozen strangers examine every detail of her home. Calm for a woman suspected of murdering her husband.

Two developments threatened to break that calm. First, Archie's $400,000 Patek Philippe watch, which was reported missing from his body the night of the crime, was found mixed in with Francine's jewelry. How do you misplace nearly half a million bucks?

And second, ammo for a Glock was found in the garage, tucked behind gardening supplies. Not exactly hidden, but a weird place for live rounds.

"Keep searching," Mickey told his men.

"Hey, Detective?" said a tech named DeNardo. Mickey couldn't remember his first name for the life of him. Something like Dan or Drew? Whatever. He was the computer forensics guy working for the Radnor PD.

"Yeah, whaddya got?" Mickey said.

"I found a text to Archie Hughes. Something you probably haven't seen before."

"I doubt that, DeNardo. We seized all of his devices, remember? We've had techs all over his cell phone, his laptop, his tablet—"

"True, but I guarantee you haven't seen this."

This turned out to be a PlayStation 5 hooked up to a flat-screen TV that took up half the wall. This was Archie's toy; the kids weren't allowed to play video games—Mom's rules, no ifs, ands, or buts. Right now, a game was on-screen. Looked like elves with machine guns...or something. Mickey wasn't a gamer.

"What's this, DeNardo? You think one of the pistol-packin' little people did it?"

"Ha-ha, no. This is Worlds of Wrath—the shared-world FPS game?"

"You're speaking Latin, only dorkier," Mickey said.

"I won't get into it, but you fight monsters throughout history while you chat with other players. What makes this game unique is the social media component. You can send screenshots and short clips as messages out into the real world, and vice versa."

Mickey's blank expression encouraged DeNardo to hurry it up.

"Anyway," the computer guy said, "at some point, Archie must have sent Francine a clip of an awesome move or something, because she responded via text. He kept that up, and at first it was all playful, but things devolved over the past few weeks. And then, just a few days before the murder..."

DeNardo thumbed the game controller and a series of text messages from Francine to Archie appeared in giant letters on the flat-screen, as if it were evidence presented in court:

I'm tired of this. So, so tired

And:

You can't hide forever. We have to deal with this

And, most damning of all:

Maybe someone will teach you a lesson someday

CHAPTER 36

8:17 a.m.

"WE'RE TOO late," Lisa Marchese said.

"No such thing as too late," Cooper Lamb replied.

"What are you talking about? This is the textbook definition of *too late!*"

To be fair, this did seem to be the case. The Hughes home was crawling with law enforcement as well as local news teams hoping to capture the perp walk of the century. News vans up and down the street, two—no, now *three* helicopters circling, live feeds picked up internationally. At this moment, there was no other breaking story in the world.

Word had spread with lightning speed: Francine Pearl Hughes was about to be arrested for the murder of her legendary husband.

Thanks to Victor—who was alerted the minute a Mickey Bernstein–friendly judge signed off on the arrest warrant—Cooper had had a half-hour head start, time enough to pick up Francine's attorney and start racing to the Main Line.

But reporters still beat them to the house, most likely tipped off by their secret sources inside the Philly or Radnor PD. They were *not* going to miss this shot.

"Why didn't she call you the moment Bernstein showed up?" Cooper asked Lisa Marchese as they climbed out of his car.

"I don't know, Lamb. My client said she had her kids to worry about."

"Well, you find her and make sure she doesn't say a word to anybody," Cooper said. "I know she's Philly's sweetheart, and she's going to want to reassure her fans, but—"

"Come on," Lisa interrupted. "This isn't my first murder case."

"Yeah, but this is your first Francine Pearl Hughes case. Besides, that's not the point. I want you to stall until I can figure out a way to keep your client from being paraded in front of the cameras. Once that happens, she's as good as guilty."

"Hold on," Lisa said. "You work for *us*, remember? I need you to chase something down."

"Whatever you're about to tell me," Cooper said, gently leading Lisa by the arm toward the house, "I can guarantee it's not as important as the next five minutes."

"Just let me say this! The rumors about the chef are true."

Cooper Lamb stopped dead in his tracks. "Tell me quick."

"Roy Nguyen was up to his puffy white chef's hat in debt. The man was a serious gambler."

"We've all had bad nights at the poker table," Cooper said, pretending like he was hearing this for the first time.

"You don't understand. I'm talking *epic* losses in Atlantic City. To the point that he started stealing from the Hughes household."

"Damn," Cooper said, wondering how long he should feign shock before urging the lawyer inside the house.

The tendons in Lisa's neck were standing out; she was clearly exasperated. "Don't you get it? This is the whole case right here. It was an inside job, engineered by Roy Nguyen. What's more valuable than a Super Bowl ring? Forget that—what's more valuable than *Archie Hughes's* Super Bowl ring?"

"You really think Chef Roy would kill a legend for a hunk of gold?"

"No. I think it was a heist that went horribly wrong, and for some reason, the Philly cops are super-eager to pin it on my client."

"Speaking of . . ."

Letting the lawyer delay things had obviously been a mistake, because here was Francine, perfectly coiffed and handcuffed, being led by Detective Mickey Bernstein down her own neatly manicured garden path, lush even in January.

CHAPTER 37

You're going to want to read these two documents right away, boss—but let me walk you through them. I yanked them from the police servers just a few minutes ago.

The first document is the full report on the gun the police found at the Hughes home. Ballistics has positively linked the weapon to the bullet in Archie's body. Nothing shocking there. I scanned it for obvious mistakes or technical missteps, but it looks solid; I'm confident this is the murder weapon.

The second document, however...now, this one took a little more digging because someone tried to erase it earlier today. But I saved the doc, and I've authenticated it. Hang on to your hat, but the murder weapon? It's been in police evidence before.

That's right. The gun that was used to murder Archie Hughes

spent the past six years in police-evidence lockup. I don't know when it was removed from the evidence room or who checked it out. Give me some time. But the attached should be enough to make it clear that someone who had access to the evidence room was involved in this murder.

CHAPTER 38

Transcript of encrypted message exchange between Veena Lion and Janie Hall

JANIE HALL: OMG.

VEENA LION: You know I hate that, Janie. Skip the drama and just tell me what you found.

HALL: Sorry, V. Mistook you for a human being for a moment there. Human beings, as you may recall, enjoy a dramatic buildup to earth-shattering developments in an ongoing case.

LION: Hate sarcasm even more than dramatic buildups.

HALL: You're no fun. Anyway, guess who lives in a penthouse apartment she can't possibly afford on the salary she earns as a high-profile yet humble nanny?

LION: Maya Rain.

HALL: Like I said, you're no fun. Anyway, I'm kind of shocked here. Based on your notes, she seemed so nice. So normal. And now she's a murder suspect!

LION: Nice and normal on the surface. But it's a carefully constructed surface, although it would probably fool the casual investigator. I need to break through all of that.

HALL: What do you need? Deep backgrounding? Dark-web stuff?

LION: The layout of that fancy penthouse.

CHAPTER 39

9:16 a.m.

"CAN I help you, miss?"

"I'm sorry, could you please just hold this?"

Veena Lion was awkwardly juggling her phone, a legal pad, a fine-tipped black marker, a large cup of coffee from La Colombe, and a mixed bunch of gerbera daisies she'd picked up at a stand on Eighteenth Street.

The overload was intentional. She had just stepped inside the swank lobby of 10 Rittenhouse, and the doorman was trained to help. This would make them instant collaborators. Possibly even allies.

The doorman carefully stabilized the coffee, then held the bouquet of flowers as Veena organized the rest of her supplies. The nervous energy radiating from her movements made the doorman all the more eager to put her at ease.

"It's okay, miss," he purred. "Take your time."

"Thank you so much...Curt," she said, reading his name tag.

"No worries at all, we've all had those days," Curt replied. "Who are you here to see?"

"My friend Yvette Rivera," Veena half lied. "I thought I'd surprise her with flowers and a Fishtown medium roast."

Veena *did* have a friend—well, a former client—who lived at

10 Rittenhouse, an ex-lawyer who was a coffee junkie and loved houseplants, even though none of them lasted long in her care.

"Oh, gosh, Ms. Yvette is out of the country at the moment! Though I know she'd appreciate those gifts."

"Oh," Veena said, pretending to be completely flustered by this information. In fact, she knew Yvette Rivera was in the Caribbean for the month; Janie Hall had double-checked. "Do you, by any chance, like Fishtown medium roast?"

"Never had it, but a hot cup sounds really good right now."

"With my compliments," she said, gesturing to the cup already in his hand. "The flowers too. I'm actually allergic."

"Wow, really? Thanks, Miss..."

"Veena Lion, and it's my pleasure. My father worked in a building like this many years ago." Veena's father had done no such thing. "The people you must see..."

Curt the doorman was sipping the hot coffee and nodding along. Within two minutes, a friendship had been cemented. Now they were just two friends chatting.

"You'd better believe it," Curt said. "Fanciest address in town."

"Yvette told me she'd seen everybody—Patti LaBelle, M. Night, even Kobe now and again."

Curt made an awkward sign of the cross, coffee cup in hand. "God rest his soul." But then he got an impish gleam in his eye. "And speaking of, you know who else I saw a lot of not too long ago?"

Veena leaned forward as if ready to receive nuclear secrets. "Who?"

"Archie Hughes."

"*Really,*" Veena said, feigning astonishment. "Oh my God. That's incredible."

"I know! Look, I'm not supposed to talk about the comings and goings of residents or their guests, but he's pretty hard to forget.

Especially with what's going on right now. You been following the news?"

"Such a shame. That family's already been through a lot."

Some sources required a team of horses to drag even basic information from their mouths. Curt was not that kind of source. He was positively gushing, and it was clear he had been dying to tell someone, anyone, about his personal connection to the murdered football legend. This segued into a story about the last time he'd seen Archie Hughes play at the Linc and what they'd cooked at the tailgate party outside the stadium, but Veena was here only for confirmation that Archie Hughes had regularly visited 10 Rittenhouse—a luxury residence well out of the financial reach of most nannies.

As Curt held forth on how to cook beer brats on a portable grill without drying them out, Veena scanned the control desk of the lobby. She finally found what she'd been looking for.

"I hate to ask you this, Curt, but would it be okay if I used the ladies'?"

Of course it was not a problem. They were friends, weren't they?

CHAPTER 40

THE HALL to the restrooms also led to the elevator bank. Veena knew this from a glance at the floor plan behind Curt's desk. She rode a car down to the subterranean garage and hoped that Curt would be too entranced by the gerbera daisies to notice her in the security camera's feed.

At least not until she confirmed something important.

The garage floor was so immaculate, you could picnic on it. Bentleys and BMWs and Audis filled about half the spaces, and carpeted walkways guided residents from their vehicles to the elevator banks. But only the rare few had access to what Veena had spotted at the lobby control desk: a private elevator leading to the penthouse.

"She can come and go as she pleases," Veena mumbled to herself. "Any visitor she wants can go up without being seen."

Awfully nice setup for a nanny from West Virginia, recruited straight out of Villanova. Definitely not everyone's grad-school experience in the City of Brotherly Love. *So who's paying your bills, Ms. Rain? And what are you giving them in return?* Surely it was something more than helpful parenting tips.

Physical spaces always helped Veena put herself in the minds of her quarries. She saw what they saw, felt the same ground under her shoes, took in the same smells. Janie liked to poke fun at Veena's slightly mystical approach, but it worked. As long as you had uninterrupted time to—

"Excuse me," an irritated voice said, breaking the spell. "What are you doing? You can't be down here!"

"Of course I can," Veena replied even before she turned around to see a tall security guard moving quickly toward her. He was trying to use his size to appear menacing. His hand even hovered near his belt, within reach of a pepper-spray canister. Veena knew she could easily outrun him if it came to that. The man's bulk would slow him down.

Not that she would give him the pleasure of a pursuit.

"How did you even get down here? You can't reach this level without an ID. Let me see yours."

Veena evaluated the man (according to his name tag, his name was Vincent—of course it was) and instantly clocked him as an extreme law-and-order type. The usual avenues of the law were most likely closed to this clod, so he had channeled all that misplaced ambition into this job. And ooh, was he itching to use that pepper spray.

"Vincent," she said, "let me stop you right there. I have an important message from the DA for you."

The man blinked. "For me? Seriously?"

Veena nodded, reached slowly into her pocket, and took out a business card embossed in blue and gold—official city colors—with the name of her sometime employer. The security guard took the business card and examined it with the same reverence a woman would give her best friend's engagement ring.

"What's the message from DA Mostel?" Vincent asked, astonished at this turn of events.

"He said to tell you to go away."

To Vincent's credit, he did as he was told.

CHAPTER 41

11:00 a.m.

IF HIS job didn't depend on his being online, Victor Suarez would never go online.

As it was, Victor left zero traces of himself on the internet. As far as the web was concerned, he had never been born.

He could not understand people who left pieces of their lives all over the place (on Facebook, in Google searches, in countless smartphone apps) for practically anyone to pick up. Did they also leave their doors unlocked and their windows wide open? It was the same thing to Victor.

But most people went through life assuming that whatever personal information they released to their banks (or their favorite online retailers or even their local pizza shops) would be guarded by the employees of those institutions with their lives. The truth was, most organizations' internet security wasn't worth a damn. And the few companies that actually bothered...well, they didn't bother to stay current. State-of-the-art cybersecurity ate into profits, after all.

Lunacy.

Victor poured himself another extra-large mug of strong black coffee—he was trying to graduate from Diet Coke—and spent an hour doing a deep dive into all things Hughes family.

He skipped the online troll stuff. That was basically useless. Anyone with an internet connection could have an opinion about anything; opinions were as common as hydrogen atoms.

No, what Victor loved were the document trails, the paperwork backdrop of the universe: Legal agreements nobody bothered to read. Direct messages that senders assumed were private. Inter-office memos that meant nothing to most people in the outside world...except Victor, who would put them aside until he found the place where each one fit.

All the information on everyone was out there. Sometimes it was in bits and pieces, like a shredded document. You just needed the mental tape and stamina to put it back together again.

Like the Google Maps search Francine had run on her phone a month ago, directions to a modest building in Center City, Philadelphia.

The address felt random until Victor realized it was *the office of the city's top divorce lawyer,* Charles "Chuck" Castrina. From there, it took only a few minutes to figure out the full story. Francine Pearl Hughes had officially retained Castrina's services that very day. Victor's boss, Cooper Lamb, was going to turn cartwheels.

Victor took another slug of coffee, thinking, *Not the same as Diet Coke, not even close,* and kept digging.

Now here was something interesting—the people trashing Francine were not the usual online trolls. These were high-end trolls. Online gamblers, mostly high rollers and whales, all of whom were none too pleased about the postponed NFC championship game. They felt like the rules had been changed; this was not the same bet it had been just a few days ago.

Conspiracy theories were abundant. Many centered on the excesses of the Eagles' father-and-son owners. And quite a lot of them linked Archie Hughes's murder to someone trying to influence the outcome of the game and, possibly, the Super Bowl. Victor believed some of the theories in these private posts; these were people with real money on the line.

Still, there was no smoking gun—nothing concrete to share with Cooper yet.

But Victor continued to dig. He put on another pot of coffee but made a mental note to restock his minifridge with Diet Coke. He could handle only so much coffee.

CHAPTER 42

12:13 p.m.

"I CAN be there by four," Cooper told the annoying jerk on the other end of the line.

"As I told you, there are no appointments available today," said the annoying jerk, who was somehow employed by the top divorce lawyer in the City of Brotherly Love despite being an annoying jerk. "Or for the remainder of the week."

"And as *I* told you, this is a professional matter, not a personal one," Cooper said. "I don't need a divorce lawyer. I'm already happily divorced."

"Doesn't change the fact that there are no appointments available."

"Tell him it's Cooper Lamb. Chuck knows me!"

"Chuck knows a lot of people."

"Do you realize how disrespectful you're being?"

"I think I'm being *extremely* respectful of my boss's time."

Ordinarily, Cooper Lamb would opt for the dripping-with-honey approach. Kindness and flattery—maybe even a harmless bribe—worked most of the time. But ten seconds into the phone conversation, Cooper had known he was up against a different type of gatekeeper. One who'd been hired because he was a sadist who took great delight in swatting away all potential distractions.

"Let me guess," Cooper said. "You're a UPenn grad. You've got that Ivy League arrogance about you."

"Insulting me won't magically open a time slot."

"No, but it might make you realize how much you don't want me showing up uninvited at your office at four p.m."

"Is that a threat?"

"You catch on quick! You *are* a UPenn grad!"

"No, but I am a former Temple running back, and I will happily escort you to the sidewalk if you even dream of showing up here without an appointment. In fact, I hope you do. Then I could skip my evening workout."

Cooper liked this guy. Of course, the dude was still an annoying jerk. But the ex-jock's passion for quick, insulting responses was admirable. Few people took such joy in their work. Even fewer threatened physical violence so eagerly.

"Listen, Mr. Temple Owl, I've gotta go pick my kids up from school. And they get cranky if I don't take them for a snack right away. But you'll be seeing me at four p.m."

"Looking forward to it, Mr. Lamb. I suspect it's been a while since anyone kicked your ass."

"You'd be surprised," Cooper replied. "Do you want me to get you anything from Reading Terminal while I'm there? Maybe a cannoli?"

"I don't want a cannoli."

"Who the hell would turn down a free Termini Brothers cannoli? There's something seriously wrong with you. See you at four."

The annoyance spiked in the assistant's voice: "Don't you d—"

CHAPTER 43

COOPER LAMB gave his best bloodcurdling Bela Lugosi impression: "Hello, children of the *night*."

"It's three o'clock, Dad," said Cooper Jr., hurling his overloaded schoolbag into the back of the car.

"Excellent point. Who's hungry for a midafternoon snack?"

"I'm guessing *you* are," Ariel Lamb said.

"Okay, you talked me into it. Though let's make it Italian pastries at Reading Terminal, since I don't have much time and I have to take you home to your mother and then slingshot back to see a divorce lawyer over at Eighteenth and Market."

"Why do you need to see a divorce lawyer? You and Mom are already divorced."

Cooper exhaled and leaned back in the driver's seat. "So *that's* why she's been so distant lately."

"Dad!" Cooper Jr. exclaimed.

"I kid, and you children know that. Your mother is so amazing, we practically didn't need a lawyer when we parted ways."

"Is that why she owns the house now?"

This was the problem with raising smart, independent-minded children: They knew *exactly* where to slide the shiv between your ribs.

"Like I said, the woman is amazing."

*   *   *

Transcript of conversation between Cooper Lamb and Prentiss Walsh,
executive assistant to divorce attorney Charles Castrina

PRENTISS WALSH: You brought your dog with you?

COOPER LAMB: His name is Lupe. He's here to make sure you
    fight fair, Mr. . . . Prentiss Walsh? Seriously? Your parents named
    you Prentiss? What, did they lose a bet with God or some-
    thing?

WALSH: Gotta be honest, Lamb, I didn't think you'd actually show
    up. But look, Chuck's not in, and I honestly don't expect him
    back the rest of the day. (*Lengthy pause*) Is there really a cannoli
    in that bag?

LAMB: Sorry. Cannoli is for closers.

WALSH: Huh?

LAMB: If you want to be a *closer,* tell Mr. Castrina I'm here, and this
    flaky, crunchy tube of Italian sweetness will be yours.

WALSH: And I told you, he's not—

LAMB: Here. (*There is the sound of a paper bag landing on a desk.*)

WALSH: Wait. I can just have this?

LAMB: Enjoy. In the meantime, Lupe! Make sure Prentiss here
    doesn't come out from behind his desk. (*Lupe growls.*)

WALSH: Come on. You can't do this. This dog shouldn't even be
    here!

LAMB: Just enjoy your snack. I'll be right out. (*A chair creaks. Lupe
    growls again. The chair creaks again.*)

WALSH: (*Shouting*) Chuck! That asshole private eye is here!

LAMB: Thank you for announcing me.

*   *   *

Transcript of conversation between Cooper Lamb and Charles Castrina, Esq.

CHARLES CASTRINA: What, no cannoli for me? I gotta say, Lamb, you bribed the wrong guy. I don't even know that guy's name.

COOPER LAMB: Lucky you. Listen, Chuck, I'll bring you a whole box of goodies from Termini Brothers if you'll be straight with me.

CASTRINA: You know I can't do that, but hey, thanks for stopping in.

LAMB: Fine. I'll show you all my cards. I'm working for Francine. So are you, apparently.

CASTRINA: See, let me stop and correct you right there. I am *not* working for Ms. Pearl.

LAMB: Interesting omission of her married name. Anyway, I hear you, Counselor. There's no need for a divorce lawyer when your spouse is dead. Thing is, Chuck, this is *exactly* why Francine needs our help.

CASTRINA: Oh, it's *our* help now? Are we teaming up? Do continue.

LAMB: They're trying to railroad Francine and I need to know why.

CASTRINA: I'd love to know too. She's a goddamn national treasure and I can't believe anyone would have the nerve to mess with her.

LAMB: So help me out.

CASTRINA: Can't do it, partner. You call it helping Francine; I call it betraying a client's sacred trust, and if she wanted me to break that trust, I'm sure she or one of the overpriced attorneys at Kaplan, DePaulo would let me know. As of right now, they haven't, so I think we're through here.

LAMB: I'm going to give you round one, Counselor. But that just makes me hungrier. I'm going to find out *everything* you know. And some things you wish you knew.

CASTRINA: How are you going to do that? Looks like you're out of cannoli.

CHAPTER 44

4:32 p.m.

FRANCINE PEARL Hughes's arrest early that morning had been met with shock all over Philadelphia; her release from jail after arranging for bail felt like a party.

There were a smattering of protesters, of course, obsessed Birds fans bundled up in Eagles sweatshirts waving posters of outrage. These were the rare Philadelphians who embraced Archie Hughes as the greatest player of all time and yet hated his wife because they blamed her for every time the Eagles stumbled. *Ah, he's distracted by his pop-star trophy wife.* Or: *She should mind her own business and not distract him so much.*

And now the latest variation: *Oh yeah, she was jealous of the team's success so she totally had him killed.*

But those "fans" were in the clear minority. Most of the people gathered outside were there to cheer on Francine. And maybe to be part of a historic moment in the city.

The only person neither protesting nor cheering was Cooper Lamb.

Somehow Francine sensed his presence in the crowd. Maybe it was because he was the only human being standing perfectly still. Once they locked eyes, Cooper began to clap. Slowly. Theatrically.

As if to say: *If you had told me the truth, and all of the truth, you might not be in this position right now.*

He watched Francine carefully, and her reaction sort of stunned him.

Francine Pearl had spent most of her life in the public eye. She knew how to smile even when she felt like dying inside. And to be sure, she smiled at Cooper.

But it was only a half smile. A weary admission that it was hard to keep a positive outlook when your entire world was burning down.

Was it possible she'd loved her husband despite it all?

CHAPTER 45

Transcript of encrypted message exchange between Veena Lion and Janie Hall

JANIE HALL: You busy, V.?

HALL: Okay, no response . . . I've got a lot to share here, so try to keep up.

HALL: Kidding!

HALL: You know how I'm always saying there are some things you're never going to find on a computer? Well, I hit the streets and did some old-school journalism, just like in the old days (three years ago, when you hired me away from the Dying Tabloid That Shall Not Be Named). You're not going to believe what I found.

HALL: I keep teasing and rambling in the hope that you'll respond, but you must be busy, so here goes . . .

HALL: Archie Hughes wasn't paying nightly visits to Maya Rain only. He had another gal pal (sorry; I cringed just typing those words) at another swank penthouse, this one in a condo in Old City. I interviewed the community relations manager. I also interviewed the guy who owns the comic-book shop across the street, and boy, was he happy to talk to me.

HALL: Comic Book Guy said he used to see Archie Hughes duck into the building from an entrance off an alley. He had a perfect view from the front window of his nerd emporium. He says he may even have a pic or two on his phone, because he bragged to his buddies. I'll forward it as soon as he sends it to me. I think he's trying to get me to go out for a drink with him in exchange for the photo; I'll have to break his heart gently.

HALL: Suzanne, the CR manager for the building, was a bit more reticent at first. But she opened up a little once I dropped the strong hint that I worked for the DA. (Not a lie, right? I mean, I work for you, you're currently working for Mostel...)

HALL: Anyway, I kept at her and she finally admitted Archie Hughes had been a frequent visitor to the penthouse. The current occupant of which is Rosalind "Roz" Cline. Somebody you might want to speak to. I'm thinking, *Kept woman*. But Suzanne didn't want to speculate on that. Didn't want to go anywhere near that, in fact.

VEENA LION: Good work, Janie.

HALL: There you are! Were you just letting me ramble on?

LION: You shouldn't ever imply you work for the DA, because that's not true. Find another way next time.

HALL: Sorry, V.

CHAPTER 46

Transcript of conversation between Veena Lion and Suzanne Hingston, community relations manager of the Villas at Elfreth's Alley

VEENA LION: Let me make myself clear. I work for District Attorney Eliott K. Mostel. So unless you and your management company want me to come back with a subpoena and a small army of investigators...

SUZANNE HINGSTON: We take our residents' privacy seriously. And shouldn't a police detective be interviewing potential witnesses?

LION: The district attorney's office routine employs its own investigators.

HINGSTON: Well, you don't even have a warrant. I know that much. I checked.

LION: Okay, fine.

HINGSTON: What are you doing? Oh, wait—*do* you have a warrant in there? Listen, I'm not trying to start something with the DA or anything—

LION: Calm down. This is not a warrant. This is five hundred dollars cash. I'll wait if you want to count it.

HINGSTON: I don't need to count it.

LION: But you're not taking it either.

HINGSTON: I'm seeing only *half* a warrant there.

LION: Ah. (*Pause*) You know, used to be I could buy some cooperation with only a quarter of a warrant.

HINGSTON: The times they are a-changing.

LION: Just make sure it's a full warrant's worth of information, Ms. Hingston.

HINGSTON: Thank you. (*Pause*) Her name is Rosalind Cline. She used to work as a hostess in one of those big casinos in Atlantic City. Don't ask me which one, because I don't know. All I know is she's still back and forth to AC all the time. I think she's there more than she's here.

LION: Wouldn't her employment history be in her rental application?

HINGSTON: If she were the one paying the bills, sure. But a private company takes care of it.

LION: Go on.

HINGSTON: What do you mean, go on? What else is there? I hardly know her, and you'd have to pay me a hell of a lot more than a grand if you want me opening up her personal files.

LION: I don't need her files.

HINGSTON: What, then?

LION: Just tell me about her.

HINGSTON: I don't know what you mean. Who cares what I think about her?

LION: When you see her walk through the lobby, what goes through your mind? Pretend I paid you a thousand dollars to tell me the truth.

HINGSTON: (*Pause*) Honestly? I think, *Who does that bitch think she is?*

LION: Well, that was candid.

HINGSTON: It's not just me. Everybody here hates her. She's a lousy tipper. And I don't care how good-looking you are, that doesn't give you permission to treat people like dirt. Swear to Christ, some of the people in this place are horrible human beings.

CHAPTER 47

REPORT TO C. LAMB BY V. SUAREZ
WEDNESDAY, JANUARY 26
(SENT WITH ENCRYPTION AND RED-FLAGGED, WITH
DELIVERY CONFIRMATION)

Take a look at the attached video clip and isolated frames, then come back to this document.

Yes, that is Francine Pearl Hughes in that video. (Rest assured, I used a facial-recognition program to confirm the match.)

I didn't start out looking for Ms. Hughes in this particular location. I had been attempting to place her near the art museum on the night of the murder. I was not successful, so I expanded my search geographically and chronologically. Within minutes, I had a match elsewhere in the city, three days before the murder.

Details on the video:

Ms. Hughes and her male companion are on the 100 block of Chestnut Street, closer to Second Street, in front of a Belgian restaurant/brewpub. This was at 9:47, according to the time stamp from the surveillance camera.

I don't know if Francine and her companion dined at the restaurant before the images were captured; a standard check on all of their credit cards came up with no record of either of them dining anywhere that evening. It's possible that they paid cash. I have a call in to the restaurant's owner; I'll update you when I know more.

While it is difficult to make out specific details from the video, I took the best single frames, enlarged them, and used image-enhancement software to bring things into focus. As you can see, Ms. Hughes and her companion are holding hands, hugging, and embracing.

Even without image enhancement, you can probably recognize the identity of her companion. He's a hard man to miss: Eagles tight end Jimmy Tua.

CHAPTER 48

COOPER LAMB / VOICE MEMO #0126-735

To whom it may concern: This evening I'm headed back down to the Linc, the very place where Eagles dare, on Sunday, to clinch the NFC championship. By my side is my faithful companion Lupe, who is expert at working the crowds. Even a crowd as hostile as the one I'm about to face.

Yeah, it's safe to say the Birds ain't gonna be happy to see me. I am definitely a distraction they don't need.

But you know what? I don't give a shit. I've got questions that demand answers. Questions for Mr. James "Jimmy" Tua. Specifically, this: Why were you fooling around with your best friend's wife just three days before he was murdered? As the kids say, it's not a good look.

What do we know about Jimmy Tua? For one, he's kind of a genius. Scratch that—he's a *certified* genius. Victor found the test results and everything. And that high-powered mind is encased in two hundred and seventy pounds of sheer muscle.

So you'd think a big guy with a big brain would know better than to step out with his bestie's best girl. Especially in public.

Yeah, I know. Chestnut Street was dark, and it was sort of late...for the Quaker City, anyway. But still, you're two of the most recognizable figures in Philly, and you're out canoodling in public?

Francine and Jimmy *had* to know what they were doing. Which tells me that they'd reached a point in their affair when they really didn't care if anyone saw them or not. You don't go waving matches and a can of gasoline around unless you're ready to burn the house down.

There are more pieces on the board than anyone is willing to acknowledge. We've got Francine and Jimmy and, possibly, Archie and Maya. Though Francine and Maya don't act as if they're opponents on the battlefield of love. They're downright chummy, in fact.

So maybe Archie and Francine were going to separate amicably, and their new lovers were waiting in the wings? That's right, ladies and germs, an Eagles pun. But if that's the case, who killed Archie? And did it have anything to do with Francine and Jimmy Tua?

There are at least two people who know the truth about them. One of them just made bail and has clammed up on the advice of her attorney—i.e., my employer. The other is currently practicing for one of the most important games of his career. And I'm about to ruin his day.

CHAPTER 49

THE FIELD was buzzing with nervous energy. Practice squads were running through passes and rushes with the active players, trying their best to imitate the Giants and impress the higher-ups. Everybody's gotta serve somebody.

Cooper Lamb found Jimmy Tua hydrating along with a handful of his teammates. His skin was slick with sweat, even in this bitter afternoon cold.

"Hey, Jimmy," Cooper said.

"Hey, it's the private eye with the cute dog," Jimmy said. "What's up?"

"Can we take this conversation to the sidelines?"

"That's where we happen to be standing, my man. Besides, I have no secrets from my teammates."

"This might be an exception. It's about Francine."

There was an instant electric-shock jolt from the burly players gathered around Jimmy Tua. It was as if Cooper had set off a firecracker at their cleats. But Jimmy himself didn't flinch. He gave Cooper a murder stare, as if daring him to go on. Naturally, Cooper dared to go on.

"More specifically, about the two of you," he said. "Being together."

Yep, check, please—that was the unspoken attitude of the surrounding players, who began to drift away from Jimmy, Cooper, and Lupe. They didn't stray too far. They didn't want to be directly involved in the ugly conversation that was about to happen, but they stayed within earshot just in case Jimmy Tua tried to rip the private eye's head off. The last thing they needed before the NFC championship game was *another* murder.

"What are you saying?" Jimmy said quietly.

"Do I have to spell it out for you? I thought you were a smart Bird."

"Yeah, you'd better spell it out, big man."

"Fine. I'm saying you've been having an affair with your best friend's wife. The same woman who was just arrested for the murder of your best friend. But I guess that's not as important as the big game this Sunday—"

By the time Cooper spoke the words *this Sunday,* Jimmy was already charging forward. But Cooper was fully aware the attack was coming. He'd watched the tension and anger building in the huge man's body from the beginning. It was as if Jimmy had been braced for this line of questioning, but Cooper was the only guy who'd been stupid enough to ask.

To the untrained eye, it probably looked as if the players were running a small drill by the sidelines. There was Jimmy Tua rushing forward like a missile and six other players scrambling toward him as if to intercept that missile.

And standing directly between Jimmy and the players: Cooper Lamb.

Cooper knew that only one thing would prevent Jimmy Tua from plowing him into the freshly cut Bermuda grass at their feet. And that one thing was Jimmy's IQ.

Jimmy Tua was a powerhouse full of rage, but he was also a

thinking man. And a thinking man wouldn't throw away his career over an insult from a PI.

(*Would he?* Cooper prayed he wouldn't.)

Right up to the last second, Cooper thought he might have made a grave miscalculation. This is how his life would end. And in front of his beloved pooch, no less.

Jimmy Tua's nose came to a sudden halt a few millimeters away from Cooper's. Only then did Cooper understand that he'd been spared. Fortunately, he'd held his ground the entire time. If he was about to be snapped in half over a tight end's knee, he'd do it on his terms—no flinching.

"You don't know what the hell you're talking about," Jimmy said.

"Didn't know you were a big fan of Belgian beer," Cooper said. "Especially right before a championship game."

There was the instant spark of recognition. Jimmy knew that Cooper knew. How Cooper knew didn't matter.

Cooper had saved this piece of information for this specific moment—it was meant to push Tua completely over the edge and get him to say something stupid. Victor had talked to the brewpub's owner as well as the bartender who'd been on duty that night.

Oh yeah, Francine Pearl Hughes and Jimmy Tua were there. Oh yeah, they were making out. But a huge cash tip was incentive enough for the bartender to keep his mouth shut.

That is, until Victor made it sound like he was affiliated with the Federal Bureau of Investigation. No cash tip can cover that kind of tab.

The rage inside Tua built to the point where Cooper thought the tight end might actually pummel him. Cooper could smell the fury on the man's breath before three linemen grabbed Tua and pulled him away. It was a struggle.

"I know exactly who you are, asshole! Where you live and what you do."

"Hey, I know who you are too," Cooper said, bright smile on his face. "You're Jimmy Tua! All-Pro, right?"

Phone call between Cooper Lamb and his children

COOPER LAMB: Kids! You're never going to believe this!
ARIEL LAMB: What's that, Dad?
LAMB: Guess who I just met—Jimmy Tua! What a great guy.

CHAPTER 50

Transcript of private conversation between Cooper Lamb and Lisa Marchese, senior partner at Kaplan, DePaulo, and Marchese

LISA MARCHESE: What the hell is that?

COOPER LAMB: This is a digital recording device. As per Pennsylvania law, I am notifying you that I am taping this conversation.

MARCHESE: I'm sitting at a bar having a late supper. Do we have to make this so formal?

LAMB: Clearly, Counselor, you're also working so that you may expense your small plates and double martinis.

MARCHESE: Are you going to update me on what you've dug up on the chef or do I have to buy you dinner first?

LAMB: No, I'll wait until you're done.

MARCHESE: What's the matter with you? I'm girding myself for a long night. People at the firm are losing their minds... not that I have to explain myself to you.

LAMB: Yeah, you kind of do. Because if you want me to help you save Francine, you're going to have to come clean with me.

MARCHESE: We're going to save Francine because she's innocent.

LAMB: Well, that's not what it looks like to the police. Unless there's something you're not telling me.

MARCHESE: Like what?

LAMB: Like *everything*. Whatever you know, I need to know it too. Which is why I brought this recording device.

MARCHESE: I truly have no idea what you're talking about.

LAMB: That's the problem we keep running into, isn't it? Everybody's tiptoeing around the truth like it's an infectious disease or something. For instance, why didn't you tell me Francine hired Chuck Castrina?

MARCHESE: Keep your voice down!

LAMB: Ooh, that got your attention. I guess I should be grateful you weren't taking a sip of your drink, otherwise I would have been treated to a shower of Grey Goose.

MARCHESE: Who told you about Chuck?

LAMB: No, Counselor. You first.

MARCHESE: Turn that thing off.

LAMB: Do you promise to tell me the whole truth and nothing but?

MARCHESE: (*To bartender*) Danny, can we move to the booth in the corner? Thanks, hon.

LAMB: I'm taking that as a yes.

CHAPTER 51

THE RESTAURANT was an old-school steak house on the first floor of the Market Street building that housed the offices of Kaplan, DePaulo, and Marchese. It had charming waitstaff in vests, portraits of local notables hung on the walls, excellent cheesy bread in a basket offered gratis. So many of the attorneys dined here regularly, it was the firm's de facto cafeteria, the place to be seen. If you wanted privacy, you headed to the fringes of downtown. Or possibly to New Jersey. For now, however, Lisa Marchese would have to settle for the quiet zone of the corner booth near the kitchen.

"Is that thing off?"

"Here you go. Powered down completely. If you want, I can dunk it into your double martini. Now, tell me what you've got."

Marchese frowned. "I'm not going to tell you, but I can show you. If you promise—and I can't stress this enough, Cooper Lamb—if you promise this information will stay inside your skull. No cute leaks to the press, none of your usual bullshit."

"If it helps Francine, then yes."

Lisa dug into her briefcase. Cooper thought she was about to bring out a file folder marked CONFIDENTIAL or something absurd like that, but instead it was an iPad. She quickly entered a password, then another one to open a vault file, and then looked into the camera to activate the facial-recognition software.

All of which was a huge relief to Cooper, because if it existed digitally, his man Victor would have no problem snagging a copy. He could pluck information from an Apple device as skillfully as a Dickensian pickpocket lifted a wallet.

She rotated the iPad toward him. "You want to know about the real Archie Hughes? Read these."

CHAPTER 52

Transcript of phone call between Cooper Lamb and his children

ARIEL LAMB: How was your meeting with the divorce lawyer?

COOPER LAMB: The dude dodged my questions like a total pro. He didn't even respond to my cannoli bribe!

ARIEL: Not everyone is a sugar monster, old man.

LAMB: Speaking of monsters, look who just showed up—it's my best frenemy, Veena Lion! Say hello to Ms. Lion, children.

COOPER JR. and ARIEL: (*In singsongy unison*) "Hello to Ms. Lion, children."

VEENA LION: (*Laughs*) They're definitely *your* kids. Hello, Coop and Ariel! My sincere apologies for taking your father away for a business meeting.

COOPER JR.: It's okay. We have homework anyway.

ARIEL: Do you always conduct your business meetings in a bar?

LION: I would like to tell you otherwise, but yeah, pretty much.

LAMB: Wait, wait—how do you know we're in a bar, young lady?

ARIEL: Only, like, about a *million* clues. Glasses clinking, murmuring voices, the sound of a cable sports channel in the background. Also, it's nine p.m. Where else would you be this time of day?

LAMB: Well, I hate to break it to you, Ms. Junior Detective, but
    you are one hundred percent wrong.

LION: (*To server*) Miss? I'd like a Hendrick's martini up with three
    blue-cheese-stuffed olives.

ARIEL: You were saying, Father?

LAMB: I was saying—ahem—you are one hundred percent wrong
    about the cannoli. Nobody turns down a Termini Brothers
    cannoli. The lawyer is clearly hiding something, and that's why
    I'm here in this church basement discussing my most recent
    case with Ms. Lion.

LION: Wow. The ease with which you lie to your poor children.

ARIEL: Uh-huh. Just make sure you take a cab home from the
    church basement. You shouldn't be driving.

LAMB: I will take all appropriate measures, children. Don't you
    worry about your old man.

COOPER JR.: See you tomorrow morning, Dad!

"I have something very important to show you."

Veena smiled and beckoned with her fingers. "Oh yeah. Gimme."

"Hang on now," Cooper said, smiling. "This stays between us. I mean, like, in *the vault,* okay?"

"Of course. *The vault.* Why would this be any different?"

The vault was their mutually agreed-upon term for a discussion that would remain completely off the record, no matter what. A free zone for private eyes. Even if those private eyes were threatened with prison by a federal judge.

"This lies deep, deep, deep in the vault."

"Fine. I'll keep it in the deepest, darkest chamber of the vault."

Cooper nodded, then slid a manila folder across the table, which was beaded with moisture from their drinks. Veena placed her fingertips on top of the folder and began to pull, but Cooper kept an iron grip on it.

"What is it?" Veena asked.

"This is ugly stuff."

"I've probably seen worse."

"Sure, but not from a national hero."

Cooper meant it. Hell, it had been painful for *him* to read. He almost wished he could bleach the memory of this file out of his brain cells. What was that old saying, about how you should never meet your heroes? It was too late for Cooper to meet Archie Hughes but not too late for him to learn what kind of man he'd been.

"It's fine," she replied. "Don't tell anyone, but I'm not much of a sports fan."

Cooper nodded and released his grip on the folder. Veena removed her sunglasses and flipped open the file.

Usually, Veena Lion gave very little away. Her frustrated opponents called her "the Sphinx." But as Veena read the series of printouts in the file, her eyes widened and her jaw dropped just a little. She might have been a stone-cold professional, but she was also a human being.

The file contained a series of screenshots of texts, each on its own page.

Where are you

    Your appointment can't be taking that long

    Hey, baby, let me know where you are, I'm worried about you, that's all

    Come on, text me back

    Baby, where are you

    You there?

    Baby, come on

Where are you, anyway? I called the salon and they said you'd left hours ago. This is NOT cool

Don't you dare ignore me, bitch

You had better call me back now, I swear to God

I can have your phone tracked, you know. You want me to do that?

F██ me

I see where you are

Really love to know what your fans would think of you right now, you f█████ whore

There's not enough fancy makeup in the world to cover up a broken nose, you hear me? CALL ME NOW

And the texts raged on and on and on. "Well, this is completely awful," Veena said, closing the file.

"Warned you," Cooper replied.

"Here's what I don't get."

"What more could you want? Archie Hughes was an abusive son of a bitch and no one knew it except Francine."

"That part is perfectly clear. What I don't get is, why would you share these with me? Do I need to tell you how much Mostel would love to get his hands on this file?"

"Because we want the same thing," Cooper said. "The truth, no matter what. Remember?"

"But I'm working for the DA, and you're trying to keep Francine Pearl Hughes out of prison. Sharing this with me doesn't help you one bit."

Cooper took a large swallow of his drink. "Normally, I'd agree with you. But in this case, the texts came directly from Francine's lawyer. Which I think is very interesting, don't you?"

"I do," Veena said, drumming her fingers on the bar. "Why would Francine's own lawyer willingly hand over a big fat motive that pretty much damns her client?"

"Lisa Marchese is one thousand percent certain that Francine didn't kill her husband."

"So what? Easy enough for her to hire someone to do it for her. A pro who turned out to be a little careless or forgot to make it look like a proper carjacking."

"No. I also believe Francine had nothing to do with it."

"You're being paid to believe her," Veena said.

"I'm working for her," Cooper replied, "but I believe her anyway. Our killer is still out there."

CHAPTER 53

11:02 p.m.

"SO WHO do you like?"

"Nobody on this planet at the moment," Veena said, stirring the dregs of her second martini with a single blue-cheese-stuffed olive speared on a wooden toothpick.

"I'm sorry," she continued. "I can't stop thinking about those texts. How can two human beings be so awful to each other? You start out with the best intentions, maybe you even think you're in love. You promise to take care of each other, be there for each other no matter what. But time passes, as it always does, and there comes the inevitable day when all of those promises are forgotten. You can't remember why you're even together. How did you end up trapped like this with a person you can barely stand? Do all relationships come with an expiration date?"

"No, no," Cooper said. "I meant who do you like for the game on Sunday? I'm waiting for a call from Red. You want in on some of the action?"

Veena didn't know if she should laugh or dump the remnants of her martini over Lamb's head. Instead, she slipped on her sunglasses and tried to force herself to sober up. They poured them strong here.

"Sure, I'll play along," Veena said. "Put me down for a thousand bucks on, um, whatever team is *not* the Eagles."

Cooper grinned. "You have no idea who's playing, do you?"

"Does it ultimately matter? Overpaid gladiators in heavy padding dancing back and forth on a lawn. I mean, what is created? What possible benefit is there to mankind? Is there a point other than distracting beer-guzzling, nacho-eating Americans for an evening of capitalism and brutality?"

"I don't know, V. Maybe it's a good thing that we channel our collective aggressions into something frivolous rather than killing each other on the streets."

"Plenty of people get killed anyway."

Cooper held up a hand as if calling for a time-out. "Hang on," he said, sputtering a little. "Rewind a sec. How can you *not* bet on the home team? How are you even a Philadelphian?"

"No idea," Veena said. "But it will be worth losing every penny of that thousand bucks for the reaction you just gave me."

Cooper smiled and leaned back. "Nicely done, Ms. Lion."

"Rowrr."

"Baaaaa."

They locked eyes. There were no more elements of the case to discuss. They'd run out of jokey banter. It was just the two of them, practically alone in this bar, with the server washing martini glasses and generally minding his own damn business.

The phone on the bar top buzzed, breaking the spell. Cooper scooped up his cell. "Hey! Red! Glad I caught you, man."

Veena watched Cooper as he placed their bets. He really did put her down for a grand! She had been kidding, but oh, well. The words coming out of his mouth were all nonsense to her. But his mouth curled occasionally into a boyish, playful smile, even though Red on the other end of the line couldn't see it. Was that meant for her? Veena didn't care. She wanted it anyway.

Without notice or preamble, Veena leaned forward and pressed her lips against his. She delighted in the surprised murmur that escaped his mouth—"Mmm, lemme get back to you, Red"—before pressing her case further. She heard his phone hit the bar top, and not gently. He cupped one side of her face with his hand and settled in for a long, searching kiss, totally unafraid of being seen.

Veena was relieved. Cooper Lamb was just as drunk as she was.

During a break in the action she whispered into his ear, "I like us like this."

"So do I. Let's go to your place."

"No," she said softly. "I mean I like us like this, at this moment in time. No expectations, just us. Nothing to complicate things. I don't ever want to hate you."

"Just keep my mouth busy so I won't say anything stupid."

Ah, but it was too late. The moment was over. Veena leaned back on her stool. The bartender busied himself with washing pint glasses and trying very hard not to notice their impromptu make-out session.

"Danny, can we get the check?"

Cooper blinked. "So that's a no to your place?"

"Right away, Danny."

She had to give Cooper credit. He tried to play it cool and gently nudge her back into the zone she'd just left: Touching her hand. Asking her to take off her sunglasses again. Suggesting they split a rideshare, you know, so they could discuss the next steps of the case. Veena gently rebuffed all these advances and gathered her things. "Give Lupe a kiss for me."

"Hang on. The *dog* gets a kiss too?"

"Just be glad you didn't bring Lupe to the bar. You would have been completely out of luck."

CHAPTER 54

REPORT TO C. LAMB BY V. SUAREZ
WEDNESDAY, JANUARY 26
(SENT WITH ENCRYPTION AND TRIPLE RED-FLAGGED,
WITH DELIVERY CONFIRMATION)

Boss—this is important. Please read this before you talk to anyone else. I have solid confirmation on the Archie Hughes abuse allegations.

This comes right from a private server in the Radnor PD. As I've mentioned before, almost every police department's intranet is a joke. They might as well pin every confidential file to the nearest utility pole. But the one in the Radnor superintendent's office is different; they spent a bit of money keeping this one locked down tight, with no connection to the internet.

Of course this is no big deal for me. I have a source inside the Radnor PD who has a way to access this server. You've told me time and again that you don't want to know how the sausage is made. Fair enough. But just know that the full cost of this particular sausage will be included in my next invoice.

On that confidential server were two reports of calls to the Hughes house, one in October, another in late December. The circumstances were vague initially but were later reported as a dispute between the gardener and the pool-maintenance man (October) and teenage kids goofing around in the neighborhood (December).

However, these calls were downgraded after the fact. The initial reports were clearly domestic violence calls, and both reports ended up on the superintendent's private server.

There is no record of who placed the reports on the confidential server, but it's fair to assume that this was the decision of the superintendent, as he is the only one with access.

I've attached the compete files, which include photos of Francine Pearl Hughes. Needless to say, they are graphic.

My contact knows what is in these reports. Don't worry; this person is rock solid and trustworthy. There will be no leaks. But my contact did pass along a warning to me to watch my back.

So I'm passing the same along to you. Keep your eyes open, boss.

THURSDAY, JANUARY 27

CHAPTER 55

COOPER LAMB / VOICE MEMO #0127-735

Once more I sit in an ice-cold car on a freezing street in downtown Philadelphia. I think I've been doing this job too long. When I die and my life flashes before my eyes, about eighty percent of it will be me sitting in an ice-cold car on a freezing street in downtown Philadelphia.

Except this time is different, because this city is on the verge of exploding and I'm watching a bunch of volatile chemicals swirl around, ready to combust at any moment.

Speaking of volatile...

Hi, Maya Rain. Your lights are on. You awake up there? Cleaning up messes? Did you fall asleep studying? Or are you entertaining someone special at this late hour? Perhaps the same someone who is paying for that condo, since I know even a top-drawer nanny couldn't afford a place like that.

Yes, I know this is sort of stalkerish behavior. Scratch that—this is *straight-up* stalker behavior. But Maya is the one piece that doesn't quite fit. Doesn't make sense that someone this special would be involved in this case by accident.

Okay, yeah, I heard what I just said about Maya being special. Victor, you can stop rolling your eyes.

Let's talk about the other volatile chemicals at play. Starting with the chemicals in my own lab.

Francine is potentially the most volatile chemical of all. In a weird way, it'd be so much easier if I knew she did it, because then I could take steps to minimize the blowback. Hell, those psycho texts from Archie would acquit her in the eyes of most Philadelphians. The bastard essentially threatened to break her beautiful face. Not a good look, Mr. Greatest of All Time.

But I know she didn't kill Archie, even if she's not telling me everything. But why is that? Is it because she's protecting her children? If so, from what? Let's say Archie and the Sables were up to some shady Super Bowl stuff. Any kind of shame associated with fraud the children might feel is nothing compared to seeing their mother sent to prison for life. Must be something else.

Who can tell me about that something?

Maybe Lisa Marchese. Wait—*of course* she knows, otherwise she wouldn't have handed me those text messages, right? Victor, redouble your efforts on her law firm's servers. I know you've already searched them, but there must be something in a file somewhere. Maybe there's a hidden server inside Marchese's office, one that requires the talents of one of your secret sausage men.

Okay, I can't believe I said that last part out loud.

Who else, who else ... well, who else is obvious. I'm parked outside of her condo right now.

Maya Rain had a front-row seat to the Hughes Family

Drama for the past few months. She's in a unique position to know most, if not all, of what Francine is so desperate to hide.

Maybe I should just climb out of this cold car, walk up to Maya's condo, and ask her in person.

CHAPTER 56

1:04 a.m.

"WHAT'S THIS?"

"One hundred American dollars, my friend. And this is the part where you nod your head, pocket the cash, sit back, and return to whatever show you're watching on your cell phone."

Curt the doorman sighed, leaning back in his chair. "I really can't do this again."

"Again?" Cooper Lamb asked. "What, do you have total strangers handing you a hundred bucks all the time?"

Lupe, waiting patiently, let out a tiny yelp as if to underscore his master's question.

"You'd be surprised what people offer me to let them sneak into this building. Look, brother, I need my job more than I need a hundred bucks."

"So now we're negotiating. Cool. Tell you what—I'm going to leave three hundred dollars with you for safekeeping. Who knows how dangerous it is up there? One of your residents might try to mug me and my dog."

"Uh-huh."

"And if I don't come back down to reclaim my money, just pocket it until you see me again."

"I've got an awful memory for faces."

"Even dog faces?"

Curt the doorman tucked the money into his breast pocket without so much as another glance at Cooper, as if to prove how bad he was with faces. Cooper walked to the elevator and rode it up to the penthouse level. Thanks to Victor, he knew exactly where to go and which doorbell to ring. And hey, the lights were on.

"Come on, Lupe, let's see if your favorite nanny is awake."

Lupe matched Cooper's pace the entire length of the hallway, though he did give him a side-eye glance: *We really doing this? Bothering this poor lady at one o'clock in the morning?*

She answered almost instantly, which both relieved and worried Cooper. Had she been expecting him? Did she catch a glimpse of him down on Eighteenth Street; was she reverse-stalking him?

"Hey, Maya," Cooper said. "Is this a bad time?"

CHAPTER 57

Transcript of private conversation between Cooper Lamb and Maya Rain, captured using an ambient recording app on Lamb's smartwatch

MAYA RAIN: Hello, Mr. Lamb. And hello, Lupe! So great to see you again.

COOPER LAMB: Great to see me or great to see the pooch? And please, call me Cooper.

RAIN: Actually I was talking to Lupe. I know you make house calls, Cooper. I just wasn't expecting you at *my* house.

LAMB: And this is a very nice house, in one of the most desirable areas of the city. Do you have, like, seventeen roommates or something?

RAIN: No. I live alone. And right now you're about to say, "Gee, the Hughes family must pay really well if you can afford a place like this."

LAMB: That would be rude, and I am nothing if not professional. I was about to insinuate that you had a sugar daddy.

RAIN: I don't have one of those either. I'm just a simple girl from West—

LAMB: Virginia, yeah, you've mentioned that. Can I come inside to talk for a minute?

RAIN: Sure, but not with your recording device running.

LAMB: I don't have any recording devices running. (*Extended silence*) Okay, fine. How did you know?

RAIN: Because you are a professional . . . or something like that.

LAMB: Fair enough, Ms. Rain. Here, I am officially turning off my top secret recording device, which no one ever notices.

RAIN: Oh, I noticed—

CHAPTER 58

"I FIGURED it was a smartwatch," Maya Rain continued. "Men don't wear wristwatches anymore, not since the smartphone came along. Come on inside. Can I get you something to drink? Some water for Lupe?"

"Actually, would you mind if I used your restroom for a moment? I spent a long time down in my car in the freezing cold working up the courage to knock on your door."

Cooper used a casual tone of voice meant to put her at ease. He was also taking a mental snapshot of her condo. Spare, high-end furniture (possibly rented), generic framed art, not much in the way of screens or electronics. If his daughter, Ariel, were here, she would tag this place a "grown-up apartment," a jab at his own cluttered digs.

"The guest bathroom is to your left," Maya said. "And before you waste too much of your time, because it's awfully late and I suspect we've both had a long day, you're not going to find anything personal in the medicine cabinet."

"I'm sorry?"

"You know—no telltale prescription bottles, no bag of heroin taped to the inside of the toilet tank, nothing like that. Isn't that what detectives do, pretend to use the bathroom and then engage in a little impromptu profiling?"

"Uh, I really just have to relieve my bladder. But thanks for the heads-up."

She's good, Cooper thought as he closed the door behind him. *Too good to be true.* Of course he intended to scour her bathroom for any revealing details. Just because she'd told him not to bother didn't mean he wouldn't try.

But as Maya had warned, there was literally nothing to reveal, except that she had a taste for expensive grooming products and furnishings. The vanity was white Carrara marble on top, solid wood below, with soft-close drawer glides and brushed-chrome fixtures. This guest bathroom was pristine enough to perform brain surgery in. Cooper felt like a heathen using the facilities.

Back in the living room, Maya was waiting for him with an ice-filled tumbler garnished with a wedge of lemon.

"I probably shouldn't," Cooper said. "I still have to drive Lupe home."

"It's mineral water, to help replace your fluids."

"I didn't have to go *that* badly."

"What did you want to talk about?" she asked, guiding him to her midcentury-modern couch, made of an impossibly soft woven fabric and supported by stubby walnut legs.

"Can I be totally straight with you?" Cooper asked as they sat down. "I'm trying to save your boss, and for whatever reason, she's reluctant to tell me the truth. I know she didn't do it. I'm just looking for evidence so I can prove it to the rest of the world. You're in a unique position to help me do that."

"You want me to betray my employer's confidence?"

"No. I just want to know what you saw."

"Which is also betraying her trust."

"Maya, I'm just going to come out and ask you: Did you see Archie hit Francine?"

For the first time, the nanny seemed speechless. This was good. Cooper pressed his advantage by pulling out prints of the photos that Victor had found. He fanned them out on her walnut coffee table. It was difficult to look at them, even though he'd seen them before.

"Oh," Maya said.

"Look, I know Francine didn't kill Archie. But after seeing these, I wouldn't blame her if she had." Instead of looking at the photos, Cooper studied Maya's face. She was taking it all in, but there was a hardness there, as if she were unwilling to *let* it all in. He saw a professional detachment in her eyes. Cooper doubted they taught that in grad school.

"Yes," Maya said after a while. "There were incidents."

"You saw Archie hit Francine."

Maya nodded. "I asked her if she needed my help finding someone to talk to. She swore me to secrecy but also assured me that this was nothing new, and she knew how to handle her husband. I knew better than to press."

"Even as a crime happened right before your eyes?"

"This is just between you and me, Cooper," she said quietly. "But Francine gave as good as she got."

"Does that include murder?"

Maya smiled and shook her head. "I should know better than to talk to a private eye at one in the morning."

"Come on, you know how this looks. And it's going to look even worse when it all comes out. I'm trying to help Francine."

"When all you've got is a hammer," Maya said, "everything looks like a nail."

"And that means?"

"You think I was Archie's side piece, that he bought me this penthouse apartment and filled it with beautiful things—a taste of the good life I'd always craved back in West Virginia. Is that right?"

"If Archie wasn't paying for it, who is?"

"That's none of your business." Maya reached out and touched the side of Cooper's face. "Don't get me wrong. I like you."

"I like you too," Cooper said, then gently took her wrist and guided her hand back to her lap. "Which is why I hope you're not hiding something. Or worse. Because I'm not going to stop until I find out what really happened."

"I know," she said. "Which is why you should be careful out there."

"Why is everyone always telling me that? Do I have a bull's-eye pinned to the back of my jacket or something? And if so, does it at least match my socks?"

Maya stood up, indicating their late-night meeting was over. Lupe took the cue and popped up from the floor expectantly.

"If multiple people tell you the same thing," she said, "it just might be the truth."

CHAPTER 59

"I NEED to see you. Right now."

"Cooper, it's two in the morning. I've got a long drive ahead of me. Don't you remember? We did this dance already."

"It's not about that. I'm talking about our case."

"I have to leave for Atlantic City in . . . ugh, like four hours."

"It will just take a minute. You and Janie hitting the craps tables?"

Veena Lion paused. She was wide awake and wouldn't be going to sleep anytime soon. She'd been at her kitchen table poring over stacks of documents and was feverishly mapping out their case and all of its possible tangents on a legal pad. She'd tried to shake off the effects of the martinis (and her bar-side make-out session with Cooper) with work and endless cups of black coffee. None of it helped. Veena felt jittery. Maybe she should just power through the rest of the night and try to catch a nap tomorrow. Even though she never, ever took naps. "How soon can you get here?"

"I'm parked in front of your building."

"Of course you are."

Cooper was at the door before Veena could decide what to cover with a blanket or push into a closet. Whatever. They'd known each other a long time. If a messy apartment was a deal breaker, then so be it.

"You know, it's been forever since I've been here," Cooper said. "I like what you've not done with the place."

"I wasn't expecting company at two a.m."

"Anyway, I just spent some time with the elusive Maya Rain."

"At her invitation?"

Cooper raised his eyebrows. "Are we jealous, Counselor?"

"No. I'm just trying to figure out her game."

"Me too," Cooper admitted. "But I think she's one of the good guys."

"Do you think that because you want to justify sleeping with her?"

"That's absurd." Cooper made a show of looking around the messy apartment. "Speaking of, do you still keep your bed in the adjoining room?"

"Cooper..."

"I just don't see a place for us to sit down and discuss the case. We're both tired, and I know I think better when I'm lying flat on my back."

Veena didn't respond. She knew Cooper's argument style; they'd dance around it and he'd try to slip something past her on a technicality. And she was honestly too exhausted to go through the steps to reach that point, so she reached out, took his hand, and led him toward her bedroom.

"Wait—is this a yes?"

"This is us lying in bed and discussing our case."

"Pants on or off?"

"Pants," Veena said, "are absolutely on."

CHAPTER 60

COOPER LAMB stared up at something he'd never thought he'd see: the ceiling of Veena Lion's bedroom.

He'd certainly hoped to gaze at it at some point. But Veena was mercurial. There was no way to confidently predict what she'd do at any given moment. For example, this: Veena leading him down the narrow hallway to her dark bedroom. Taking him by the shoulders. Leveling her gaze at him, her eyes almost glowing in the dark, so close he could feel her warm breath on his neck.

And then Veena shoving him backward until he bounced onto the surface of her bed, which was covered in stacks of clean laundry.

Veena spun around and dropped backward too, bouncing him— and the tumbled stacks of laundry—a second time.

"Was it good for you?" Cooper asked, deadpan, as they lay next to each other.

"The case," Veena reminded him.

"We should move in together," Cooper said.

"We've had this conversation on a number of occasions, remember? We determined there was no way we could be with each other all the time."

"Right, right. Because one of us would end up trying to hide the other's corpse and attempt to get away with the perfect, untraceable murder—"

"Even though we both know there is no such thing as the perfect murder."

"Well, that's only when we are investigating them," Cooper countered. "If one of us is dead, and the other is determined not to get caught, then I think that person would have a strong chance of getting away with it."

Veena sighed. "See, this conversation right now is why we could never live together. I'm literally dizzy."

"Good, because now that you're weak and swooning, it's my turn to ask a question."

Lupe naturally chose this moment to jump onto Veena's bed. He selected a location near her head and curled himself into a ball. It had been a long, cold night for him, much of it spent outside in a cold car or inside a stranger's apartment. Veena's home, however, was one of Lupe's favorite places. He adored her and everything associated with her.

"Hi, loopy Lupe," Veena whispered, giving him scritches behind his ears. "Such a good boy."

"So, um, back to my question. It's serious. A matter of life and death."

Veena rolled over and gave Cooper affectionate scritches behind his ears too. "Aw, is someone jealous?"

"Not in the least. But my belly could use some rubbing."

"You said something about a serious question?"

Cooper hesitated. He never let his guard down completely with anyone. Not with his ex, certainly, not even when she was his wife, which might have been the root of their problems. And not with his children, because they deserved a steady, stable presence and he was a grown-ass man; they didn't need to know when he was worried or stressed.

With Veena, however, it was different. Sure, they joked and sparred and flirted. He drove her more than a little nuts. But a rock-solid trust had developed between them over the years, probably because they were variations of the same animal. He loved that she took off her sunglasses for him. So what the hell, right?

"There's a strong chance that someone will try to kill us if we keep going with this investigation," Cooper said.

Veena narrowed her eyes. "What makes you think that?"

"People keep warning me away. Even Victor is telling me to watch my step, which is an astounding display of emotion for him."

"Since when does Cooper Lamb listen to warnings?"

"Since the warnings are coming from witnesses and suspects involved in this case. Even Maya the nanny told me to watch my back. And when a childcare provider is telling you to be careful..."

"So do you want to stop?" Veena traced a thumb along Cooper's jawline.

"Hell no. I just wanted to let you know that I would still respect you if *you* decided to stop."

"Well, I'm not stopping until we find the truth."

"Even if it kills us?"

Veena removed her hand from Cooper's face. She extended her pinkie and waited until Cooper got the hint and wrapped his pinkie finger around hers.

"Pinkie-swear that if one of us gets killed," Veena said, "the other won't rest until the killer is brought to justice."

"Pinkie-swear," Cooper said, gently shaking her pinkie twice. "But what if they get both of us?"

CHAPTER 61

Transcript of encrypted message exchange between Victor Suarez and Cooper Lamb

VICTOR SUAREZ: Sorry for the early wake-up text but I've got three important items for you, boss.

COOPER LAMB: New phone, who dis?

SUAREZ: [No response]

LAMB: You're no fun, Victor. Go ahead, what do you have for me?

SUAREZ: Item one: Just received confirmation Detective Mickey Bernstein was already en route to Eakins Oval *before* Archie Hughes's body was discovered by the P/Os who called it in.

LAMB: WHAT? That means... you have this absolutely nailed down?

SUAREZ: [No response]

LAMB: Okay, okay, dumb question. But how do you know? I need to be sure this is rock solid before I go gunning for Dick Mickey. If I'm going to have the entire homicide department wedged sideways up my ass, it has to be for a good reason.

SUAREZ: I traced Bernstein's complete movements starting twelve hours before the crime. Confirmed by his personal phone's own GPS, backed up by traffic cams both here and in New Jersey.

LAMB: Tell me about Jersey.

SUAREZ: That's item two. Bernstein was in AC earlier in the evening.

LAMB: Blackjack? Baccarat?

SUAREZ: Poker. High rollers' table. I've got house footage detailing how much he lost and exactly how he lost it. He only left because of a phone call, at approximately 7:18 p.m.

LAMB: Who?

SUAREZ: That would be item three. The call came from the Eagles' business office.

LAMB: From Papa Sable or Younger, Fatter Sable?

SUAREZ: Still running down a record for that call . . . if it hasn't been scrubbed.

LAMB: You have to find that call, Victor. That could be the key to everything.

SUAREZ: Which leads me to believe it's already been wiped. But I'll try. Also, your suspicion about Bernstein working for the Sables turned out to be accurate.

LAMB: He's their fixer, right?

SUAREZ: They're making sizable deposits to a secret account of Bernstein's. No one, not even his wife, has access to this account.

LAMB: Damn it, I hate being right. There's no way Bernstein should be allowed anywhere near this case, yet somehow, he's the guy calling all the shots.

SUAREZ: I'm working on that too. A source tells me there's a memo somewhere in which Bernstein spells out exactly why he's the man for the job.

LAMB: Stellar work, as usual.

SUAREZ: Rain has a very faint digital trail. She's either a true no-body or a ghost.

LAMB: I'm not sure which disturbs me more. Anyway, time to turn up the heat under Tricky Mickey.

SUAREZ: You're going to have to settle on a nickname for him, boss. I can't keep up.

LAMB: Ha-ha-ha. Get back to work.

CHAPTER 62

Transcript of call from Cooper Lamb's phone to Detective Michael Bernstein

ARIEL LAMB: Hello, I would like to speak with Detective
    Bernstein, please.
MICHAEL BERNSTEIN: Uh, yeah, this is…wait, who is this?
ARIEL: (*Muffled*) Dad, he's on the line.
BERNSTEIN: Hello? Hello?
COOPER LAMB: (*Muffled*) Oops, thanks, honey. (*Pause*) Hey,
    Detective! Glad I caught you. This is Cooper Lamb. Got a
    minute? I have something very important you should know.
BERNSTEIN: Hang on—was that one of your kids just now?
LAMB: Yeah, that was my daughter, Ariel. I'm driving her and her
    brother to school, but I thought it was super-important to
    reach out to you right away. Don't worry, they understand.
    Kind of goes with the territory.
BERNSTEIN: What do you want, Lamb?
LAMB: I mean, I imagine you share a little shop talk with your
    youngsters now and again. "Boy, you kids should have seen the
    floater we pulled out of the Delaware this afternoon, talk about
    fleshy bloat—"

BERNSTEIN: I don't have time for this.

LAMB: Kids, the detective says he's too busy to speak to someone involved in the case he's investigating. Does that sound right to you?

BERNSTEIN: Lamb, I swear to God . . .

ARIEL: I think he should at least talk to you.

LAMB: Do you hear that, Detective? Out of the mouths of babes.

BERNSTEIN: Make it quick.

LAMB: This is too serious for the phone. Let's meet up in one hour. You pick the place.

BERNSTEIN: Can't do it.

LAMB: Are you serious? What, do you have to drive down to Atlantic City this morning? Or are the Sables expecting you to report in?

BERNSTEIN: The f█ did you just say to me?

LAMB: Whoa, whoa, whoa! Detective! I've got you on speakerphone. Do you really want to curse like that in front of my kids?

BERNSTEIN: Kids, I sincerely apologize for the profanity. But your dad is a scumbag who shouldn't have you on speakerphone during a work call, so I'm hanging up now.

LAMB: Come on, Mickey! Be a mensch, meet with me! I can help.

BERNSTEIN: You know how you can help? Do better by your children, ass█.

"I believe the homicide detective just hung up on me," Cooper said as he negotiated the busy traffic circle around Philadelphia's City Hall.

"Admit it," Ariel said, "you wanted him to hang up on you, didn't you?"

"I wanted to see what he would do when I said key words such as *Atlantic City* and *Sable*."

Cooper Jr., who was sprawled out in the back seat, had been listening to everything with a bemused smile on his face. But now he couldn't resist. "Is that cop working for the owners of the Eagles?"

"Yeah," Ariel said, "is he like their bagman or something?"

"Where did you learn about bagmen?"

"We are your children," she replied. "We pick up everything."

"I'm so proud I could weep."

CHAPTER 63

Transcript of recorded interview with Rosalind "Roz" Cline conducted by Veena Lion and Janie Hall

ROZ CLINE: Jeez, do you always wear those things inside? You look like you're with the Secret Service or something. All I see is myself talking to myself.

JANIE HALL: I assure you it's nothing personal, Ms. Cline. Veena is light-sensitive.

CLINE: What do you mean, light-sensitive? You're inside a casino. It's practically midnight in here all the time.

VEENA LION: Let's not talk about my boring sunglasses. I want to hear all about you. I'm fascinated how you keep one foot in Philly and one foot here. Kind of the best of both worlds?

CLINE: Nobody uses the word *best* in connection to either Philly or Jersey. I'm guessing you two didn't grow up here.

LION: Where did you grow up?

CLINE: Blackwood, New Jersey. Pretty much right at the beginning of the expressway.

HALL: Did you attend college nearby too?

CLINE: College? I didn't even finish high school. That's the big lie they push—work your ass off so you can graduate from high school, and don't you dare miss a day or you won't get the perfect-attendance award! And God forbid you're not accepted to the right Ivy League school—you're doomed to a lifetime of failure. Never mind that if you go to college, you're chained to a lifetime of debt. No, I knew it was all a racket from a young age.

LION: How young, exactly?

CLINE: Finished ninth grade and that was all I could stand. Can I get another coffee? Maybe with a little Irish in it this time?

HALL: I'll take care of that for you right away.

LION: Thanks, Janie. While we're waiting, I wanted to ask you about Archie Hughes. How long did you know him?

CLINE: Who said I knew Archie Hughes?

LION: Of course you knew him. He was paying for your apartment.

CLINE: I don't believe . . . that is utter bull█! Who told you that? I'm serious. I want to know a name.

LION: It's not important. Especially if it's not true.

CLINE: Is that why you're here? To drag me into this whole murder mess? No, thank you. And you can keep your coffee. I have things to do.

LION: Please, Ms. Cline, wait. You have to understand something. I'm buried in bull█ from everyone around Archie. I'm talking his wife, the cops, the lawyers. I need someone to tell me the truth about the man. Someone who has nothing to gain.

CLINE: Is that what you really want? The truth?

LION: Absolutely.

CLINE: You're one of the few. (*Sighs*) I can't tell you how tired I am of this city. Everybody's always making assumptions about everybody else. *Ooh, how can that dirtbag possibly afford that Lexus? Ooh, look at that stuck-up b█ in her Old City condo, she must have a sugar daddy somewhere.* They never think, *Huh, maybe that lady did it all for herself.*

LION: Tell me how you did it, then. I'm one of those suckers who
   has a perfect-attendance certificate in a drawer somewhere,
   and I'm still paying off my law school tab. What do you know
   that I don't?

CLINE: I know plenty. (*To Janie Hall*) Oh, thanks, hon. (*Sips*) Wow.
   You did Irish this up.

HALL: I told them to give me an Atlantic City pour.

LION: You were saying, Ms. Cline?

CLINE: The trick is to figure out what people want and come up
   with a way to give it to them. No guilt, no shame, no fuss,
   none of that nonsense.

HALL: And you've figured this out?

CLINE: Oh, sweetie. A long time ago. And if you can give people
   want they secretly want and make sure they never, ever feel
   bad about wanting it . . . well, they will reward you.

LION: I'll bet poor Archie needed that kind of escape now and
   again.

CLINE: Oh yeah. I don't think people appreciate what it's like to be
   in the spotlight all the time. Sure, there are perks. But the
   stress and pressure and constant scrutiny can be awful. And
   that wife of his . . .

HALL: Francine?

CLINE: I can't hear one of her old songs on the radio without
   feeling homicidal. Nobody knows what Philadelphia's so-called
   sweetheart put that poor man through. She's a real pill.

LION: And you'd make Archie feel better.

CLINE: I know what you're thinking, and no, he didn't pay for my
   condo. I can afford it all on my own. Money is not one of my
   worries.

HALL: So your thing with Archie was for real.

CLINE: I'm gonna pretend you didn't just imply that I'm a whore.

HALL: No, it's sweet! Sorry, that came out all wrong.

CLINE: Everybody knew the NFL superstar, but very few people knew the real Archie, the sweet kid from Detroit. I don't even think Princess Francine saw that part of him. When something struck Archie as funny, he laughed with his whole heart, you know? God, I loved spending time with him. Wasn't nearly enough, but it was enough. It had to be.

LION: Do you think his wife knew about your relationship?

CLINE: He only stayed over a few times…she watched him like a goddamn hawk during the off-season.

LION: How have you been coping with your loss?

CLINE: I'm drinking Irish coffee first thing in the morning, what does that tell you? Speaking of, if I could trouble you for another…

CHAPTER 64

_10:18 a.m._

JANIE STEERED their rented Honda Civic down the Atlantic City Expressway toward Philly as Veena, in the passenger seat, furiously scribbled notes—underlining phrases, drawing arrows to related ideas, circling key words.

Janie loved watching her boss work. It was like Veena was spilling the contents of her brain onto a series of yellow legal pads. Janie ordered them in bulk and sometimes had a hard time keeping up with the demand.

"What did you think of Ms. Cline?" Veena asked.

"I wish I could down a shot of her confidence," Janie replied. "She seems to have life pretty much figured out."

"She's a mess, and her so-called confidence is yet another mask she wears. She's still that same frightened ninth-grader who turned people-pleasing into a way of life."

"Whoa, V. Kind of harsh, don't you think?"

Veena shrugged and continued making notes.

"But yeah, I guess I can see that," Janie said. "What tipped you off? Was it the Irish coffee?"

"No—the constant need to impress us. Only people who feel inferior do that."

"Well, one thing was clear," Janie said. "Roz was totally into

Archie Hughes. She spoke of him like he was the love of her life, not a casual fling."

Veena nodded. "She also knows a lot more than she's saying. She probably thinks she's protecting his memory, but I'm sure she's also treading carefully. Above all else, Roz Cline is a survivor, and she doesn't want to get sucked into the whirlpool."

"So what's the plan?"

"We stay on her until we learn what she knows. Roz was wary of me, but maybe she'll cozy up to you, my underling and her potential enabler."

"Me?"

"You're the trusted underling. She'll want an inside track on what I'm looking for, and you're in a unique position to give it to her. Drop her a text. Tell her you loved what she said about living without shame, and gee, you really wish you could do that too. Maybe offer to buy her a drink, see where it goes."

"I'm still hung up on the word *underling*, V. Is that how you see me?"

"Good—you can use that!"

Janie frowned. "Not exactly what I meant, but point taken."

"Meanwhile, Cooper Lamb will be watching Archie's other romantic entanglement, Maya Rain."

"Cooper? I didn't realize we'd partnered up with the opposing team."

"We're both trying to figure out the truth. That puts us on the same team."

CHAPTER 65

COOPER LAMB / VOICE MEMO #20127-735

The kids have been safely deposited at school and I'm back in front of Maya Rain's condo like a real creep. It's been only a few hours since I saw her, but it feels like a lifetime.

Victor, if you're listening..., ah, who am I kidding, you're the only person who listens to these things. But please ignore all of this stuff about me pining away for someone who's a possible witness in the biggest murder case in Philadelphia history. Because that would be wrong, and I would never, ever act on it.

Anyway...

Maya isn't scheduled to be at the Hughes house until noon, which means she'll probably be headed downstairs to her car around eleven fifteen. I slipped the garage security guy a crisp hundred-dollar bill to let me know the moment she calls down for her ride.

At first he was weird about it, but then I casually mentioned that I was trying to stop this annoying lawyer chick working for the DA from hassling Maya. Garage Dude was all too happy to help after that. I probably didn't even need to slip him the hundred. Thank you for being you, Veena.

My plan is to follow her until we reach the Hughes home, then come up with some pretext to knock on the door . . . some detail I forgot to follow up on. I don't know. Maybe you can help me with that, Victor.

Speaking of, I'm finding it hard to believe that you're coming up with zilch on Maya Rain. I mean, this is *you* we're talking about here, Victor. Keep trying. I need to know everything about her.

Okay, *need* is a strong word. I *want* to know everything about her.

For the case!

I think Archie was paying for Maya's apartment despite what she says. I think she and Archie had some kind of relationship that was extramarital but also somehow had the blessing of Francine. Hey, it's the twenty-first century, people are gender-fluid and relationship-fluid these days. Maybe Archie and Francine allowed each other to have little dalliances . . . just as long as they cleared them with each other first.

For all I know, Francine hired Maya as a nanny and trusted her, liked her, and then Archie expressed an interest, and Francine thought, *Sure, why not? I trust her, I like her, and I could literally destroy her if she moves in on my husband for real.*

I'll need to watch the Francine-Maya dynamic a little more to know for sure. But Victor, if you can find any kind of document trail regarding Maya's employment at the Hughes house, that would be huge. A high-profile gig like that would definitely require a state background check. You have any sources in Harrisburg who could help us out?

I just can't believe someone as amazing as Maya popped out of the West Virginia woods and into a multimillionaire's Main Line mansion without leaving some traces.

CHAPTER 66

COOPER LAMB / VOICE MEMO #20127-735 (continued)

Okay, now that I've been thinking about it some more...

Here's the lame and obvious version: Francine was tired of being abused by her ultra-famous, ultra-wealthy husband and used some of that wealth to hire a hit man to take him out and make it look like an accident.

The problem with this take? It ignores all of the shady characters and circumstances surrounding Archie's murder. There are too many moving parts that don't fit into this neat, tidy narrative.

For example, there's the NFL factor and another obvious version. A hack private eye would say, *Duh, somebody wants to throw the Super Bowl. What better way than killing the Birds' star player? It takes him off the field, shakes the confidence of the team.*

The problem with this theory is that Archie's death seems to have had the opposite effect on the team. They've been galvanized into winning this one for Archie, and the city is more Eagles-crazy than ever. And it also ignores the other shady circumstances and characters.

Mickey Bernstein, for one. Unless he's moonlighting as a hit man, what's his role in all this? Why was he speeding to the crime scene before anyone knew it was a crime scene? What do we know about Mickey?

We know that Mickey Bernstein is a bagman for the Sables. We know he was headed to Archie's body before anyone officially reported it. We know that he lobbied the commissioner and possibly even the mayor to run this investigation. All of this speaks to someone who (a) knew about the crime in advance, and (b) wants to completely control the investigation of said crime.

But why?

Now I'm starting to think this does have everything to do with the Super Bowl. Sometimes the obvious and lame theory is correct, because crooks and killers are often obvious and lame.

I need to see if this theory has legs...

Transcript of Cooper Lamb's phone call to Red's Bar and Grill, Atlantic City

COOPER LAMB: Let me speak to Red, please.
BARTENDER: I don't know anybody named Red.
LAMB: Let's not do this again, sparky. Put him on.
BARTENDER: Fine, whatever.
LAMB: Don't stop being you.
RED DOYLE: Yeah, what's the good word, Cooper?
LAMB: I was hoping you could tell me.
DOYLE: It's a s███ show here, if I'm being perfectly honest. All of

the heavy guys are jittery. I feel like I'm talking all of them down off the ledge. It's like I'm a friggin' therapist instead of your friendly neighborhood bookie.

LAMB: And that's exactly why I'm calling. Who has the most to gain from the championship game being delayed?

DOYLE: Nobody. This whole thing sucks and it's freaking everybody out.

LAMB: Come on. You telling me there's no angle to be played with the delay?

DOYLE: This isn't like throwing a fight or something, Lamb. It's too public. Everybody knows what happened.

LAMB: Yeah, but once you place a bet, there's no changing it. I mean, that's the first thing you told me once we started doing...uh, business together.

DOYLE: That's right. Except in this case, the game was pushed back a week, and whenever you go past seventy-two hours, all bets are literally off. So people can adjust their wagers accordingly. Look, I know you're working some private-eye angle here, but I just don't see it. If there were a way to make some bank from this whole mess, believe me, I'd be doing it.

CHAPTER 67

Transcript of phone call between Maya Rain and Glenn Sable

MAYA RAIN: Hello, Glenn.

GLENN SABLE: Hey, yeah, just checking in... er, Maya. Seeing how you're doing and all. It's been a crazy ███ week, hasn't it? What are you up to?

RAIN: Just getting ready for work. And you?

SABLE: Did I catch you heading into the shower? Or maybe out of it? In which case, maybe we can FaceTime or something.

RAIN: About to step out the door in a minute, actually. Francine and the kids need me at noon today. Something I can help you with?

SABLE: Ah, no, nothing like that. I was just worried about you, kid. And it's been a while.

RAIN: The Hughes family have been through a lot, and I'm doing my best to keep the kids happy and distracted.

SABLE: What? Oh, yeah. Right. But that's not exactly what I meant, Vanessa.

RAIN: I'm sorry?

SABLE: I mean Maya. Apologies. I've got so many names running through my head.

RAIN: That's okay, but I really have to go. My ride's here.

SABLE: I understand. Hey, if you get the chance, maybe you could stop by after work. It would be great to catch up. Maybe have a drink or three.

RAIN: I'm going to be with Francine and the kids fairly late.

SABLE: Well, maybe I'll stop by there. I haven't been down to Rittenhouse Square in a while.

RAIN: That might not be the best idea, with all of the media attention lately.

SABLE: You're not giving me a lot to work with here. (*Laughs*)

RAIN: I really have to get going, Glenn.

SABLE: No, sure thing. But listen to me, and I'm deadly serious here. Be careful out there. You see anybody following you or acting weird, I'm your first phone call, you hear me?

RAIN: I appreciate that, Glenn, I really do. Talk to you soon, okay?

SABLE: Especially if it's one of the private investigators on the case. There are two of them—one working for your boss, the other for the DA.

RAIN: I'm not worried about them at all.

CHAPTER 68

11:29 a.m.

COOPER ALMOST didn't see her.

He had been expecting a tip-off call from Garage Dude. He'd also kept an eye on the front entrance. If Maya Rain darted out for a prework latte, he wanted to know about it. But that commanded only a small part of his attention. The rest of his brain was busy running through the scenarios and possibilities of the Archie Hughes murder—mostly to distract himself from the scenarios and possibilities with Maya Rain.

And then Cooper glimpsed something in his peripheral vision that forced him to sit up behind the wheel and take a closer look.

There—in the alley. A side entrance to the building meant for employees, deliveries, and trash pickup. There stood Maya Rain, carefully dressed for a day in the nanny trenches and still managing to look obscenely beautiful.

Cooper rubbed his eyes. He'd slept so little that he felt like hammered garbage. Yet Maya, who'd also been up late, appeared perfectly refreshed, ready for anything. He'd have to ask her for her beauty secrets one of these days.

But first, he wanted to ask Maya what she was doing standing in the alley next to her condo.

"You should be down in the garage, climbing into your sensible

Subaru like a good nanny," Cooper muttered to himself. "What—
or who—are you waiting for?"

Cooper realized that this was a perfect opportunity to look at
her, *really* look at her, in an unguarded moment. What did her face
reveal when she thought no one was paying attention?

But from his vantage point parked on the east side of Eighteenth
Street, he couldn't make out her features. Not in much detail.

He reached under his seat for the hard case resting there. Years
ago, in a completely different universe, his then-wife had made
a then-outrageous purchase for him: high-end Canon binoculars.
"Doesn't every private snoop need a quality set of snooping gog-
gles?" she'd said at the time, a little woozy with vodka martinis and
still very much in love. Cooper couldn't believe it; he'd promised
to treasure them always. A bittersweet memory. Like so many from
back then.

Cooper flipped open the case and saw the shape of the high-end
binoculars in dark gray padding, but no binoculars. *What?* A thief
would have smashed the window and then stolen the case too, for
maximum resale value. So what had happened to them?

If Cooper had to guess, he'd say they were at the bottom of Cooper
Jr.'s underwear drawer. The boy did love to "borrow" his dad's PI
gadgets. "Memo to self," Cooper muttered, even though he wasn't
actively recording. "Discuss with son how 'borrowing' works."

Cooper squinted. Didn't help. Then inspiration struck. He
pulled out his phone, hit the camera app, pointed the lens out his
window, then used his fingers to zoom in on his target. Not perfect,
by any means. But better than squinting.

He tapped the RECORD button, telling himself this was just him
being a professional investigator, not a creep.

Maya's face was as placid as the top of a cool lake. If she had
troubled thoughts, she wasn't allowing the tension to bubble to
the surface.

And then Cooper's view was obscured by something large, pale, and blurry.

He lowered the phone, rubbed his eyes, and took a better look. A late-model white Ford Bronco was slowly making its way down the alley. Something pricked at his brain—he *knew* this car. But from where?

There was something on the rear panel, a sticker of some sort. Cooper pointed his phone camera at the Bronco and used his thumb and finger to enlarge the image.

It was an FOP sticker—Fraternal Order of Police. And the black license plate frame had a discreet motto running across the top and bottom:

OUR DAY BEGINS

WHEN YOUR DAY ENDS

Cooper couldn't believe it. This was Mickey Bernstein's car.

CHAPTER 69

COOPER'S MIND was reeling with the possibilities even as Maya slid into the Bronco's passenger seat, pulled the belt over her shoulder, and clicked it in place. All without paying much mind to what she was doing, as if she'd done it dozens of times before.

Maya and Mickey the detective? Now, that was a pairing he never would have predicted.

Sure, he could imagine Bernstein making a few clumsy moves on the hot nanny, figuring she was anonymous enough not to matter. But this was something different. And it was not the usual business of a cop picking up a witness either. For one thing, that would never involve just one detective. No, this was friendly, familiar. Which meant they were allies...right? Or maybe Maya knew something, and Tricky Mickey was coaxing it out of her with false promises of police protection—all of it off the books, because Bernstein was working his own angle.

Cooper hurriedly opened the city streets app on his phone to see where this alley led so he could pick up their trail. He couldn't pursue Bernstein directly down the alley; the veteran cop would spot him in a microsecond.

The app offered some good news: The alley ended at a side street that would take you north to Sansom Street or south to Walnut.

But the bad news: He didn't know which direction Bernstein might be headed. That depended on where he was taking her.

A left turn onto Walnut could mean he was headed to the Roundhouse at Eighth and Arch for something official—or something meant to *seem* official.

A right turn could mean Bernstein was giving her a lift to the Main Line for work…or perhaps taking her to the Sables' head office at the Linc.

And if Cooper chose wrong, he would lose them.

Cooper put his hand on the gear shift, ready to spring into action whenever Bernstein hit the gas. But he lingered. Bernstein and Maya were talking about *something,* their faces only inches apart.

He wished he could go back in time and have Victor wire Bernstein's car for sound. "Memo to self," Cooper mumbled. "Have Victor invent time machine, then travel back and bug Mickey's ride."

For a fleeting second, Cooper considered the direct approach—running up to the car, pounding on the windshield, smiling, and making a *Roll down your window* gesture—just to see where the conversation took them.

But Bernstein would most likely give him the finger and peel off down the alley. Besides, Cooper's sole advantage was that neither Mickey nor Maya knew Cooper was there. So he would flip a coin at the end of the alley and try to follow them. Maybe their destination would tell him everything he needed to know.

But there was one thing Cooper Lamb wasn't prepared for.

Maya moving closer to Bernstein and giving him a long, slow, deep kiss.

A nuke went off in Cooper's skull, and his senses fuzzed out for a moment. Was he actually seeing this? Son of a bitch!

Okay, there was no way Detective Mickey was Maya's sugar daddy. Not unless he had a small fortune tucked away in a metal box under some floorboards somewhere. Cooper knew what homicide detectives took home, and he could not float Maya's apartment on top of his own house.

But forget all of that for now.

Why the hell was Mickey Bernstein heading up this investigation?

Before Cooper had a chance to consider that question, the white Bronco rocketed down the alley.

This was it.

Time to toss that coin.

CHAPTER 70

COOPER LAMB / VOICE MEMO #20127-735 (continued)

I am currently in hot pursuit of Mickey Bernstein, big-deal homicide detective.

I'm recording all of this just in case something...well, weird happens. This is Philadelphia, after all. And everybody's been telling me to watch my back. So maybe a recording of these next few minutes will come in handy for the person investigating my murder.

Please, don't let me be murdered.

Victor, if I am murdered, avenge me.

I guessed correctly, by the way. Mickey turned right, heading toward Sansom Street, which means he's going to the Linc or the Main Line.

Victor, I don't know if you're listening to this in real time or not, but in case you are, work your magic. Tell me where Bernstein is headed.

Okay, you must be busy. No magic for now. I have to do this the old-fashioned way.

Bernstein is continuing down Sansom Street. At some

point he has to turn, otherwise he's headed into the river. I am following close behind. But not too close. Bernstein is police, and he knows when he's being followed.

Okay, he's taking a right on Twenty-Second Street, which makes sense. This will take him to the on-ramps for the interstate and then to everybody's least favorite highway, the Schuylkill Expressway. Ah, Mickey, but are you taking the freeway west, out of your jurisdiction and into the chilly embrace of the Main Line? Or are you taking it east, down to the Linc?

The next few minutes will tell us everything...

Oh, s██.

I think he spotted me.

S██, s██, s██.

This is *not* good, Victor.

If Bernstein saw me, all he has to do is call it in, and within a minute I'll be pulled over, and who knows how that might go? At best, I'll be slapped with a dozen tickets for fictional violations. At worst, I'll end up...

Okay, he definitely sees me. I'm turning around now.

CHAPTER 71

AS COOPER Lamb drove home, he expected that any minute he'd be pulled over, arrested, and possibly shot. His name would be added to the hundreds of murder victims in Philadelphia every year, because when it came down to it, what was one more?

None of those things happened.

Cooper obsessively checked his rear- and side-view mirrors, looking for any hint of a police vehicle, marked or otherwise. No such hint appeared, which worried him even more. What if Bernstein had someone *else* coming for him? Some shadowy player from the underworld—someone who Cooper wouldn't hear coming until it was far too late?

But he made the short drive back to his brownstone at Twentieth and Green without incident. He even successfully parallel-parked. (Again, without anyone around to appreciate it.)

Cooper went upstairs to take a shower. This was where he did his best thinking, and he had a lot to think over. He undressed, stuffed his clothes in the hamper, knelt down, and pulled out the Browning Black Label 1911-380 clipped to the underside of his bed. He carried the weapon into the bathroom, twisted on the shower water, and adjusted the temperature to just shy of scalding. Cooper needed to shake the chill from his bones and the adrenaline from his muscles. The Browning was just in case someone broke in and tried to kill him while he relaxed.

Only twice before had he felt compelled to bring a firearm into the bathroom, and both times he'd debated the best place for the weapon. Top of the toilet tank? No, because then it became a race between himself and an intruder. Resting on the water pipe? Too precarious, and Cooper couldn't stand the idea of the inevitable *Philadelphia Daily News* headline: "Private Eye Shoots Self in Shower." (*Does it hurt, getting shot right in yer shower? Ha-ha-ha-ha.*)

Cooper tucked his Browning into his mesh shower caddy, which he'd purchased mainly as a place to keep his gun. The fact that it also held soap and shampoo was a bonus.

But now it was time to sort out the facts. Maya and Mickey. Rain and Bernstein. How did that happen? And what did it mean? Bernstein worked for the Sables. Had Bernstein and Maya met at some Eagles event where all the members of the Hughes family (and, of course, the nanny) were present? That would be the innocent answer. But there was nothing innocent about this situation.

So most likely the murder had brought them together . . . but the murder had just happened on Sunday. Bernstein and Maya looked like they'd known each other a lot longer than a few days.

Cooper lowered his head, allowing the scalding water to pummel his neck and shoulders. He needed sleep. But the Maya Rain situation felt like a thorn in his brain; he couldn't properly relax until he plucked it out of his gray matter.

Fortunately, Cooper didn't have to leave his brownstone to pick up the kids; they had a half day at school, and his ex was picking them up early to catch an afternoon matinee. "You're not the only fun parent," his ex had said. Cooper wanted to tell her not to worry about that. He was the opposite of fun right now.

The detective spent the rest of the day brooding. Lupe followed his master's lead and seemed extra-contemplative as well. Cooper set up camp on the sofa, which gave him views of both his front door and the window overlooking Green Street. Lupe perched next to him, head on Cooper's lap.

At some point Cooper must have fallen asleep, because Lupe's sharp series of barks jolted him awake. His hand grabbed the Browning tucked between two cushions, and his brain tried to fix on a target—the door or the window?

But nothing was happening inside or out of the brownstone. The sun had set a while ago, and the neighborhood was dark...

Except for the flashing lights that danced across the window.

Cooper crouched down low, listened, then peered outside. A white Bronco was crawling down Green, flashing its headlights, followed by the piercing, repeating electronic chirp of a portable siren. The driver gunned it down the block.

"Hello, Detective Bernstein," Cooper mumbled. "What brings you out this evening?"

Clearly Bernstein wanted to send a message. But was it just a warning or a prelude to something else? Maybe it was a distraction to keep Cooper's eyes on the street while someone came through his front door.

"Lupe," he whispered. "Eyes sharp."

Lupe gave a quiet, low growl in response. He was on the case.

The second drive-by happened a few minutes later, and Cooper tensed up all over again. But the third, a minute later, with a constant flutter of electronic chirps, just annoyed him. If Bernstein was going to do something, he should just do it already.

On the fourth drive-by, which was a full half hour later, Cooper realized this was the point. To keep him on edge, to let him know he'd crossed a line.

FRIDAY, JANUARY 28

CHAPTER 72

2:11 a.m.

"VICTOR? GOOD, you're up."

"What's up, boss?"

Cooper wasn't surprised Victor Suarez was awake in the middle of the night. A true surprise would have been finding Victor asleep or—even more shocking—out somewhere enjoying himself.

"Can you shake down an address for me?"

"Sure," Victor replied. "Just as soon as you stop talking like a 1950s private eye."

"Be kind to your favorite employer. I've had a rough day."

"Mickey Bernstein, right?"

"How did you know?"

"How did I know what? Mickey's been the puzzle piece that hasn't fit this whole time. I figured you'd eventually want to go knocking on his door. Okay, got a pen?"

"Hang on. You found it that easily? What, do you have access to the home addresses of all Philly cops?" Cooper knew quite a few guys on the force, and they were super-cautious about any scraps of personal information leaking out on the internet. They often came to him looking for the name of a good web cleaner, a high-tech private eye (of sorts) who would scrub all traces of them off the web. Not that this helped them when dealing with a specialist like Victor Suarez.

There was a strange sound on the other end of the line, like an elephant clearing its throat. Cooper quickly realized this was the sound of Victor Suarez *laughing*.

"Good one, boss."

"Whatever. Let me have the address."

"You want the rundown on his wife and kids too?"

Cooper knew Victor was kidding. At least, he *hoped* he was kidding.

CHAPTER 73

FOR DECADES, Northeast Philadelphia had felt almost like a suburb, a place somehow *apart* from the city, even though it rested firmly within the city limits. The lawns were wider, the houses slightly bigger. For years, it had been a haven for middle-class families fleeing the blue-collar neighborhoods of the inner city. But recently it had become a glorious melting pot, much like the rest of Philly.

Except for this part of it.

Mickey Bernstein's slice of Northeast Philly held on to that 1950s white-flight feeling—outsiders most certainly *not* welcome. This neighborhood was so far to the northeast, it was practically Bucks County.

Cooper pulled up in front of the homicide detective's house. A massive lawn crawled up to the main entrance of the Colonial-style home and its three-car garage, from which hung a tasteful Eagles flag, the new white Bronco parked outside. Whatever job Bernstein was doing on the side clearly had its perks.

What was Cooper thinking, taking the fight to Bernstein? He knew this was a total grade-school move: *You showed up at my place, I'm gonna show up at yours. Only I'm not going to hide in a white Bronco.*

No, it wasn't that. Cooper wanted to talk to Bernstein face-to-face. He was tired of being brushed off and chased away. He wanted straight answers.

Cooper pounded on Bernstein's door with the side of his fist. Inside, a dog yip-yip-yip-yipped like it had lost its fool mind. Cooper pounded again. *That's right, pooch, wake up your owner. And the owner's wife and kids while you're at it. Let's get the whole family down here to talk about Daddy Detective's afternoon with Maya Rain.*

Slowly the house creaked to life. An upstairs light switched on. Blinds were parted with fingers, then shut again. The dog continued to express its very strong feelings about the visitor at the front door. Slippered feet slapped their way down a hardwood staircase. A vestibule light flickered to life. The door opened. A blinking murder cop looked at him.

"You gotta be kidding me," Bernstein said.

"Clearly you had an urgent need to see me," Cooper said. "Figured I'd save you the trouble of coming to my place again."

"It's two in the goddamn morning. Who gave you my address?"

"Tell me, Mickey, back in the academy, didn't they teach you that dating the nanny of a murder victim's family might not be the *best* look?"

"Get the hell out of here."

Bernstein was wearing a robe, but Cooper could tell that was for show. The homicide detective had none of the telltale signs of sleep, and his breath carried the sweet-sharp odor of whiskey.

The yipping dog—some indeterminate breed that reminded Cooper of a dust mop—appeared between Bernstein's legs to complain a bit more. Cooper forced a smile as he locked eyes with the noisy little bastard and reached into his jacket pocket.

"Hey!" Bernstein said. "Keep your hands where I can see them!"

"Easy," Cooper replied. He pulled a small plastic baggie of dog treats out of his pocket. "Lupe loves these things. I think your pooch will go crazy for them."

Before Bernstein had a chance to protest, Cooper was taking a knee and grabbing one of the nuggets ("Paw-Lickin' Chicken"). The Yipping Dust Mop was suspicious but also intrigued by the scent.

"Don't you give my dog anyth—"

The protest was cut short because Cooper made two moves in rapid succession. He dropped the treat for the Dust Mop, then he clenched his right fist and sent it rocketing skyward on a collision course with Bernstein's face.

The homicide detective was caught completely off guard. Usually, a person taking a knee in front of you doesn't have the advantage in a close-quarters fight. But Cooper didn't intend this to be a fight. He was betting that his strength, speed, and weight would knock Bernstein for a loop.

Which it did. Blood gushed out of the detective's nose and mouth, and the blow had the bonus effect of rendering Bernstein unconscious. Cooper had heard people say this was difficult to do in real life. He supposed that was true, but the army had taught him many ways to do exactly that.

"Good dogs deserve treats," Cooper said.

Cooper pushed Bernstein's body all the way into the vestibule and dropped a few more treats for the Dust Mop before he pulled the door shut. Cooper wasn't a total monster.

CHAPTER 74

7:41 a.m.

"WOW, DAD."

"'Wow, Dad' what?"

"You look like you slept rough in the street," Ariel said.

"You're not too far off the mark, daughter. And who taught you about sleeping rough?"

Truth was, Cooper hadn't slept at all since assaulting the city's most famous homicide detective. He was pretty sure that single uppercut had placed a target firmly on his back. Bernstein hadn't been goaded into a fevered response, but Cooper knew for sure there would be a response. Maybe Bernstein would slip up, and it would be something he could use to help Francine.

"What's on the agenda today, old man?"

"Glad you asked," Cooper said. "Today's goal is convincing my own client to help me save her life."

"You're seeing Francine Hughes again?" Ariel asked.

"Why, yes, I am. Private eye to the stars, that's your dear old father."

Cooper Jr. leaned in from the back seat. "Do you think Francine could get us tickets to the game on Sunday?"

"You mean you want me to ask the grieving widow for tickets

to a game her late husband should have been playing? That might not be the smartest move, my boy."

Ariel shook her head. "That would be unethical."

"Yeah, but this is *Dad* we're talking about," Cooper Jr. said.

"Hey, Dad is sitting right here! And by the way, private eyes have a very strict ethical code."

Cooper Jr. frowned. "But you told me you became a private detective because you didn't want anyone telling you what to do."

"Plus you can set your own hours," Ariel added.

"Don't you two have schoolwork to finish or something?"

Transcript of conversation between Cooper Lamb and Francine Hughes

COOPER LAMB: Thanks for taking the time to see me, Francine. I wanted to ask you about Maya.

FRANCINE HUGHES: You're too old for her.

LAMB: Um, that's not what I'm asking.

HUGHES: Sure, sure. I see the way you look at her.

LAMB: If I'm looking at her in a particular way, it's because I'm trying to figure out how she fits into this case.

HUGHES: What do you mean? Maya looks after the kids. I have no earthly idea why you're trying to drag her into this.

LAMB: I'm not dragging her anywhere. She seems to live at the center of this thing, Francine. Did you know she's dating Mickey Bernstein?

HUGHES: (*Pause*) What she does in her time off is none of my business.

LAMB: You have no problem with your nanny being in a relationship with the man investigating your husband's murder?

HUGHES: I think we're through here, Cooper. You should probably go.

LAMB: If you want me to help your defense team save you, you're going to have to tell me everything you know about Maya and Bernstein.

HUGHES: I said we're through. I need you to leave.

LAMB: Hey, I'm on your side here!

HUGHES: Well, it doesn't feel that way. Sometimes you're no better than those reporters who call and text and e-mail all damn day. What does my nanny's personal life have to do with anything? It's all just gossip.

LAMB: Francine, it's clear we have one tiny problem between us.

HUGHES: And what's that?

LAMB: You're constantly lying to me.

HUGHES: (*Sharply*) Excuse me?

LAMB: Hey, it's okay. Sure, it makes my job a bit more challenging, but it ultimately doesn't matter, because I'm going to find the truth, no matter what. It's what I do.

HUGHES: Well, here's some truth for you. I didn't murder my husband. Maybe the prick deserved it, but I didn't kill him.

LAMB: Now we're finally getting to the truth.

HUGHES: I should fire you.

LAMB: *Please*. Put me out of my misery.

CHAPTER 75

"NICE ARM!" Cooper shouted with real delight, cradling the football to his chest.

And it was true, there had been surprising power behind the toss. But Cooper had to stop himself before continuing the thought: *An arm just like your father's.*

Cooper had found the twelve-year-old Archie Hughes Jr. outside alone, lost in his thoughts, toeing a Wilson Duke NFL football around the frosty lawn. The sight broke Cooper's heart. Cooper knew he should be down at the Linc, squeezing the Eagles' owners for answers. But he had never been a guy who could turn his back on a kid. He'd asked Archie Jr. how far he could throw that ball. And damn, did Junior show him.

"Let's do that again!" the boy shouted.

"Give me your worst," Cooper said, tossing him the pigskin. The kid caught it effortlessly and with a grace that belied his age. Cooper hoped that was because Archie had spent time out here practicing with his kid. Those memories would mean everything down the line.

Cooper knew this from personal experience. He clung to the few memories he had of his own father like faded wallet photos.

After Cooper and Archie Jr. had tossed the ball around a few times, with Lupe serving as their cheerleader, Maddie Hughes and Maya Rain emerged from the house. Maddie roared with delight when she saw Lupe.

"I love the Lamb's doggy!"

Lupe, the little glory hound, bounded over to Maddie for some chin scratches.

Cooper's attention was all on Maya, so much so that he failed to notice that Archie Jr. had hurled the football. Cooper caught it at the last possible second, and the blow took his breath away.

"Nobody taught you to keep your eye on the ball, Cooper?" Maya asked.

Cooper coughed, then tossed the ball back to the kid. "I thought I was."

"He's pretty amazing, isn't he?"

"It's good to see you again, Maya."

"I don't seem to be able to shake you," she said.

"Exactly how hard are you trying?"

Was that shyness on her face right now? Or flirtation? Whatever it was, Cooper didn't want to ruin the mood just yet by mentioning her boyfriend the homicide detective. "Is there somewhere we could talk?"

Maya glanced over at the Hughes kids playing with Lupe. "Not here. Let's talk in the pool house."

"Because sure, talking inside the pool house in the middle of a freezing January day isn't suspicious at all."

"Or we could do this another time."

"Pool house it is."

Cooper told the kids to look after Lupe, and he let Maya lead the way.

CHAPTER 76

Transcript of private conversation between Cooper Lamb and Maya Rain, captured using an ambient recording app on Lamb's smartwatch

COOPER LAMB: This place is huge! You could fit my entire brownstone inside here. Twice.

MAYA RAIN: Interesting you mention that. Why were you outside my apartment yesterday morning?

LAMB: You saw me down on Eighteenth Street, huh?

RAIN: I was waiting for you to come upstairs and tell me whatever was on your mind, but you never did.

LAMB: Maybe I was working up the courage until your boyfriend showed up in his white Bronco.

RAIN: Ahh, so you saw Detective Bernstein pick me up. Is that what this is about?

LAMB: Detective, huh? So formal. Especially considering you two started kissing after you climbed into the passenger seat.

RAIN: You know, Cooper, I didn't think you were one of those sleazy private eyes who goes around taking photos of married men with their younger lovers. Guess I was wrong about you.

LAMB: Is Bernstein your sugar daddy? Because I have no idea how he swings your Rittenhouse Square condo on his police salary.

RAIN: Bernstein has nothing to do with where I live. I'm not dating him. You have the wrong idea about so many things.

LAMB: Maya, this is f█████ hopeless. I already know who's paying for that place of yours. In fact, I'm going to pay him a visit this afternoon. I just wanted you to tell me the truth. Just one time.

RAIN: You're free to speculate however you want.

LAMB: By the way, who's Vanessa?

RAIN: Are you just throwing random names at me to see if I'll react?

LAMB: It's either your real name or another identity you use. I'm leaning toward the former.

RAIN: I don't have an alias or a pseudonym or an alternate identity. Just being me is enough.

LAMB: If only I knew who you really were.

RAIN: You're looking at her.

LAMB: (*Pause*) I'd better go before Maddie and Archie Jr. decide to formally adopt my dog.

CHAPTER 77

Transcript of private conversation between Cooper Lamb and Eagles co-owner Harold Sable in his office at Lincoln Financial Field

COOPER LAMB: Honestly, Harold, I don't know how you keep all of these plates spinning on all of these poles.

HAROLD SABLE: What're you talking about, plates and poles?

LAMB: I mean you must be crazy-busy right now, but you seem perfectly calm in the center of the storm.

SABLE: Is this why you had to see me right away? You want free lessons in time management?

LAMB: Just the expenses alone. I mean, how do you keep track of it all? Cars here, travel there, all of those luxury suites...

SABLE: Oh, I get it. You're delivering some kind of private-eye monologue. Well, go ahead, don't let me stop you.

LAMB: Not to mention all of the condos and apartments around town. I've seen Maya Rain's pad. That place can't be cheap.

SABLE: And now we come to the point. Only there's one prob-lem—who the f███ is Maya Rain?

LAMB: You know exactly who she is.

SABLE: Maya, Maya...oh, right, the nanny. You think *I'm* paying for Archie's nanny's apartment? Isn't she living at Villanova or something? I still don't see how this is any of my business or why you're wasting my f████ time with this nonsense.

LAMB: Nonsense? You were covering for Archie by taking care of his mistress's penthouse. Anything to keep your star quarterback happy, right?

SABLE: If Archie had anything on the side—and I'm not saying he did—he could certainly have afforded to pay her living expenses on his own.

LAMB: Not if he wanted to keep it supersecret from Francine.

SABLE: You actually think Archie and this Maya were a thing?

LAMB: I *know* Archie and Maya were a thing.

SABLE: (*Laughs*) No, a████. Maya and the *detective* are a thing.

LAMB: (*Pause*) Really.

SABLE: You just don't get it. I know you're zipping around town trying to connect the dots and all. But you can't make it fit, can you? That's because there are no dots to connect. People are gonna do what they wanna do whether or not it's convenient for you. So he's banging the nanny. Who gives a s██? People do all kinds of crazy things.

LAMB: Crazy things like work for you?

SABLE: What's this, now?

LAMB: I know Bernstein's on your payroll.

SABLE: Unbelievable. Where'd you get that?

LAMB: You denying it?

SABLE: Yes, I'm denying it. Bernstein wishes he were on my payroll—he'd do a lot better than what the city gives him. No, I like Mickey because I was pals with his old man, and yeah, I might throw him some tickets now and again, but I throw a lot of tickets around. See, there you go again. Connecting dots that aren't even on the same page.

LAMB: (*Pause*) I really have this all twisted around, don't I?

SABLE: That's the first smart thing you've said today.

LAMB: Well, thanks for setting me straight, Harold. You're actually saving me a lot of time.

SABLE: Tell you what, Lamb. Just to show you what an outstanding guy I am, I want you to be my guest this Sunday at the game.

LAMB: You think I can be bought with a ticket to the game everybody in the world wants to see?

SABLE: I'm not trying to buy anything. I'm just a generous guy by nature.

LAMB: In that case, can you spare three tickets so I can bring the kids?

SABLE: Like I said before, you're unbelievable.

CHAPTER 78

12:25 p.m.

THE TRAFFIC on Third Street just above Market was slower than usual up to Arch Street. Something was off; Veena had an uneasy feeling. She looked up at the skyline for black smoke or news choppers or both but saw nothing out of place. That made her worry all the more.

"Driver, please pull over," Veena said. "We'll get out here."

Their rideshare driver seemed stunned by the very suggestion. "But I'm supposed to take you to Second and Arch."

"Charge us for the whole trip, and I'll add an obscene tip," Veena said. "Come on, Janie. We're walking the rest of the way."

"You got it, V."

They hurried east on Market. The brutal winter winds chilled by the nearby Delaware River blasted their bodies as if trying to push them away.

"Why did we get out here? What's going on?"

"Hopefully nothing, but ..."

"But what?"

"Traffic is never this slow. To me, that means police activity."

"And Roz Cline lives nearby ..."

They hurried down Market Street, fighting the cold wind. At the far end of the block, near the ramp leading to Penn's Landing, there were two police vans blocking traffic, and street cops were steering pedestrians away. As they closed the distance, even more police cars arrived, lights flashing, along with an EMT truck that squawked and squeezed through the blockade, forcing its way up Second Street in the wrong direction.

"This is such a huge response," Janie said. "What the hell is going on?"

"There are no fire engines," said Veena. "Just police and EMTs."

"I don't like this."

"You still have your old press pass, right?"

"Five years out of date."

"They probably won't pay too much attention. We should head up the walk to Church Street. Maybe we can sneak past the police along Christ Church."

Veena was right; nobody paid them much mind as they wound their way through the police vehicles toward Roz's condo. A crowd had gathered outside. Veena could hear snippets of conversation that chilled her blood even more than the January cold:

"Can you see anything from here?"

"Trust you me, you don't want to look."

"I need to get back to my apartment. This totally sucks."

"Anybody actually see her jump?"

CHAPTER 79

Transcript of conversation between Janie Hall and Stephanie Weddle, captured using an ambient recording app on Hall's personal phone

JANIE HALL: Oh my God. I can't believe this. We were just with her yesterday...

VEENA LION: Before we let our imaginations run wild, let's find out for sure.

HALL: Hang on. Oh, I know that cop over by the condo entrance. Let me see if she can tell us what's going on. (*Pause*) Hey, Steph! It's me, Janie Hall.

OFFICER STEPHANIE WEDDLE: Huh? Oh, hey, Janie. I didn't know you were still on the beat. Thought you'd retired a few years ago when that rag of yours folded.

HALL: Wasn't *my* rag, thankfully. I just gave them words in exchange for money. And yeah, I'm still at it. Hey, what happened here? I was trying to make my way up Third when everything just ground to a halt.

WEDDLE: You don't wanna know.

HALL: Come on, Steph. Of course I want to know.

WEDDLE: Heh-heh. Off the record?

HALL: As always.

WEDDLE: What about your friend over there, the elegant-looking lady you walked up with?

HALL: That's Veena. She's a lawyer, so we have that confidentiality thing going.

WEDDLE: Is that right?

HALL: That's right.

WEDDLE: Okay, well ... we don't know if this is a suicide or something else. A resident on the top floor tumbled off the balcony and landed in the alley.

HALL: Oh God.

WEDDLE: Yeah, it's a mess. And I mean that literally. The poor man who found her is having a real hard time of it.

HALL: Who is it?

WEDDLE: The man who found her?

HALL: No, the victim.

WEDDLE: I don't know if I should tell you that. Even off the record—you understand.

HALL: Of course, Steph, I totally get it. But the thing is, we were headed over here, to this building, to visit a friend of Veena's. She wasn't feeling too good, and we were worried about her.

WEDDLE: I don't know, Janie. I'd better ask someone ...

HALL: Just give me a first name so my heart stops racing. Please?

WEDDLE: Damn it, Janie. (*Lengthy pause*) Okay, her first name is Rosalind. But the building super says everyone calls her Roz. Please tell me that's not your friend's friend.

HALL: Thank you, Steph. I really appreciate it. You've just put my mind at ease.

CHAPTER 80

"IT'S HER."

"Uh-huh," Veena said, staring off into the distance.

Janie Hall blinked. "Did you hear me, V.? It's *her*. Roz Cline. I just got confirmation from my cop friend. They found her body on the sidewalk. I pretended I didn't know her to get information from Steph, but it's looking like—"

"I already knew it was Roz."

"—she either jumped or was...wait, how did you know it was Roz?"

Veena wasn't looking at Janie. She was focused on the alley next to the building. Janie followed her gaze and saw burly guys in suits stepping out of the side entrance. She recognized most of them from her police-beat days. They were homicide.

Veena said, "I knew because of him."

Among the murder cops: Mickey Bernstein. He seemed to be running the show, instructing his colleagues on the next moves.

"This freakin' guy is everywhere," Janie murmured.

"And he shouldn't be anywhere near this."

"Why's that?"

"Because he's currently my number one suspect in the murder

of Archie Hughes. And who was our most promising lead? The woman who was just shoved from her balcony."

"We don't know for sure that's what happened, V."

"She sounded like she was in love, not suicidal. Either way, Bernstein is the last person who should be investigating Roz Cline's murder, because he's probably the one who did it."

"Come on, V. I know he's a scumbag, but that's a huge line to cross."

The two of them took in the bustling crime scene together. Janie tried to absorb the details like a newspaper reporter. That meant looking for the *telling* details—the small things that would bring this scene to life for a reader later. The body language of the police (upset, blasé, confused). The behavior of the lookie-loos gathered on the sidewalk (rowdy, sad, suspicious).

And, of course, anything striking about the murder victim herself—anything to bring her to life for a few more seconds. Janie was no longer a reporter, but she still found the technique useful, especially when Veena asked for her take. And her boss *always* asked.

Veena Lion, however, took in crime scenes in a different way. Instead of using her eyes and ears like recording devices, she analyzed the scene like it was a life-size board game. Who were the key players? What did this recent move mean strategically? Who had been in the best position to make that move?

And sometimes, Veena just stepped right onto the game board and started playing along.

CHAPTER 81

Transcript of conversation between Veena Lion and Detective Michael Bernstein, captured using an ambient recording app on her phone

VEENA LION: Detective Bernstein! You got a minute?

MICHAEL BERNSTEIN: Not really, Veena.

LION: Fine. You don't want to talk to me, I'll find people who will.

BERNSTEIN: Hey! Wait up and listen to me for a sec. You're gonna want to stay away from this one. I'm not saying that as a threat. I'm saying it as your friend. Just be patient. You and the DA are going to get the outcome you want.

LION: All I want is the truth, Bernstein.

BERNSTEIN: Oh, you'll get the whole story. Don't worry.

LION: I'm not so sure. Are you going to tell your superior officers about the connection between this murder and the Archie Hughes murder?

BERNSTEIN: Who said this was a murder? And what does one have to do with the other?

LION: Thought as much. See you soon, Detective.

BERNSTEIN: What do you mean, soon?

* * *

Transcript of interview with James Papaleo, doorman at the Villas at Elfreth's Alley, conducted by Veena Lion and Janie Hall

VEENA LION: Excuse me, are you the employee who found the body?

JAMES PAPALEO: God, I wish I hadn't. You have no idea. There are some things you can never erase from your brain.

JANIE HALL: I'm so sorry, Mr. Papaleo. I know how hard this is. But we're just trying to figure out what happened here.

PAPALEO: Like I told the other cops, I just heard it. I didn't know what I was hearing, but it sounded like a ton of produce fell off the back of a truck, you know? A loud, wet . . . *cracking* sound.

LION: Did you know Roz Cline pretty well?

PAPALEO: Yeah, I did. Everybody did. She was the life of this place. Really nice girl, very popular. I don't understand this, I really don't.

HALL: When you say *popular,* what do you mean exactly? Did she entertain a lot of friends?

PAPALEO: Nah, not a lot. She wasn't a partyer like that. Really classy lady, real discreet. And the people she—what did you say, *entertained*? Well, they were classy people too.

LION: People like Archie Hughes?

PAPALEO: No offense, Detectives, but I think I should be discreet too. I mean, Archie obviously had nothing to do with what happened to poor Roz here.

LION: But Archie *did* visit often, right? Never mind, you don't have to answer that. I have all the sign-in logs from the management company.

PAPALEO: Don't know what good that'll do you.

HALL: What do you mean?

PAPALEO: People like Archie Hughes pay a visit, their names don't go into the sign-in logs. Too many crazy Eagles fans out there.

Somebody sees his name on the log one day, and before you know it, you've got a crowd camped outside. The poor guy didn't want to be bothered.

LION: Or caught.

PAPALEO: What was that?

LION: Never mind. I'm guessing their friend Maya Rain wouldn't be on the visitor logs either.

PAPALEO: I don't know any Maya Rain. Who's that?

HALL: What about Roz's other friend...ah, sorry, I'm blanking here. What's her name...(*Snaps fingers*) Super-pretty, in her twenties...

PAPALEO: You probably mean Vanessa. Yeah, she and Roz were really close. Really sweet ladies...oh no. You're asking because you have to break the bad news to Vanessa, right?

LION: I have a feeling she already knows.

CHAPTER 82

Transcript of encrypted message exchange between Cooper Lamb and Veena Lion

VEENA LION: What's the latest?

COOPER LAMB: Oh, nothing, just a leisurely day avoiding the police, sparring with a nanny, and trying to wrestle information out of an obese multimillionaire. Right now I'm waiting for the young ones to finish their pricey Quaker education for the day so I can feed them sugar and regale them with tales of violence before dropping them off at their mother's place.

LION: Roz Cline is dead.

LAMB: You've gotta be s█████ me! Okay, you have me beat. What happened...oh, wait. Was Roz the Old City jumper? It's all over KYW.

LION: I'm down here right now. Guess who else is here?

LAMB: Bernstein.

LION: Yep.

LAMB: Thank God.

LION: ?

LAMB: If he's there, that means he's not stalking me and looking for an opportunity to have me arrested or shot.

LION: ??????

LAMB: Long story. But wait, why is he there?

LION: We have a dead NFL superstar, a dead celebrity chef, and a dead Atlantic City hostess. The first two are murders, and I'm pretty sure the third is one too.

LAMB: And Mickey Bernstein just happens to be there in record time for every killing. You should ask him why that is.

LION: Tried that already. He told me I should steer clear of this for my own good. He said he was telling me because we're old friends.

LAMB: I didn't know you two were close.

LION: I didn't either. I'd be tempted to ask him out if it weren't for that triple-homicide thing.

LAMB: Seriously? You think Bernstein killed all three of them? I mean, Mickey had a head start on Archie's murder, but I don't think he pulled the trigger himself. Victor tracked his movements.

LION: Even detectives have partners.

LAMB: So now it's a conspiracy?

LION: It already was, by definition.

LAMB: Touché. But we have nothing solid tying Mickey to any of these killings. If anyone has a reason to show up at a murder scene, it's a freakin' murder cop.

LION: So you think Bernstein is innocent?

LAMB: Hell no. He practically has a neon GUILTY sign over his head. But we need to prove it.

LION: Two potential witnesses have been killed. Who else is left to squeeze?

LAMB: We make the rounds again. And this time, we squeeze harder.

SATURDAY, JANUARY 29

CHAPTER 83

CONFIDENTIAL DOCUMENT FROM JANIE HALL TO VEENA LION, FOUND ON AN ENCRYPTED SERVER

Okay, V., consider this file extremely private and incredibly confidential. This is why I'm not texting you this information. If you have a place where you keep supersecret information—stuff so secret you don't even tell me about it—put the contents of this entire folder in there. RIGHT NOW.

This is because I'm about to admit to a crime.

First, my justification for the crime, then the crime itself.

I went home yesterday thinking a lot about Roz Cline. The woman who was about to become my new best friend. Her sudden death...her murder...hit home in a way I wasn't expecting. I didn't want it to be for nothing. She deserves better than that.

But the truth is, she's just a bit player in the murder of the century. And the people on the other side—whoever they may be—aren't playing fair. So why should we? This, then, is the motive for my crime. (Crimes, actually.)

Now to the means and opportunity for said crime(s).

I know you like to tease me about my tortured dating life. And it is tortured. But it used to be tortured with a purpose. Since I'm in a confessing mood, and since this document will never see the light of day (right, V.?), I'll admit that when I was a tabloid reporter, I preferred to date useful individuals.

"Useful" meaning in a lowly position yet connected to the halls of power. (It didn't hurt if they were a little hot too.)

A few years ago, before I came to work for you, one of my useful dates was a guy named Prentiss Walsh. A bit of a smacked ass, to be honest, but ambitious. He'll probably be mayor someday. And he just so happens to be the executive assistant of Charles Castrina, divorce attorney to the Philadelphia stars.

Well, last night I called Prentiss. He was very happy to hear from me. He suggested I go to his place. I told him I was a little tipsy and happened to be at a bar right around the corner from his office. He told me he'd be right over. I told him I'd have another drink while I waited. He told me to have two. I had nothing stronger than a club soda with lime.

Well, hellos led to flirtations, which led to more drinks (whiskey for him; club soda masquerading as gin and tonic for me), which led to my bold suggestion that we raid his boss's high-end liquor cabinet. I mean, it was just around the corner, and I knew Prentiss had the pass card and keys . . .

I know what you're going to say, and believe me, I already said those things to myself. But remember what I told you about the other side not playing fair?

Anyway, this wasn't a long shot; I know a few things about Prentiss. For one, he has a larcenous streak, so the idea of getting hammered on Chuck Castrina's expensive scotch while possibly making out with a former reporter on Castrina's ten-thousand-dollar Chesterfield leather sofa . . . well, this would be too great a temptation to resist. And the other thing about Prentiss? He's pretty much a lightweight. We made it to the sofa . . . and that was it before he passed out.

I helped myself to the file cabinet. The keys were on Prentiss's ring.

I found Francine Hughes's file.

And V., let me tell you, I wish I'd had a few drinks before opening that folder of horrors.

I scanned everything and dropped it into this folder. Take a look for yourself. Just be warned—it is entirely awful.

CHAPTER 84

REPORT TO C. LAMB BY V. SUAREZ
SATURDAY, JANUARY 29
(SENT WITH ENCRYPTION AND RED-FLAGGED, WITH
DELIVERY CONFIRMATION)

Some quick but extremely vital updates. Please read carefully, boss. I'm going to call you after I end this to follow up.

And I know you're going to ask me about sources, and I'll share what I can with you at a later date if you really need to know. But in the past, you've expressed strong disinterest in all of my "dark-web geek stuff," as you call it. So it's up to you. Just know that this information comes with the usual caveats.

I have a very solid lead on Roz Cline's killer. Yes, killer. Her death was no accident; this was a one-hundred-percent professional hit.

What's interesting is who they hired. The job didn't go to local muscle—and that upset the local muscle a great deal. Instead, the job went to an upper-echelon gunman who works out of both Vegas and Atlantic City. Expensive as they come, and absolutely bold and brazen. My sense is that he's the guy you bring in when you have champagne problems. The local muscle grumbled about it, but it's clear they're afraid of him, so they didn't grumble too loud.

Why bring in a hitter this expensive for a casino hostess like Roz Cline? It stands to reason she must have had some expensive information about Archie Hughes in her head.

I'm still working on identifying this hit man. Even an alias will help me track him, although I doubt he's still on the East Coast.

I'm also searching for who hired him, though the clients in these situations are always very well shielded (as you can imagine). But even if I can't find the client's identity, knowing what channels he or she used will be helpful. There are only so many ways you can find a killer for hire, and the method of communication will tell me a great deal about the client.

More updates as I learn them.

But I can't stress this enough: Watch your back out there. You know me, boss. Very little frightens me. Well, I am very frightened by the types of people who are involved in this investigation.

Keep your head low. You know your tendency to take a wild leap, maybe piss off the wrong person? Yeah, don't do that. At least not until you hear from me again.

CHAPTER 85

6:03 p.m.

VEENA LION found herself sitting across from Cooper Lamb in his backyard (although *backyard* was a stretch for the concrete slab behind his brownstone), both of them on rickety beach chairs, knees touching, passing a cold bottle of Yuengling Lager back and forth. There were four more holstered in the cardboard carrier at their feet. The beer would stay perfectly cold. The sun had set, and outside felt like the inside of an industrial freezer.

"Can't we take these to your kitchen table?" Veena asked.

"I don't spend nearly enough time in my backyard," Cooper said. "I thought it was one of the selling points of this place."

"This is a glorified alley, my friend."

"Yeah, but it's *my* alley; no one else has access but me. I was thinking this spring I could put a grill out here, maybe hang a few twinkle lights. You think the kids would like that?"

"I think this alley is so narrow, the kids will have to watch from inside as you flip burgers."

"The other selling point?" Cooper continued as if Veena hadn't spoken. "No one would think to plant a bug out here."

Veena's eyes narrowed. "You think somebody wired your place?"

"I have to assume so, yes. Yours too."

"It doesn't matter," Veena said. "I won't need words to explain what I've found." She removed the folder from her briefcase and handed it to Cooper, who in turn handed her the Yuengling. Veena finished the bottle, slid the empty into a slot, and removed another beer from the cardboard carrier.

Cooper quickly read Janie's memo, then flipped to the next page. It was a printout of a photograph, just like every other item in this folder.

Cooper was puzzled. He flipped to the next. And the next. And the next, and soon, the images fell together into a complete picture. Just as they had for Veena.

Cooper looked up and locked eyes with her. His eyes were wet. Veena passed the beer over to Cooper. He nodded his thanks, drained half of it, passed the bottle back, and continued flipping pages.

Veena pulled out her phone and did a quick search for *Francine Pearl Hughes* and *Kennedy Center*. The video was the first to appear in the search. It was a concert from last summer, with the president and his wife in the audience. Critics ranked her iconic performance as right up there with greats like Aretha Franklin, Beyoncé, Patti LaBelle, and Pink.

Veena pointed at Francine's arms on the screen.

"Yeah, it's a nice dress," Cooper said.

"But look at the style. That dress? On a hot summer evening?"

Cooper squinted, then slowly understood. "He hit her only where clothes would hide the bruises." He said it softly, not because he was afraid of being overheard, but because he was still reeling from what he'd seen in the folder.

The abusive texts were bad enough. But the violence inflicted on Francine's body earned her abuser a special place in hell.

The bruises somehow looked raw and tender, even though he was seeing them in two-dimensional, black-and-white images. He felt as if touching the photo would make the subject flinch.

Big powerful hands inflicted that damage. You could make out the dark purple finger marks from where he'd grabbed her and decided to make her suffer.

The folder was stuffed with similar images from all over Francine's body—where no one else would see.

No one except Archie.

"Keep flipping," Veena said.

"I don't know if I can."

"You have to."

"What am I going to see?"

"Just keep flipping."

Cooper continued flipping, and soon the images changed. Were these bruises shot at a different angle? It looked like Francine Pearl Hughes had somehow shrunk, as if the savage beatings had diminished her, made her a frail shadow of herself.

But the photos weren't of Francine. Once Cooper understood, he felt an atom bomb explode in his chest.

"He hit the kids too."

SUNDAY, JANUARY 30

CHAPTER 86

2:57 p.m.

"I CAN'T believe we're actually doing this!" said Cooper Lamb Jr.

"Me too," replied his father, although without quite the same level of enthusiasm.

That they were attending the NFC championship game wasn't the surprise. Harold Sable had honored his promise; a cream-colored envelope with the team logo had been waiting for *Mr. Cooper Lamb and Family* at the will-call window. But there were no tickets inside.

Instead, Cooper had pulled out a handwritten note instructing him to take the enclosed green plastic card to a particular luxury box and swipe it through the reader. Cooper led his children to the elevators per the instructions.

Cooper was reasonably sure that Harold Sable wasn't the one who'd written *XOXO* at the bottom of the note.

"Isn't this just a wee bit unethical?" asked Ariel Lamb as the elevator doors closed. "I mean, taking championship-game seats from someone who might be implicated in a murder?"

"Accepting seats may be a little unethical," Cooper replied. "But it's not as if we're hanging out with the owners in their luxury box or anything."

"Dad," Cooper Jr. said. "These are the elevators to the luxury boxes."

Cooper turned to his children and winked.

One swipe of the card led them into Glenn Sable's lair, which was directly next to his father's (bigger) box. The reactions from those gathered inside told Cooper everything he needed to know. A look of shock—perhaps even fear—flickered on Glenn Sable's face before he covered it up with a scowl.

The Hughes children were there, and they squealed with delight the moment they saw Cooper, thinking he had Lupe with him. Alas, he had left his constant companion with his ex-wife; a stadium full of screaming fans wasn't the ideal place for the pup. After hearing that, the Hughes kids waved shy hellos and turned their attention back to the pregame festivities taking place on the field.

But Maya Rain was there, and she wore a warm, knowing smile as she locked eyes with Cooper. Of course she was the one who had arranged this.

"Thank you," Cooper told her.

"For what?" she replied.

"X-O-X-O?"

"Mea culpa," she said, smiling. "I like you, Cooper. I couldn't have you and your family sitting out there in the cold. What good is a personal connection to the team if you can't exploit it every once in a while?"

"Well, I appreciate it. So do my children."

"They are very welcome. Your wife couldn't join us?"

Cooper smirked. "I'm divorced. But I think you knew that."

"How would I know that?"

Cooper had a half dozen responses to that question: *Because you're super-observant, and I'm not wearing a ring. Because we've been walking a flirtatious line for days and never once did you bring up other partners. Although you don't seem to have a problem with married men.* But he let it go. "Speaking of personal connections, where's Francine?"

"She wasn't feeling up to this today," Maya said. "And I don't think anyone could blame her. But the kids wanted to see the game, so I agreed to take them."

"Another tough day at the office, huh?"

Maya leaned in close, as if she were about to reveal something dark and personal. She touched the top of Cooper's hand; her fingertips were cold. "I'm not exactly a sports fan," she whispered.

Cooper, pretending to be scandalized by this confession, held his hand to his mouth. He saw Glenn Sable throwing eye-daggers his way. Apparently this particular private eye was most unwelcome in Glenn's luxury box.

Not that his children noticed. They were too busy joining the Hughes children in a raid on Glenn's Eagles-themed dessert bar. There was plenty of Stock's pound cake with green frosting, Termini Brothers cookies in the shape of the team logo, and ice-filled coolers holding tubs of Breyers mint chocolate chip.

"I don't think the little big man likes that we're speaking," Cooper said.

"Little big man doesn't like a lot of things."

"Such as?"

"Let's just say that Francine isn't here right now with her children because she's not exactly welcome."

"Glenn has a problem with Philadelphia's sweetheart?"

Cooper was suddenly aware of the lack of space between them. Good thing his children were laser-focused on the overflowing buffet of sugar.

"The Sables thought Francine was bad for Archie's career. That she distracted him from his commitment to the team. Pulled him closer to show business instead of the game."

"God forbid Archie make someone *else* money," Cooper muttered.

"I guess they wanted to squeeze every dime out of their investment before he retired."

"It's not just that," Maya said. "The Sables even tried to block Francine's halftime performance at this year's Super Bowl."

Cooper couldn't help himself—he threw Glenn Sable some eye-daggers of his own.

CHAPTER 87

TAKE AWAY the shocking murder. Take away the unprecedented weeklong delay. Take away all of the naysayers who said the Eagles wouldn't go any further without Archie Hughes's almost supernatural touchdown passes.

If you had been dropped down into a stadium seat and told absolutely *nothing* about this game, you'd still quickly realize you were watching the greatest nail-biter of all time. Despite everyone believing that the Giants would humiliate the Birds, the Eagles stood firm. New quarterback Terry Mortelite held his own, working well with receiver Lee McCoy. By halftime, the Eagles were down by only three points.

Ordinarily, Cooper Lamb would have enjoyed such an exciting nail-biter. But his focus stayed on the occupants of the luxury box, most of whom were cheering and shouting and absolutely giddy with the thrill of possible victory. Even those who weren't jacked up on sweets had delighted expressions on their faces; they all looked like they'd been handed a surprise gift from the football gods.

All except one person—the man who should have been the happiest. Instead of celebrating along with the rest of the box, Glenn Sable looked like someone had urinated all over his fancy dessert table.

Cooper decided to wander over to Glenn for a mood check. And maybe get some long-overdue answers.

"Jimmy Tua is an absolute madman on the field," Cooper told the younger Sable. "I can't believe what I'm seeing. You must be turning cartwheels."

"Game's not over yet," Glenn grumbled. He refused to look Cooper in the eye.

"Ah. You're being cautious. I can respect that."

"That ain't it, Lamb. Archie should be down there right now. None of this feels right without him."

"Your players are honoring him the best way they can. They're clawing their way back."

"Yeah, yeah."

"Though I'm not sure Archie deserves it."

That got Glenn's attention. He didn't seem able to process what he'd just heard. Was it a joke or an insult or something else? Cooper let the little big man sort through his very big feelings for a moment before leaning in close.

"I saw what that monster did to his wife and children," Cooper snarled. "And you're a monster for protecting him."

"You think you can go around saying whatever you want," Glenn said quietly. "But that's not the way the world works."

"I want no part of a world where cruelty to children is not only accepted but rewarded."

"Speaking of, why don't you take your kids and leave."

"What, did they finish your favorite ice cream?"

Glenn could no longer keep his voice quiet or calm. "You want me to call security? Let Cooper Junior see Daddy get his ass royally kicked?"

Maya Rain appeared between them with the stealth of a boxing referee. "I'll take the kids down to your car, Cooper."

"Ha, look at that!" cried Glenn with fake delight. "You need a nanny to bail you out. Yeah, real tough guy. You're as soft as your last name!"

"I am soft, you're right," Cooper said with a smile. "Ordinarily if someone said that, I'd threaten to break his bones, but I'm too lazy to wade through all that fat."

Maya slowly closed her eyes. "Oh, boy." She opened her eyes and placed a hand on Cooper's chest. "We should go."

"What did you say to me?" Glenn said, as if he were preparing to fight Cooper.

"You can't bury the truth forever," Cooper said. "That's not the way the world works."

CHAPTER 88

Transcript of conversation between Cooper Lamb and Maya Rain, captured using a recording app on Lamb's smartwatch

COOPER LAMB: Thanks for being the cooler head up there.

MAYA RAIN: All part of the job. Cleaning up messes—

LAMB: Is what you do, right?

RAIN: Something like that.

COOPER LAMB JR.: Dad, can we turn on the radio so we can at least *hear* the second half of the game?

LAMB: What? Oh, right. Hand these keys to your sister and turn on the power. Do *not* turn on the engine, you got it?

COOPER JR.: Got it.

RAIN: Smart idea. Because we need to talk.

LAMB: Well, there isn't a pool house handy, so I had to improvise.

(*Ambient sounds of power windows being raised, and a muffled sports broadcast behind the recorded voices.*)

RAIN: I can't believe what you said to Glenn.

LAMB: I'm tired of everyone lying. Did you know what that monster did to Francine and the kids?

RAIN: I didn't know . . . everything. Not until after, when it was too late to do anything about it.

LAMB: Sounds like Archie deserved some cosmic payback. Part of me is glad he's dead.

RAIN: Don't say that.

LAMB: That's not going to stop me from finding out who killed him. The Sables know a lot more than they're saying.

RAIN: Sure, but I thought you would have been a *little* more professional. Especially considering you were a guest.

LAMB: To steal your favorite line: It's all part of the job. It's what *I* do.

RAIN: What *are* you trying to do, Cooper?

LAMB: Some people don't tell the truth until you push them out of their comfort zone, make them a little miserable. But I'm sure you knew that, otherwise you wouldn't have invited me into Sable's luxury box.

RAIN: No good deed goes unpunished.

LAMB: Is that why you were surveilling Roz Cline? You were trying to do a good deed?

RAIN: Who told you about...never mind, it doesn't matter.

LAMB: We'd save each other a lot of time if we were honest. I don't know how you fit into all of this, and I can't tell if you're trying to help me or throw me hopelessly off track.

RAIN: You think way too much of me.

LAMB: Here's some honesty: I think about you a lot.

RAIN: (*Pause*) Cooper...we can't do this.

LAMB: Because you're with Mickey Bernstein? How did you even meet him?

RAIN: I should get back to the kids.

LAMB: Give me one more minute. Tell me why you were watching Roz Cline. You know she's dead, right? Pushed right off her penthouse balcony in the middle of the afternoon.

RAIN: I know, Cooper.

LAMB: Of course you know. Bernstein is investigating that murder too, even though he should be a million f█████ miles from all of these cases.

RAIN: I don't ask Mickey about his business, and he doesn't ask about mine. How we met doesn't matter, but it has nothing to do with Archie's murder.

LAMB: So why keep tabs on Roz Cline?

RAIN: I did it for Francine. I know this may not make sense to you, but she's become my dearest friend. I was hired to care for her children, but I came to care for her too. That's the way it happens sometimes. And the thought of anyone hurting her . . . I just couldn't let that happen.

LAMB: How could Roz hurt Francine?

RAIN: Cooper, my friend, I think you know exactly how.

LAMB: None of this makes sense. You know that, right? Help me out here.

RAIN: That's what I've been doing, whether you believe me or not. Kids' messes aren't the only messes I clean up.

LAMB: Who's looking out for you?

RAIN: That's sweet. And I truly mean it. So few people look out for each other these days. Especially in this city.

LAMB: So let me protect you.

RAIN: Go listen to the rest of the game with your kids. I think the Birds are going to give people a big surprise.

LAMB: Says the non–sports fan.

RAIN: Call me an optimist.

CHAPTER 89

"WOW, DAD, game of the century and we're sitting in your car," Ariel said. "Can't wait to tell my grandkids someday about the epic championship game I *almost* saw."

"Ingrate. Up until an hour ago, you were feasting on sugary sweets in one of the owners' boxes! Tell your grandkids about *that*."

"This is so lame."

"Shhh, quiet for a second."

Cooper didn't want to care about the Eagles or the game or anything else that wasn't related to the three murders he was investigating. But he couldn't help it; the game *was* one for the record books. It was a nail-biter right up to the very end, when the new quarterback managed some kind of insane Hail Mary pass (and oh, did Cooper regret not being able to see it) and, with just *seconds* to go ... clinched the Eagles' victory.

"Dad."

"Wow, wow, wow," Cooper said, stunned.

"*Dad,*" Ariel said. "I can't believe we missed that!"

His daughter was right. He should have waited to squeeze Glenn Sable until after the game was over. Maybe that would have revealed another piece of the puzzle, because one thing was clear: Glenn Sable had not been happy about the prospect of an Eagles victory.

Did he have Archie murdered to ensure the team's loss? And if so, why? A winning team was far more profitable than a runner-up. None of this made sense.

"Well," Cooper said, "at least there's the Super Bowl to look forward to."

"Where are we going to watch that?" Cooper Jr. asked. "In a dumpster behind the stadium?"

"Keep joking, kid," Cooper replied. "Wiseasses don't go to Chickie's and Pete's for a celebratory dinner."

"We'll never get a table there. Not on a day like this."

"You're lucky to have a father who knows a guy who knows a guy. There's a table waiting for us."

"Don't drink too much beer when we're there," Ariel said. "Mom doesn't like it when you drink too much beer, then drive us home."

"I promise I will drink an entirely appropriate amount of beer," Cooper assured his daughter. "Now, let's beat the crowd and feast on some Crabfries."

CHAPTER 90

REPORT TO C. LAMB BY V. SUAREZ
SUNDAY, JANUARY 30
*(SENT WITH ENCRYPTION AND RED-FLAGGED, WITH
DELIVERY CONFIRMATION)*

Here's what I've been able to learn about this hired killer.

He has no real name (or aliases) that I can pin to a driver's
license or passport. But he has two nicknames: "the Quiet One"
and "Tesla." The names are a nod to this hit man's silence and
speed. If you want a hit done fast and clean with zero traces, you
pay extra for the Quiet One.

No law enforcement agency, domestic or foreign, has been
able to gather more than scraps about the Quiet One. (I know; I
looked.) The FBI won't even acknowledge he exists, attributing his
work to various other people. As if it would be bad form to admit
total defeat.

But for the Archie Hughes and Roz Cline killings, the Quiet
One seems to fit. There was zero forensic evidence left behind; no

cameras caught the murder; and the killer eluded the authorities despite police officers being on the scene almost immediately.

The missing Super Bowl ring is the only part of this that feels off. The Quiet One would not bother with such a souvenir—unless his client had insisted on it. That said, it still feels out of character.

Under my own alias, I tried to reach out to arrange some kind of meeting with the Quiet One or one of his associates. I was pretty much laughed out of the dark web. The kind of people who can afford to hire the Quiet One are way above my pay grade...or even one that I can reasonably fake. Every overture I made was quickly shut down.

And I'll be honest: I'm worried about trying again, because I'd rather not catch the Quiet One's attention. You treat me fair, boss, but I don't want to die for this job.

This should tell you a lot about who might have hired the Quiet One to kill Archie Hughes. These are not ordinary wealthy people. They look down on new-money types like the Sables. We're talking about the highest echelon of the wealthy, individuals who reshape the world as they like. You have to ask yourself, why would these people want Archie dead?

Hope you and the kids had fun at the game. I'll admit to being incredibly jealous that you were able to witness firsthand the Hail Mary pass they'll be talking about for decades to come.

I'll send more as I learn it.

Oh, one more thing—this just came in. It's about Maya Rain. See the document attached to this message.

CHAPTER 91

9:48 p.m.

COOPER DRANK more than an appropriate amount of beer.

Not with the children, of course. He had his two standard bottles of Yuengling Lager and enough crab fries to soak up every last ounce of that beer. The mood at Chickie's and Pete's was festive, and of course Cooper loved celebrating with his kids. But he was very distracted.

One distraction was Victor's most recent report, which was even more alarming than the first. The Quiet One, huh? Why were they working so hard to find a killer who could disappear without a trace, eluding the FBI, Interpol, you name it? How could two private eyes from Philly possibly hope to find him?

But that was academic for now. The second, and bigger, distraction was Maya Rain. Cooper couldn't help but think he'd missed an opportunity back at the Linc. Maybe there was something he could have said to unlock her mental vault. Cooper liked her a lot but didn't trust her; maybe she felt the same way about him. Behind the flirtation, they were both cautious, professional people.

Maybe he should try again, convince her that he was worth her trust.

While settling the tab at Chickie's, Cooper bought a six-pack of Yuengling and stashed it in the trunk of his car. After dropping off

271

his children—and once again hearing the story of how Dad had ruined the championship game for them—Cooper drove across Center City to Eighteenth Street. As it was Sunday, there were parking spots available. He parked in essentially the same spot he had a few days ago and nursed his beer while waiting for Maya to return home. Although maybe she had plans with Mickey Bernstein.

At the tail end of Cooper's fourth lager, Bernstein dropped Maya off. They kissed goodbye. Maya went upstairs.

Cooper was nowhere numb enough. It still hurt.

He thought about drinking the fifth and sixth beers. Instead, he went into Maya's building. The two lagers were enough of a bribe for Curt the doorman—hell, the entire city was in a celebratory mood. Besides, Curt recognized Cooper. "Go on up. I'll let her know you're on the way."

While consuming beers one through four in the driver's seat of his car, Cooper had planned his speech—this was how he'd earn her trust and work his way into her heart. But when Maya opened the door, his brain refused to cooperate, so he said the first thing that came to mind, an item he'd just come across in Vincent's latest file: "You own a Glock forty-four."

"Good to see you again too, Cooper. Do you want to come in?"

So much for trust. Well, in for a dime, in for a dollar. "That's the same model that killed Archie Hughes."

Maya closed the door behind him. "You think I killed my own employer?"

"No," Cooper said. "I'm just following the evidence. Did anyone have access to your gun besides you?"

"Before I start talking about my personal firearms—which, by the way, are perfectly normal in West Virginia—can I offer you something to drink?"

"I've had enough to drink," Cooper said. "Schuylkill punch will be fine."

"I don't know how to make that cocktail."

"Just turn on the tap."

Where was he going with this? Cooper didn't know, but the document that Victor had sent while Cooper and the kids were at Chickie's and Pete's clearly showed a Glock .44 registered to Maya Rain at this address. Recent permit too; Victor said it had been pushed through the system in record time. Why would a nanny suddenly need to pack heat?

When Maya returned from the kitchen, she was holding a gun.

CHAPTER 92

"I'M NO expert," Cooper said, "but I'm fairly sure that's not a glass of water."

"I'll get that in a minute," Maya said.

"Would that be *after* you kill me?"

There was one of those horrible, elongated moments—a second or two in actual time that feels like an eternity when you experience it. Both of their lives could hinge on what happened next.

"You really do think the worst of me," she replied, breaking the tension. "No, I brought this out to show you my high-school graduation present from my father. Very ladylike, isn't it?"

Maya snapped open the wheel of the small pearl-handled revolver and showed him the empty chambers. She moved with the grace of a person who had grown up with guns. Cooper was simply relieved he wouldn't be forced to pull his own piece and engage in a gun battle with the most beautiful woman he'd ever met.

"Adorable," Cooper said. "But that's not the gun I was talking about."

"But this is my point," Maya said. "I don't know how you learned about the Glock, but that was a gift from Detective Bernstein. I guess he thinks I'm just some rube from West Virginia, so I need to have some personal protection."

"Where is the Glock?"

"That's the weird thing—I don't know. Maybe he took it back when he realized I had my own gun and a permit to carry? I honestly hadn't thought about it until you mentioned it."

Cooper's mind spun with possible explanations, all of them sinister. Among the worst was the idea that Bernstein was trying to frame Maya, taking advantage of her kindness and her proximity to the murder victim. Could be that he wasn't dating Maya; he was merely getting close enough to tighten the noose around her slender neck.

"I know where the gun is," Cooper said. "It's booked into evidence."

Maya's face twisted with revulsion. "Are you saying *that* gun was used to kill Archie?"

"Possibly," Cooper said. "If we knew for sure, we'd be that much closer to finding his killer."

"I'll get that water now. And a drink for myself."

Cooper followed her into the kitchenette. She opened the tap to fill a tumbler, then turned around to find Cooper very close.

"There's no one else here," Cooper said. "It's just the two of us now. If you tell me what you know, I'll do everything in my power to protect you."

"I'm not the one who needs protecting."

"What do you mean by that?"

Maya sighed. "Archie had enemies on and off the field. You don't want to provoke them."

"What, you don't think I can handle myself?"

"Clearly that's what you think about me."

Cooper had to admit she had a point.

"Listen," he said. "All I'm saying is, if you let people like Bernstein and the Sables into your life, they're going to want something in return. They always do. Maybe it's something as simple as sex. But sometimes it's more. A lot more. I don't want you getting hurt."

Maya smiled. "Look, I have my eyes open. Mickey is just . . . we're having fun. We both know what this is. And the Sables, yeah, they're sleazebags, but they're mostly full of bluster. They're harmless. I've had to deal with guys like them all my life. I know how to handle them."

"The same words have been spoken by every victim," Cooper said, "right before she realizes she *can't* handle them."

"Do I look like a victim to you?"

Maya Rain filled the tumbler with water and gave it to him. And in that instant, Cooper saw her mask slip a little. He saw a fierceness in her eyes, and it caught him by surprise. Maybe it was anger, maybe it was lust, maybe it was something else. Cooper could have responded with another question. Or a kiss . . .

But his instincts told him to go in the opposite direction. So he dumped the water into the sink, walked out of the apartment, took the elevator down, and left the building.

CHAPTER 93

THE WALL exploded just to the left of Cooper Lamb's face. Hot fragments stung his cheeks as he dived to the sidewalk. Without even thinking, he pulled his Browning from his underarm holster and returned fire.

The shots came from the service driveway next to Maya's building. The same driveway where Bernstein had picked her up the other day.

That you, Mickey? You jealous bastard.

Cooper kept firing at the shadows as he ran, hoping his would-be killer would seek cover and allow Cooper to reach his car on Eighteenth Street. And Cooper almost did. But the assassin was quick and clearly unafraid. Return fire chewed up the asphalt under Cooper's feet. He was already moving fast, but he dug deep and found the fuel to move faster. Cooper's wartime responses kicked in—he made it to the other side of his car without being hit. Bullets shattered the window over his head. Beads of glass rained down into his hair. This assassin meant it.

Yeah, but so did Cooper.

He reloaded quickly and returned fire over the hood of his car. Six shots, all aimed at the killer's center of gravity—based on his best guess of where that was, of course. The killer was still hidden in the shadows. But Cooper had had plenty of experience in the army firing into the shadows at people who wanted him to die.

Cooper crouched down and listened closely. Total silence except for the far-off wail of a siren. Gunfire in this part of Philadelphia was rare; someone had called it in.

Either he'd hit the gunman or the gunman had fled the scene.

That meant that with every second, the shooter—and potential witness—was either slipping farther into the afterlife or putting more distance between himself and Cooper.

Do you think you hit him, Cooper? There was a third possibility: the shooter was waiting for him to stick his head up so he could blow it away.

Nobody lives forever, Cooper told himself. He darted out from behind the car and ran toward the service driveway. At the other end, he spied a vague form running away, pumping his arms and legs and moving with preternatural speed.

Damn it.

CHAPTER 94

COOPER REMEMBERED exactly where the service driveway led: to a side street that took you to either Sansom Street or Walnut Street, depending on which way you turned. As he approached the driveway's end, he flipped a mental coin, then hung a right toward Sansom.

It was the correct move. Cooper caught sight of the shooter as he raced to the left, headed west down Sansom.

Whoever this guy was, he had the speed of an Olympic sprinter. Cooper was surprisingly fast too, especially given his height. But he had to ignore the pounding of his heart and the screaming of his muscles to keep pace with the shooter.

Cooper hoped this guy would hop into a car at some point so he'd have a legitimate reason to give up the pursuit. But no. The shooter continued to run. So, what, had he taken public transportation to the hit?

By the time the shooter reached Twenty-Second and Market, Cooper realized that he might have done just that. The guy was headed down a set of concrete stairs to the underground trolley line.

Cooper skidded to a halt just before the stairs. Could be a trap. Shooter could be waiting at the bottom for Cooper's silhouette to appear, and then *blam-blam-blam*—slaughtered Lamb.

He waited. The seconds piled up again. Cooper hated this. The shooter was probably catching a trolley right now.

Except...wasn't it too late for that? These lines ground to a halt around eleven p.m. Most likely, the shooter was down there waiting for him.

Screw it.

Cooper crouched and peered down the stairs, Browning in his hands. Fluorescent lights flickered on the grime and litter. There was no shooter.

He bounded down the stairs, ready for an ambush. *Where are you?* He listened carefully.

The tiled walls of the station echoed with a peculiar sound. Something slapping. It was faint, but it was fast and consistent in its rhythm. Cooper turned the corner and saw that he was right, the station was closed. But there was enough room above a security gate for someone very determined to scale it and jump down to the other side.

Down to the tracks. And that's when Cooper understood the slapping sound. They were footsteps.

The shooter was escaping through the trolley tunnel.

CHAPTER 95

THIS WAS probably one of the worst ideas in the long, troubled history of bad ideas. Cooper knew this. But he scaled the gate anyway.

The army had prepared him for these kinds of insane activities. Climbing tall barriers. Hunting prey in the dark. Running until you thought your heart and lungs would burst in your rib cage.

But none of those activities usually took place in a cold urban environment like this one: a freezing, grimy commuter tunnel that plowed under the Schuylkill River.

Yep. A seriously bad idea, for sure.

But Cooper knew he couldn't turn around and make the loser's march back to his car on Eighteenth Street. When someone tries to blow your brains out, you don't just turn the other cheek so he can take another shot. Cooper needed to find this bastard and make him explain.

So into the tunnel he went, pumping his legs as fast as he could.

The terrain was dark and treacherous. He had to avoid the rails and trash and vermin (yeah, he could hear them complain and squeak) while still matching the speed of the shooter, who was barely visible at the far end of the tunnel. Why did he have to be so fast? Why couldn't they have dispatched a weight-challenged hit man, some dude named Mel or Irv who could be caught easily?

Cooper couldn't help thinking about what Victor had told him about the Atlantic City hit man, aka Tesla or the Quiet One. The assassin notorious for speed (check) and stealth (check). Is that who Cooper was chasing through this damn tunnel?

On top of all that, Cooper idly wondered (as he ran, ran, ran) how wide the Schuylkill River was, how long this tunnel went on. Did the Quiet One have an end point in mind? Or did he think there was no way Cooper would be stupid enough to pursue him down here?

Sorry, Tesla, Cooper thought. *I am that stupid.*

The tunnel seemed to go on forever. Cooper wouldn't have been surprised to see signs for Pittsburgh. But he turned a bend, and the dim glow of the next station appeared in the distance. Thirty-Third Street, right in the heart of the University of Pennsylvania's campus. Maybe the Quiet One was returning to his dorm in the quad.

The sharp crack of a push bar on a metal gate told Cooper that his quarry was headed to the surface.

Ignore your pounding heart. Ignore your burning lungs. Get up there, Cooper. Go bag yourself a hit man.

When he reached the street, he saw a surprising number of students around. Probably coming home after a long night of post-Eagles-win revelry. Cooper scanned the slowly moving bodies for the one body who looked out of place. *Come on, Quiet One, show yourself...*

"It's a cop!" someone cried.

Cooper spun around to find the tipsy student was talking about *him*.

"You don't belong here!" the doughy-faced kid in John Lennon glasses shouted. "Get off our campus, pig!"

"Did you see a slender man with a gun run through here?"

Cooper asked him and his friends. But they either didn't hear him or didn't care to answer. They closed ranks around Cooper, feeling emboldened by the lager or cider or shots in their systems.

"Defund the police!"

"'I can't breathe!'"

"Blue lives suck!"

Cooper tried to ignore them as he looked around for any trace of the Quiet One. If the shooter was smart—and clearly he was—he would have slowed down and blended into the crowd. But Cooper would recognize him. Not that he had a description, but he'd spent the past twenty minutes watching the shooter *move*. He was pretty sure he could identify him by body language.

The students, however, were determined to give him as much grief as possible. They blocked his attempts to look around them and continued shouting slogans at him.

"All cops are bastards!"

"Defund the po-po!"

"I don't believe this," Cooper said. "You've got a problem with me, but you guys are cool with a professional killer roaming the campus?"

The Quiet One—if indeed that's who Cooper had been chasing—was nowhere in sight. Cooper had lost him. He holstered his Browning and willed himself to take slow, steady breaths.

A young woman with blue hair practically spat in his face. "When's the last time you murdered someone, *pig*?"

"Ask me again in a couple of days," Cooper replied.

CHAPTER 96

COOPER LAMB took the long way home.

Not because he wanted to. He would have loved nothing more than to crash for a few hours and allow his stressed body to recharge. But that might be a fatal mistake. The shooter had known exactly where to find Cooper tonight, so he most certainly knew where Cooper lived. Cooper could be stumbling right into an ambush.

Okay, part of him didn't care—an early death would let him catch up on his sleep. But Cooper needed to see this case through to the end. And, if nothing else, get a little payback after that guy had tried to remodel Cooper's face with a bullet.

The long way home meant a meandering route up Thirty-Fourth Street to the Philadelphia Zoo (*Hello, lions, I'll say hi to Veena for you*), then across the Girard Avenue Bridge and past Girard College, the nearly two-hundred-year-old boarding school originally opened for fatherless boys. This reminded him of Archie Hughes Jr. Strange to think that in another era, he might have ended up here.

From there, he took Corinthian Street down to his own neighborhood, skirting along the east side of the Eastern State Penitentiary. Its guests had included Al Capone and Willie Sutton; today, the former prison catered to history buffs and haunted-building freaks.

Cooper liked the place because the Dead Milkmen shot the video for "Punk Rock Girl" inside its walls.

On Green Street, he saw no obvious signs that anyone was watching his brownstone. Still, Cooper hopped a fence and made his way to his backyard—what Veena had dismissed as a glorified alley. Okay, maybe this *was* an alley. The place felt extra-claustrophobic now that he was steeling himself for a possible attack.

Cooper checked all possible entry points in the back of his brownstone, looking for anything out of place. Everything seemed fine except for one detail.

No excited Lupe noises.

Lupe always greeted him eagerly when he arrived home. In fact, whenever Cooper entered through the back, he always saw Lupe's excited face looking down at him from the bedroom windows.

He wasn't there now.

Cooper doubled back and made his way around to the front of his building. He slid his key into the lock with surgical-level care and precision to avoid making any noise. He kept his front door well oiled with WD-40 specifically for moments like these. Stealth was everything; some old army habits died hard.

The front door opened into a foyer and long hallway. His Browning was empty, but his possible attackers didn't know that. If it came to it, he could use it as a distraction while planning his next move.

But if they'd hurt Lupe, there would be no planning needed. Cooper would punish them. Punish them *permanently*.

Cooper moved down the length of his hallway, taking care not to step on the floorboards that creaked.

Gun in hand, he slowly opened his bedroom door to find . . .

Lupe staring back at him from the bed. *Oh, you're home.*

Next to him was a slender form wrapped up in his comforter. The form stirred, then rolled over into a new position.

Cooper felt all the tension in his body dissolve at once. He undressed and slipped into bed next to Veena. The world was a dangerous, screwed-up place, but somehow this made it okay. For tonight, anyway. Veena stirred, pushing her body back into Cooper's.

"Love you," she whispered, then went back to sleep.

MONDAY, JANUARY 31

CHAPTER 97

7:13 a.m.

ON A few occasions, Cooper Lamb had felt the need to shower with a gun close by. But walking his dog with a gun? This was a first.

One hand he kept on the leash, the other in his jacket pocket, fingers wrapped around the grip of his fully loaded Browning. His would-be killer was still out there, and Cooper would be foolish to venture outside without protection.

Lupe knew something was up. Cooper was sure the pup could feel the tension because he kept an extra-vigilant eye on Green Street, scanning for possible threats. Of course, to Lupe, a threat usually meant a squirrel. With the energy Cooper was radiating, the poor dog must have thought a fifty-foot squirrel was rampaging up the Ben Franklin Parkway.

No squirrels attacked. No gunmen either.

When Cooper returned home, Veena was already in the shower. Cooper unhooked Lupe's leash and walked into the kitchen to start breakfast. This Monday demanded something huge and greasy to soak up all that anxiety. Lupe kept a close eye on Cooper's movements in case a spare treat might be thrown his way.

In one oversize pan, a pile of sliced potatoes and bell peppers for Cooper's world-famous epic hash browns. In another pan, four thick slabs of scrapple, a Philly favorite. It was misunderstood by the world at large but incredibly delicious when grilled to perfection. Who cared that scrapple was essentially a gray block of all the parts of the pig that couldn't be sold separately and that most people put it in the same category as haggis? With the right amount of Pennsylvania Dutch seasoning (which Cooper suspected was largely pepper), it became a delicacy right up there with caviar.

"Oooh, scrapple," Veena said with honest delight as she sat down at the table. She was freshly scrubbed, and you would never know her clothes had been draped over Cooper's desk chair all night. Cooper, however, looked as if he'd rolled down a hill and slept in a gully. A shower was definitely in order.

"So what's next?" Veena asked as they were finishing breakfast.

"What, this artery-clogging feast wasn't enough for you? Should I put some baby backs on the grill?"

"With the Archie Hughes case," Veena clarified.

"Oh, what's next with *that*," Cooper said, then added with a note of solemnity, "Well, considering I was almost killed last night in pursuit of the truth—"

"Whatever," Veena replied. "What's next?"

"I'm actually being serious here, V. Someone took a few shots at me outside Maya Rain's building. I trailed him all the way to Penn, but I lost him in the crowd."

"Maya Rain's place. Huh."

"Yeah. She said something that's been knocking around in my skull all morning."

"I'm sure she did."

"No, not like that. About Archie having more enemies than just the ones on the field."

"You're thinking Archie himself was in some kind of trouble. This is interesting. Maybe our focus is too narrow. Let's think outside the NFL."

"Sure, but the NFL was Archie's entire life. To the point that the Sables were jealous when Archie spent time with his family."

"That's not entirely true," Veena said. "Janie found some financial breakdowns that... well, never mind that for now. But Archie's credit cards say that he spent a lot of lazy afternoons at the Merion Golf Club."

"You think his golfing buddies got mad and ordered a hit? What, did he play multiple balls on the same hole?"

"I doubt that's punishable by death." Veena polished off the last of her hash browns, then walked her plate into the kitchenette. "I'm just saying it's something we should look into."

Cooper pondered this. "Fair enough. I'll do it."

"But you made this lovely breakfast."

"And almost took a bullet to the brain! I don't know why you're not making a bigger deal out of that."

"Well, he missed, right? I'm going to bring the leftovers to Janie." Veena was already scooping eggs and hash browns into a plastic container.

"Anyway, I know the club a little," Cooper said. "It'll be easier for me to slip inside and ask some questions."

"Hmm. I don't think she's much of a scrapple fan. That's all you and Lupe."

"Generous of you! I'll let you know what I find."

"Bye, Lupe, sweetheart!" Veena called.

Bye, sweetheart, Cooper thought. He groaned as he dragged himself to the shower; he hated having to dress up and look semirespectable.

CHAPTER 98

Partial transcript of Cooper Lamb's conversation with Richard Gard and Loren Feldman, longtime members of the Merion Golf Club

COOPER LAMB: They really pour these bottomless Bloody Marys stiff here, gentlemen. (*Palm slaps a tabletop*) Hoo-ah!

RICHARD GARD: That's one of the best perks of the club, if you ask me. And thanks for this round, Cooper. Mighty kind of you.

LOREN FELDMAN: Jeez, stop pushing the kid. If he wants to join, he'll join.

LAMB: You know, I think you guys are talking me into it. And that's not just the rail vodka talking. (*Pause*) Tell me one thing, though. Archie Hughes was a member, right?

GARD: Boy, was he.

FELDMAN: Hey, enough of that. You want to get us kicked out?

GARD: What? It's not like it's a state secret or anything.

LAMB: What's a state secret? Ah, come on, guys! I'm, like, the world's biggest Birds fan. You gotta tell me!

GARD: Archie liked to gamble. Like, on everything. You could be standing on a street corner flipping a quarter, and he'd show up and want to make a wager.

FELDMAN: Yeah, but that wasn't the problem.

LAMB: What was the problem?

FELDMAN: The problem was, he was the worst gambler I ever met. He lost all the damn time! Whatever winning Archie Hughes had in him, he saved it for the football field. Which is good, because that's how he could afford to do all that losing.

GARD: Aw, Archie wasn't that bad.

FELDMAN: Wasn't that bad? How do you lose *half a million bucks* during so-called friendly rounds of golf?

LAMB: Whoa. He lost *how* much?

GARD: Look at who's spilling state secrets now.

FELDMAN: You started this! But yeah, he lost that much. Easy. I know a guy who pretty much financed his Margate summer home with what he took off Archie Hughes. Guy called his place the Eagles Nest. Which I think is pretty hilarious.

GARD: If you want some good Archie Hughes stories, you need to talk to Ben E.

FELDMAN: Oh yeah, Ben E. has all the great stories. Not only from here but down in AC too.

LAMB: Who's this Benny?

GARD: Come on, you're not that young! I'm sure you've seen Ben E. Franco. Legendary seashore comic. For a while there, he had a couple of men's clothing shops down on South Street. Maybe that was before your time.

FELDMAN: The old prick did have the best commercials! Remember the one where the models in bikinis came out and whipped him because he was selling his suits for too low a price?

LAMB: Sounds like my kind of guy. How can I get hold of Benny?

FELDMAN: No, it's not *Benny*. It's *Ben E*. E., like a middle initial.

LAMB: How can I get hold of Ben E.?

GARD: I don't know. Can you walk straight?

LAMB: If it makes you gentlemen feel better, I'll call a cab before heading over to him.

GARD: No, no. That's not why I'm asking.

LAMB: Then what does it matter if I can walk straight or not?

GARD: Because he's sitting right across the room.

CHAPTER 99

Transcript of conversation between Cooper Lamb and Ben E. Franco, semiretired Atlantic City entertainer

COOPER LAMB: Mr. Franco?

BEN E. FRANCO: If Mr. Franco owes you money, he said he'll be right back after he visits the cash machine.

LAMB: Ha-ha, nothing like that, Mr. Franco.

FRANCO: So formal! Call me Ben E. As long as we're so close, why don't you pull up a chair and buy me another mimosa.

LAMB: You got it. (*To waiter*) Excuse me, could you bring Mr. Franco another?

FRANCO: So what can I do for you, young man? You want an autograph for your sweetheart? Because, you know, she can have the real thing for next to nothing. Hell, at my age, I might even pay *her*.

LAMB: Heh. Your friends Rich and Loren over there said you had some good Archie Hughes stories.

FRANCO: Rich and who? Oh, the *alte kaker* over there with the lady's first name? Ah, they ain't my friends. They're hangers-on. Rich made a lot of money gouging people one billable hour at a time. I should know. He was my entertainment lawyer for years! And as for Loren Bacall, Christ on a cracker. The man can't handle his liquor. One time he was hauled in front of a judge. The judge says, "You've been brought here for drinking." Loren says, "Okay, let's get started."

LAMB: Ha-ha-ha, that's good, Ben E. But I'd really love to hear about Archie.

FRANCO: God rest his soul.

LAMB: You two were close, I gather.

FRANCO: You gather? What are you, a migrant field worker? No, we weren't close. That big bastard owed me a lot of money.

LAMB: Archie owed you money?

FRANCO: Are you kidding? Archie Hughes owed *everybody* money.

LAMB: How much money are we talking? Loren said it was something like half a million.

FRANCO: Ha! Don't listen to that souse, he has no idea what he's talking about. Archie owed a lot more than that. (*Whispering*) I'm talking *millions*.

LAMB: Come on.

FRANCO: Kid, you know I'm a kidder, but I ain't kidding about this. I've been around this town for way too many years and never saw anyone throw money away like Archie Hughes. He did it here, and I heard he owes millions out in that desert town too.

LAMB: Vegas?

FRANCO: No, the Gobi Desert. Yeah, Vegas! Where else do people go to hand over their hard-earned cash in exchange for the cheap flash of a leg and a piece of rubber chicken at a lousy buffet? Come to think of it, his buddy was in just as deep. And look where it got them.

LAMB: Which buddy?

FRANCO: You know, that ass█ chef who got himself killed last week.

LAMB: So you think their gambling debts had something to do with their deaths?

FRANCO: (*Long pause*) We've been joking around, kid, but listen to me. And listen to me carefully. This is serious business. Always has been. This is the way of the Mob. They want you to have a good time, drink their wines, feel up their girls, watch their ponies run. Whatever. But when the bill comes, you'd better be ready to open your wallet and pay. The entire organization runs on this principle. If people don't pay, the Mob goes away. And let me tell you, they're not going anywhere.

LAMB: Makes sense. But how do you get someone like Archie Hughes to pay?

FRANCO: If someone serious decides to welsh on a bet, you send someone serious to speak with him.

LAMB: What kind of serious are we talking about?

FRANCO: I think you know exactly the kind of *serious* I'm talking about. Look how Mr. Greatest of All Time ended up. Nobody's untouchable, Mr. Lamb.

LAMB: (*Slight pause*) You know who I am?

FRANCO: You've been asking a lot of questions around town. People have noticed. *Serious* people.

LAMB: I'd be happy to speak with these people. Maybe they can help me straighten all this out.

FRANCO: You don't understand. I am trying to help. I know this Mob guy. Capo. Friend of mine. Keeps a collection of other guys' balls in his man cave. He'd be happy to add yours to the collection. You're pissing off people. You're pissing off the *wrong* people. (*Pause*) Now, if you'll excuse me, I have to go shake the dew off my lily. Watch your back, kid. And your front.

CHAPTER 100

2:01 p.m.

VEENA COULD drive...technically. She just wasn't comfortable driving. But even though Cooper had tried to pace himself at the country club, he was in no condition to rocket down the Atlantic City Expressway. The mix of vodka and subtle death threats had clouded his mind. Which meant he handed his keys to a very reluctant Veena.

Cooper tried to keep her calm as she weaved in and out of traffic. "Look, it's a sleepy Monday in January. We'll have the whole city to ourselves."

"Yes. Just us and the gangsters you count as friends."

"Hey, Red is *not* a gangster," Cooper said. "At least, I don't *think* he is. Though if you're in business with a bunch of gangsters, I suppose that, strictly speaking—"

"And what about the associates of this Ben E. Franco guy?"

"He didn't name names. He didn't have to. But don't worry. I know the usual suspects—the next generation of the old Philly Mob. I'm not going to approach them until I vet them with Red."

"You couldn't have just called Red?"

"Some conversations need to happen face to face. Besides, I thought we deserved a little break. We'll talk to Red, then rent a penthouse for pennies and knock back some complimentary glasses of wine."

"Don't you have to be back in time to pick up the kids from school? And Lupe from your ex?"

"The Eagles just won the championship. Do you think anybody—let alone teachers—is in school today? Hey, keep your eyes on the road."

"You know what? Before we drive home tomorrow, I'm getting hammered, so you'll have to drive."

"Fair enough."

CHAPTER 101

CASINOS WATCH YOU.

There are no blind spots, no hidden corners—nothing is left to chance. If you ever want to record a few minutes of your life in complete detail (and from multiple angles), simply walk onto the main floor of a casino.

But Cooper and Veena weren't feeling *that* kind of watching.

When casinos watch you, it's like a mama bird making sure you aren't trying to run off with one of her chicks. This was a different kind of watching. More like a bird of prey sizing them up for the kill.

"Am I crazy," Cooper said, "or do you feel all kinds of eyes on us?"

"Oh, good. I thought it was just me."

"Well, Ben E. did say the Mob was well aware of our activities. I'm sure they're all wondering why we just checked into Caesars on Monday afternoon."

"Maybe we just can't say no to the slots," Veena said.

"Ben E. would have a crude double entendre to share off that one."

"And you don't?"

"I think I'm hungover. Let's get settled, then go have an early cocktail with Red Doyle."

"Didn't you just say you were hungover?"

"No better way to avoid crashing to the ground than by pulling back on the stick."

"Your best friend Ben E. would have a crude joke about that one too."

"I think he's my new hero." As Cooper spoke, the phone in his jacket pocket vibrated. "Hold on. Got a message from Victor."

REPORT TO C. LAMB BY V. SUAREZ
MONDAY, JANUARY 31
(SENT WITH ENCRYPTION AND RED-FLAGGED, WITH
DELIVERY CONFIRMATION)

A quick heads-up, boss. I know you're in AC with Ms. Lion. Just keep your eyes open. I confirmed this with three different sources (including the New Jersey Turnpike Authority): Mickey Bernstein's in AC too.

CHAPTER 102

"RED, MEET Veena. We're working the Archie Hughes case together."

"Yeah, yeah. Before I say a word, if the two of ya are secretly recording me right now, that would be a violation of New Jersey law."

"Come on, Red," Cooper said, "I wouldn't do you dirty like that. Besides, Jersey has a one-party consent law. We wouldn't need your permission."

"You for sure would do me dirty," Red replied. "I'm giving the lady the benefit of the doubt."

"We are not recording this conversation, Mr. Doyle," Veena said.

They were sitting in the cocktail bar of a hotel originally known as the Boardwalk Regency; it was one of the area's oldest hotel-casinos, opening in 1979, just after gambling became legal in Atlantic City. There had been a dizzying series of owners over the years and flirtations with a dozen different themes and styles, each one trying to find the secret mix of ingredients that would lure Philadelphians to AC instead of Vegas. None of them quite worked, so now the place was capitalizing on its old-school status—1979 was all the rage again, apparently.

Red Doyle had grown up in Atlantic City, and it showed. His

prematurely aged face seemed chiseled from granite and cured with years of alcohol and tobacco. He was off the cigarettes now, though; he contented himself with his whiskey sour. Veena had already polished off a glass of chardonnay and ordered another. Cooper stuck to a mug of Yuengling Lager.

"I need your confirmation on something," Cooper said.

"Unofficially," Red said. It was a demand, not a question.

"As always," Cooper said. "We know Archie owed quite a bit of money around town. We're trying to figure a ballpark estimate."

"Heh. A *bit* of money, huh? Whatever your guess might be, I guarantee the actual amount is way higher."

"Half a million," Veena suggested.

"Honey, please." Red waved his hand like he was trying to swat away the very notion. "Archie *wished* he owed me only half a million bucks. He was into me for about a million three."

"Wait, wait," Cooper said. "One point three million just to you alone?"

"Easily that much," Red said. "Word was that he owed something like seven million between here and Vegas. Mostly here."

Cooper whistled in horror or surprise—or maybe both.

"Why didn't he just pay?" Veena asked. "The man's contract with the Eagles earned him at least fifty million a year."

"That's the funny thing about high rollers like Archie," Red replied. "They really, really don't like to pay."

"And what happens when someone like Archie doesn't pay?" Veena asked.

"That's the thing. Nobody would be stupid enough to put out a hit on the GOAT. I mean, that's just bad for business."

"Ben E. Franco seemed to think that's what happened."

"Ah, Ben E. Franco is full of shit. That guy has been recycling jokes since the days of JFK, and half of those were lifted from Joey Bishop."

"Okay," Cooper said. "But let's take your case, Red—how do *you* make your displeasure known?"

"Well, for one thing, I stop taking their bets."

"Let's say you do that. What's next? I mean, no offense, Red, but you're up my ass sideways when I'm, like, a day late."

"I can't believe I'm listening to this," Veena said. "What are you two, thirteen?"

"Small-timers like you, Lamb—no offense—always pay up quick. They know that word travels fast, and if they screw up a few times, they're done."

"And with Archie?" Veena asked. "Plenty of people were still taking his bets."

"Yeah, how could they refuse, right? I mean, they were counting on him paying up eventually."

"Except he died before he paid up," Cooper said. "Can't imagine you're too happy about being down a million and a half bucks."

"Eh, it'll sort itself out. Always does."

"I don't think the Mob was so philosophical about being owed millions of dollars by Archie when he was alive."

"No, they weren't."

"So what did they do?"

Red shook his head. "Look, they wouldn't send a shooter. No way, no how. But they would send someone serious. Someone who specialized in reluctant clients, let's put it that way."

Veena leaned forward. "You're talking about the Quiet One."

CHAPTER 103

RED TURNED pale. "How do you know about that?" he whispered.

"You think you're my only source?" Cooper said, taking the baton from Veena. He kind of relished these moments when he had a leg up on know-it-all (and seen-it-all) Red Doyle.

"You two—you really like sticking your pricks in the hornet's nest, don't you."

"That's what I'm known for," Veena said, deadpan. "Sticking my prick wherever I want."

"I'm sorry, Ms. Lion. But seriously, you have no idea what you're doing."

"Oh, I don't know," Cooper said. "We've met the opposition. I'm pretty sure this Quiet One tried to silence me last night."

"Nope," Red said. "If someone sent...*that one* after you, we wouldn't be talking right now. I would be trying to decide whether or not it was worth driving to Philly for your goddamn funeral."

"You don't think the Quiet One killed Archie?" asked Veena.

Red frowned, then signaled the bartender for another whiskey sour. "Is it possible? Sure. But it wouldn't make no sense. The professional you're talking about would cost too much, even for a debt as sizable as Archie's. Just wouldn't make sense."

"What about Roz Cline?" Veena asked.

"What about her?"

"Why did she have to die?"

"I have no earthly idea, but she kind of put herself in that position. Once she sank her hooks into Archie, she was sure to parade her fatted calf all around town. You ask me, she got what she deserved."

"She deserved to be thrown off her balcony?"

"Buy the ticket, take the ride."

Cooper watched Veena struggle to contain the rage simmering inside her. Not that anyone else could tell, especially Red. But Cooper knew she was using all of her willpower to keep from knocking Red on his ass. "Speaking of tickets, what's our favorite policeman Mickey Bernstein doing in town?" Cooper asked.

"How would I know?"

"He works for you, right?"

"Nice try, Lamb. No, Mickey is not currently in my employ. He's down here all the time. Maybe he's a big fan of the Knife and Fork, I don't know."

"You've been a big help, Red."

"I'm not sure what you want from me. But hey, one more thing, just between the three of us—"

Cooper interrupted. "I know, I know, we should watch our backs."

"Oh, no, you two are way past that point. I'll do what I can, but you keep screwing around with hornet's nests, you're gonna get stung."

"You're a big fan of that metaphor, Red."

"I don't know why you came here showing your faces around town. You could have picked up the phone, you know."

Cooper wasn't facing Veena, but he could practically feel the heat from her eyes. There would be an *I told you so* later on.

"In fact, if you two were smart, you'd drive back to Philly right now. Don't worry about the room, I'll take care of it."

"Trying to scare us off, Red? You nervous about where this investigation is headed?"

Red smiled. "Please. I'm just trying to keep one of my small-timers from getting killed."

CHAPTER 104

4:04 p.m.

"LET'S HIT the boardwalk and think," Cooper said.

Veena nodded and led the way out of the hotel and onto the nearly empty boardwalk outside. The sky was slate gray, and the winter Atlantic Ocean was restless, pummeling the khaki sand like it had a grudge against it. This was not a place you wanted to be in the off-season. But Cooper liked the salty air, always had, going back to the days when his parents would bring him to AC. The scent brought back happy memories because even the most troubled families could call a truce on vacation.

But something felt off. And not just because they were in Atlantic City in late January. They reached the steel railing on the far side of the boardwalk and looked out over the sand.

"Red knows more than he's telling," Veena said.

"To be fair, though, we've always had a strange dynamic. He enjoys holding things over me. He's like a creepy uncle or something."

"And yet you place bets—large amounts of money—with this man."

"Hey, you heard him. I'm just a small-timer."

The boardwalk wasn't entirely empty. There was a man in a clear rain poncho and a fedora lingering by their hotel's entrance. Taking a break between shifts at the slot machines, most likely.

"Do we take his advice and leave?" Veena asked.

"Hell no," Cooper said.

"That's what I was hoping you'd say. So how do we find these mobsters you claim to know?"

Out of the corner of his eye, Cooper saw the man in the clear rain poncho start walking toward them.

"Cooper?"

Something off about his face. Distorted features, like he was a burn victim and had endured months of skin grafts. Or maybe it was the winter sun playing tricks on Cooper's eyes.

But then Cooper saw the stranger in the clear rain poncho take aim.

There was no time to cry out. He slammed into Veena with his left shoulder as he pulled the Browning out of his jacket pocket. His intention was to push Veena out of harm's way—push her all the way to friggin' Ventnor, if he had to—and return fire on this bastard.

The bad news was that Cooper moved too suddenly and powerfully to stop his own momentum. He fell on top of Veena, and his gun went skittering across the boardwalk.

The good news was that this probably saved their lives, because the man in the clear poncho wasn't anticipating this and fired above their heads. Bullets sparked against the steel railing.

"Shit!" Cooper yelled. They were defenseless and completely out in the open. The only play he had left was to scramble to his feet and charge at the man. Sure, Cooper might take a bullet. He might take multiple bullets. But if that gave Veena time to find cover, it would be worth it.

Cooper tensed, preparing to sprint. But something grabbed the collar of his jacket and jerked *hard*. Immediately he was reminded of a seashore attraction: the Hell Hole, a ride where you're spinning so fast, you almost don't feel the floor fall away from your feet.

For two seconds, Cooper had no idea how or why he was falling.

When sand exploded in his face, and he saw Veena still clutching the collar of his jacket, he understood.

She had pulled him off the edge of the boardwalk—and out of the line of fire.

Maybe Cooper had saved her life a few moments ago, but she had absolutely just saved his life.

"Thank you," he said, struggling to catch his breath.

"Thank me later," Veena said quickly. "Crawl under the boardwalk *now*."

They scuttled like crabs under the wooden walkway as bullets chopped into the sand. The killer in the poncho was intent on seeing this job through.

Veena dragged Cooper across the sand, back toward the casino.

"Wait!" Cooper whispered.

He looked up at the underside of the boardwalk. Hazy light poured through the gaps in the planks. Creaks in the wood revealed the gunman's path. The man knew they were hiding down there, so he was following them, keeping pace with them, lining up his next shot.

There was a peculiar melody cutting through the silence, not far away. The man was whistling a tune. Familiar, yet out of place, given the circumstances. What the hell was it? Cooper wondered.

"Under the Boardwalk"—the Drifters' hit from 1964. That's what it was. This scarred-up hit man had a peculiar sense of humor. Cooper Lamb did not want to die under the Atlantic City boardwalk listening to that goddamn song.

He reached for Veena's arm, but a bullet punched through the boards and cut through the patch of sand between them. The shooter knew exactly where they were hiding!

Veena was digging in her purse, most likely for her phone. He wanted to tell her not to bother—even if the AC police responded, they'd arrive just in time to load his and Veena's shot-up bodies onto a meat wagon. But he didn't dare make a sound.

"Cover your ears," Veena said. She pulled a COP .357 derringer from her purse and started firing toward the boards above them. *Blam-blam-blam-blam!* She blasted four shots through the weather-beaten wood. A moment later, they heard a heavy thud, like a sack of potatoes hitting the boards.

When enough time had passed, Cooper and Veena climbed back onto the boardwalk and walked up to their assailant. All four bullets had blasted into the man's chest. Now that Cooper was closer, he could see the man's face wasn't scarred. It had been hidden behind a clear plastic Halloween mask.

Veena crouched down and pulled away the mask. Cooper expected to see Mickey Bernstein, but for the umpteenth time today, he realized he'd made the wrong assumption. The man's face wasn't familiar to either of them.

"Is this the Quiet One?"

"No idea."

"Is he the one who tried to shoot you last night?"

"Roll him over so I can see the back of his head; maybe I'll recognize him," Cooper said. "Are you okay?"

"I'm okay."

"I didn't know you had a gun."

"I live in the city, what do you expect?"

"You used to be famously anti-gun."

"I used to be someone who wasn't on the Mob's hit list."

CHAPTER 105

THE SURPRISE punch knocked Red Doyle out of his chair and set off a noisy chain reaction in the nearly empty lounge. Red's cocktail tipped over and flooded the tabletop; his chair flipped over in the opposite direction and bashed into a chair at another table.

Cooper didn't care. He kicked all of the furniture out of the way so that Red couldn't hide from the ass-beating he was about to receive.

"The hell's the matter with you!" Red cried out, half worried and half furious.

"You sent a killer after us," Cooper snarled.

"I didn't send anybody after you!"

That earned Red a literal kick in the backside, which flipped the man over onto his belly. Cooper planted a knee in Red's spine and twisted his right arm behind his back.

"Agh!" Red screamed. "You lost your damn mind?"

"I want you to think about spending the rest of this year without the use of your arms," Cooper said. "And that's just the beginning unless you start telling me the truth."

"I'm not saying another word to you, asshole. I'm going to let the police do all of the talking. You forget—this is *my* town."

Cooper was so focused on deciding which of Red Doyle's joints he was going to dislocate first that he didn't notice Veena crouch down in front of the bookie and place the barrel of her petite handgun against his bony forehead. She lowered her sunglasses.

"I was just forced to kill someone," Veena said calmly. "This is something I'm going to have to carry with me forever. But let me tell you this: I have zero problem doing it again."

Cooper could feel the fight leave Red's body. Whatever he saw in Veena's eyes, he believed it.

"I'm telling you the truth," Red said softly. "Whatever just happened to you, I had nothing to do with it. I was trying to *warn* you. You two have big fat targets painted on your backs."

"Why?" Veena asked. "Because someone shot a football player in downtown Philadelphia and we're trying to find out who pulled the trigger?"

"No. Because you're poking around at one little corner of a very dangerous situation."

"Detail it for us."

"Take that gun off my head."

Veena took the gun off his head, and Red exhaled before continuing.

"The Sables bet huge on the NFC game yesterday."

"Illegal, but not surprising."

"No, you don't understand. They bet against the Birds."

"What?"

"You're finally getting it, aren't you? This has the makings of the biggest gambling disaster in ages, and the Mob wants no part of it. They want to shut this down completely and bury anyone who knows about it. What happened to Archie is sad, but they don't want any loose ends."

"So they *did* send the Quiet One after him."

"No! I'm telling you, that would be the opposite of what they'd

313

do. It only brings more attention to this whole thing. I mean, look at you two. You wouldn't be sticking a gun in my face if Archie were still alive."

"There's more, isn't there?"

"If I tell you more, we're all dead."

CHAPTER 106

"IT'S ALREADY over, Red. Everything's going to come out sooner or later. You might as well tell me now."

"Goddamn you, Cooper. Get me a drink first."

"Tell me, then I'll buy you a bottle."

"You're going to owe me more than that. Too bad I'll never have the chance to collect, because my body will be rotting in the Pine Barrens." Red ordered a drink anyway. Another whiskey sour. The bartender made a half-hearted attempt to intervene, maybe show those two the door. But Red waved him off, grumbling about the bartender not stepping in a few minutes ago when Cooper Lamb was kicking his ass. Neither Cooper nor Veena cared for another drink. Bad idea to pour alcohol on top of all that adrenaline.

"In a way, you two were right. This *was* about Archie Hughes."

"How?" Veena asked.

"Archie was supposed to throw the NFC game, and—*poof!*—his debts would vanish. Complete reset."

"The Sables agreed to this deal?" Cooper asked.

"The Sables came up with this deal! The way they tell it, it was the only solution to an impossible situation. Yeah, the team loses, boo-hoo. Philadelphia is used to losing. Nothing new there. But Archie has the boot taken off his neck, the Mob gets its money, and the Sables recoup their losses and then some, so it all should have worked out fine."

"But it didn't," Veena said. "Because someone killed Archie before he could throw the game."

"Do you finally see what I mean? Why would the Mob kill the man at the center of the plan? No, this was something else. A fluke, dumb freakin' luck, punishment from God, who the hell knows. The rest of us have to deal with the aftermath. Including you two."

"What do you mean? Why us two?" Cooper asked.

"You two are loose ends. And now maybe I'm a loose end too."

Cooper realized Red Doyle wasn't being a prick—he was terrified. In his own way, he had been trying to steer them away from this situation before it was too late. But now, with a dead (alleged) Mob triggerman rapidly cooling outside on the boardwalk, there was no turning back. They would have to see this through to the end.

Cooper put a hand on Red Doyle's shoulder. "Hey, we still good?"

Red turned to Cooper and opened his eyes wide in genuine surprise; he looked as if Cooper had just told him that he'd won the Pennsylvania Lottery and then that he had terminal cancer.

"You're unbelievable, Lamb. You know that?"

TUESDAY, FEBRUARY 1

CHAPTER 107

5:02 a.m.

THE TROLLEY Car, out on the fringes of Northeast Philly, was open twenty-four hours a day, seven days a week, cash only. Cooper Lamb had always thought this was the perfect setup for armed robbery. Hit 'em right after Sunday brunch and walk away with a mint. Well, maybe not a mint. The prices were so reasonable, that stolen dough would get you as far as Allentown. Maybe.

Cooper chose the place and extended the invitation; Mickey Bernstein accepted it.

Yeah, Cooper was still stunned by that. He'd assumed he'd have to go knocking on the homicide cop's front door once again, and it was very likely such an encounter would end with a fistfight and handcuffs. A diner was a neutral spot and a clue that maybe Bernstein was willing to share some information.

Either that or Bernstein wanted to lure Cooper to an isolated parking lot at crazy o'clock in the morning so he could finish what he'd started a few nights ago outside Maya's apartment building.

After all, it wouldn't be the first time Mickey Bernstein showed up early to a homicide.

Cooper was pretending to study the menu when Bernstein arrived a few minutes before the appointed time. He slid into the booth across from Cooper, who had arrived even earlier to choose this table: right in the middle of the dining room, in full view of pretty much everybody, next to the battered upright piano and microphone.

Yes, the Trolley Car featured live entertainment, although Cooper had never witnessed it himself.

"Need a minute to look over the menu?" Cooper asked.

"Pretty sure I have it memorized by now," Bernstein said, then gestured to a waitress, who changed course immediately to take care of the celebrity cop's order. "Black coffee, sweetie, and a toasted bagel with cream cheese. Thanks."

Cooper hadn't been planning on ordering anything, since he wasn't hungry, and this meeting would most likely not be a pleasant one. But he mirrored Bernstein's order, substituting a Diet Coke for the coffee.

"I'll level with you," the homicide cop said. "On everything."

"That's very kind of you."

"Just one rule," Bernstein said. "No tapes."

"I promise, I'm not taping anything."

"Yeah, I hear you saying the words, but I'm dead serious about this. I know all the tricks. Don't make me dunk your watch in your Diet Coke."

"Bernstein, I'm not even wearing a watch. I could give a crap about recording you. I just want to know the truth."

"Fine. And I'll give you the truth. But I don't think you're going to be very happy when you hear it."

"Why's that?"

"Because you're going to realize what a freakin' idiot you've been."

CHAPTER 108

THERE WERE three reasons Cooper Lamb had chosen the Trolley Car for his meeting with Mickey Bernstein.

One: The physical location. Close enough to I-95 for Cooper to make a quick getaway if he had to, but the diner was also in Bernstein's neck of the woods (the so-called Great Northeast), so it was in his comfort zone.

Two: The crowd. Plenty of potential witnesses in case things went sideways.

Three: The piano.

And this was key. Cooper remembered it from a long-ago trip here with the kids; they were mortified when he waved a lighter and shouted, "'Free Bird'!" even though no musicians were around. ("Dad, you seriously need a therapist," Ariel told him.) But the piano and microphone were perfect hiding places for secret recording gear.

Which was why he'd brought Victor here three hours earlier and promised him a heart-stopping omelet if he'd wire the piano and mic for sound.

As Cooper had said, Bernstein wouldn't find any trace of a recording device . . . unless he decided to lift the lid of that upright and start poking around.

Transcript of conversation between Cooper Lamb and homicide detective Michael Bernstein

MICHAEL BERNSTEIN: Yeah, I gave Maya Rain a gun. And yes, that gun turned out to be the murder weapon.

COOPER LAMB: Why would you give Archie Hughes's nanny a gun?

BERNSTEIN: Because of Archie Hughes! Come on, you know what kind of company he kept. Take away the gambling lowlifes and rappers and street gangs and God knows who else, and there were still plenty of criminals who would've loved to pick Archie's bones clean. I wanted her to be able to protect herself, just in case.

LAMB: Are you in love with her?

BERNSTEIN: Who, Maya? Yeah, maybe I am. But who the hell isn't?

LAMB: Bernstein, come on. Why the hell are you still on this case? You should have recused yourself a week ago.

BERNSTEIN: What, because I'm having a little fling? Grow up, man. Do you know how small this town is? If I had to recuse myself every time I knew someone on the fringes of a homicide investigation, I wouldn't investigate any murders. Don't be like those idiot reporters who look for gossip when at the end of the day, it doesn't matter.

LAMB: You just told me you gave your secret girlfriend the murder weapon used in the highest-profile murder in the city's history. Would we call that the *fringes*?

BERNSTEIN: Clearly, someone lifted it from her bag at some point, hoping to do exactly this—confuse the issue.

LAMB: And what is this issue?

BERNSTEIN: Archie traveled in some rough company, and it caught up with him. I'm trying to find out who was behind it.

LAMB: Is that why you took on the Roz Cline case?

BERNSTEIN: Cline definitely set Archie up with some of this rough company. I think they wanted to silence her so nobody would be able to trace it back to them. So, yeah, it's a related case.

LAMB: You any closer to finding out who "they" might be?

BERNSTEIN: The investigation is ongoing.

LAMB: Please. You're telling me you have no idea at all?

BERNSTEIN: In my experience, you either know who did it right away or it's a long slog to figure it out. This is one of those long-slog cases.

LAMB: Huh. I thought you'd have a hunch or something. Like your old man.

BERNSTEIN: (*Through a mouthful of bagel*) What can I tell you.

LAMB: Well, I've got something to share with you too.

BERNSTEIN: Yeah?

LAMB: Veena Lion probably killed the Quiet One yesterday. I helped out a little, but she did the heavy lifting.

BERNSTEIN: The quiet who? What the hell is that supposed to mean?

LAMB: For a little while, I thought *you* might be the Quiet One. But now I see that I'm completely wrong about that.

BERNSTEIN: I don't know what you're talking about, but look, I gotta go. Hope this clears things up.

LAMB: You didn't finish your bagel.

BERNSTEIN: Hey, I've gotta work on that case you want me to solve so bad.

(*Long pause; there are diners murmuring and the clatter of silverware on plates in the background.*)

LAMB: Please tell me you got all that, Victor. (*Pause*) Also, I need you to hit an ATM for me. Mickey stuck me with the tab, and I didn't bring any cash.

CHAPTER 109

"ANYWAY, SO, yeah, I was listening in the whole time. Bernstein is full of crap."

They were driving south on I-95, headed toward Center City. Cooper dodged rush-hour traffic as Victor crouched in the passenger seat with a laptop on his knees. He was still hacking as he maintained his end of the conversation.

"What specifically was crap?" Cooper asked.

"Pretty much everything that wasn't self-serving," Victor replied. "But what was most interesting were the things he left out."

"Such as?"

"His other two jobs, aside from the Philly PD."

"Two jobs, huh? Well, we already know one of them. He works for the Sables."

"Yep. And I found a digital trail leading from the Eagles' head office to Bernstein's secret bank accounts. He's been working for them for three years now."

"Doing what, though?"

"It's not like there's a memo line on the checks that says *Fixer* or anything. But the amounts vary, so I'm guessing that's what he is. If the Sables have any problems, then Bernstein is there to take care of them."

"Who's the other employer?"

"This was a little trickier, because the amounts deposited were more infrequent, and I had a hard time tracing them. At first."

"And..."

Victor was silent except for the clacking his fingers made on the laptop keys. Cooper didn't push him. The man was doing his research in real time.

"Okay, this isn't locked down as tight. But as I'm reading through some older clips about Bernstein's father, I'm starting to figure out the connections."

"Victor, what are you talking about?"

"The Mob."

"Philly or Atlantic City?"

"Boil it down and it's all the same Mob, has been since the 1920s. One big screwed-up family, and the Bernsteins have been their silent fixers going back decades. Mickey is just following in his father's footsteps. And his grandfather's, for that matter. Mickey's grandfather used to run errands for Joe Ida and Angelo Bruno."

Cooper watched the skyscrapers of Center City slide into view. Old knockaround guys like Ida and Bruno wouldn't recognize Philly anymore. Their sons and grandsons had transformed it— with the help of the police and the politicians they kept in their pocket. It wasn't new corruption; it was the same corruption with a twenty-first-century sheen.

"Hold on," Victor said suddenly. "Pull over."

"What—right here on I-95? Are you crazy?"

"Boss, pull over! Now!"

CHAPTER 110

SOMEHOW, COOPER LAMB defied space and time (and the morning rush hour) to force his way onto the highway's shoulder. Which wasn't much of a shoulder. Officials had been rebuilding I-95 almost since they'd first slammed it through the river wards back in the 1970s, and now they were expanding it by another two lanes. Construction gear and debris littered the side of the road. It was a miracle Cooper hadn't crashed into an asphalt spreader.

"I hope this is worth almost dying for," Cooper said.

"Oh, it's worth it," Victor told him.

"What is it?"

"A page of high-end escorts."

"If you're lonely, Victor, I recommend a Dungeons and Dragons club or some other nerd-friendly gathering."

"Yeah, funny, boss," Victor said in a way that made it plain he did not find Cooper's joke even remotely funny. "No, these pages were heavily protected in the first place, top-notch encryption, then scrubbed from the internet."

"How did you find them?"

"Avid fans collect this stuff in the hopes of catching someone famous on their way down," Victor said, "or on their way up."

"There's always a screenshot."

"Funny you say that. This is why I had you pull over." Victor turned his laptop so that Cooper could see the screen. If Cooper had been watching himself, he would have seen a classic Hollywood double take.

"Is that Maya Rain in a slutty Halloween costume?"

"No," Victor said. "This is Vanessa Harlowe in her work clothes."

"A long way from West Virginia," Cooper mumbled, staring at the image and trying to square it with the flesh-and-blood woman he'd come to know. She was gorgeous in real life. On-screen, she looked like a CGI character, like someone had attempted to capture her natural beauty but produced a cheap caricature instead.

"What does that mean?" Victor asked.

"Nothing. So she was a hooker."

"Five years ago, in AC. Based on what I'm seeing, Vanessa Harlowe was at the top of her game. Fifteen hundred an hour, ten grand for the night. She worked with someone else you know— Rosalind Cline."

"Let me guess. Her madam."

"They don't call it that anymore, boss."

"Well, she's not a madam anymore either."

CHAPTER 111

12:27 p.m.

FOR MAKING a discovery this huge, Janie Hall thought she deserved lunch at the Sansom Street Oyster House.

While waiting for her boss, Janie sat at the raw bar and ordered a dozen assorted oysters from up and down the East Coast. Wellfleets from Cape Cod; Glidden Points from Maine; stormy bays and sugar shacks from Jersey. *And* a double shrimp cocktail.

This was just for starters.

The food was its own reward, but Janie also enjoyed knowing that her reporter's instincts were still strong. When something nagged at her, it was the reporter inside her brain urging her to follow up, ask another question, keep pushing.

The ring. Like a Tolkien fantasy novel, it all came down to the ring. In this case, the missing Super Bowl ring.

It bothered Janie and fit none of the narratives Veena had been entertaining (professional hit man, personal grudges). A stolen ring made no sense with any of those. Why would a hit man take a Super Bowl ring when that would serve as a blinking red arrow pointed right at him? Maybe someone with a grudge would take the ring as a trophy, but again, to what end? The moment someone discovered it, the killer was as good as exposed.

No. A stolen ring meant a robbery.

As her boss and Cooper Lamb took a trip down to the shore, Janie called up one of the useful individuals in her life, this one from about five years ago.

The name he'd given Janie was Travis, but she knew it was fake. Travis was a kind of dark alternative-universe version of Cooper Lamb—a fellow shamus, but completely amoral and perfectly at home in the underworld. (Janie *did* enjoy the occasional bad boy.)

She had been writing a piece on high-profile art heists on the Main Line, and her reporting led her to Travis, a private eye who specialized in recovering stolen goods (for a steep fee), as long as the police were kept out of it. Only one of his quotes—on background—made it into the piece, but Janie and Travis had ended up downing more than a few martinis at the Continental over the years.

Which was where they'd met up the night before.

"Tell me who would try to fence a stolen Super Bowl ring," Janie said.

"Somebody really stupid," Travis replied.

And she would have left it at that if Travis had not followed it up with "You know, it's funny you say that. Last week I had some idiot reach out through one of my associates trying to sell Archie Hughes's ring. Even if it was real, the ring is radioactive. I can't imagine who would buy it. If someone is selling it, it'll be on the street, for crackhead prices."

A noise next to Janie snapped her out of her reverie—the legs of the next stool over scraping against the tile floor.

"Did you start with a dozen oysters or did you order only three?" Veena asked.

"When you hear what I've got, you're going to buy me another dozen," said Janie. "And a chilled lobster tail."

CHAPTER 112

JANIE SLID the slip of notebook paper to her employer. Veena lifted it from the counter, unfolded it, read the name and address Janie had scribbled on it.

"Who's this?"

"Quite possibly the guy who killed Archie Hughes."

"Some random guy from Kensington is now our lead suspect?"

Janie walked Veena through her conversation with Travis, the recovery specialist from the previous night. It had taken another two martinis, but Travis finally agreed to give Janie the name and address of the moron who claimed he had Archie Hughes's Super Bowl ring and wallet.

Travis was convinced this was a dead lead; a man smart enough to evade every surveillance camera in the Museum of Art area wouldn't go shooting his mouth off about having the missing ring.

"But the guy might not know there is footage," Veena said.

"Exactly," Janie replied. "Which made me think, what if this was just a carjacking gone wrong?"

Veena started riffing. "This guy thinks he's just boosting a fancy car but then sees who he's robbing, freaks out, and shoots him."

"He doesn't want to go away empty-handed, so he takes what he can carry."

"Archie's wallet. And his Super Bowl ring."

"It's possible, right?"

"Only one way to find out."

Veena pushed her stool back and prepared to leave. Janie grabbed her arm. "Wait."

"Don't worry, just put the tab on the company card," Veena said. "Good work."

"No, it's not that. I don't think you want to be going up to this guy's apartment alone. That neighborhood is rough—I covered crime up there for two years. And with your painted nails, fancy shades, and expensive shoes, you're kind of a target."

Veena smiled. "Yesterday I shot and killed a professional hit man. I also threatened to put a bullet in an elderly man's face. I don't think I'll have a problem."

Janie started to laugh, but the sound died in her throat as she clocked Veena's expression and realized she wasn't joking. Before she could form a follow-up question—she had several—Veena was adjusting her shades and heading out the door.

CHAPTER 113

WHEN CRAZY Percy Marshall had woken up this morning, he hadn't thought he'd open his front door and find a gun pointed at his heart that afternoon. For one thing, he didn't know that anyone knew (or cared) where he lived. Big difference from a week ago, when he thought his luck had changed. But now, as Crazy Percy looked at the pretty lady holding the tiny gun, he realized it was worse than ever. He sighed.

Transcript of conversation between Veena Lion and Percy Marshall

VEENA LION: May I come inside, Mr. Marshall?

PERCY MARSHALL: Can I just say no?

LION: No.

MARSHALL: Then, sure, make yourself at home. Want a beer?

LION: No, thank you. I'd like you to give me the Super Bowl ring and the wallet.

MARSHALL: Yeah, yeah. Figured that's why you were here. Why didn't Bernstein come down here himself? Hey, wait—you didn't show me your badge. I don't think that's legal. You're supposed to show me your badge.

LION: The ring?

MARSHALL: Okay, okay.

(*Long pause as Marshall leaves, pulls open a kitchen drawer, returns.*)

LION: Tell me how you got these.

MARSHALL: You know how I got these.

LION: Tell me anyway.

MARSHALL: I was walking, minding my own business, when I saw this crazy-ass car just sitting in front of the art museum. I got closer and realized who was inside it. I figured he was passed out or something, in which case I would have called for help. But no—he was shot, man. Someone killed him! I didn't want any part of that.

LION: But before you ran away, you helped yourself to his Super Bowl ring and wallet.

MARSHALL: But I just gave them back to you! So it's kind of like I borrowed them, right? Or held on to them for safekeeping?

LION: And you have no idea who killed Archie.

MARSHALL: Oh, I didn't say that.

LION: Excuse me?

MARSHALL: Yeah, I know who killed the quarterback. And for the right price, I'll tell ya.

LION: For a price, huh? Okay. How much is your life worth to you?

MARSHALL: What do you m—? Hey, come on, now, you don't have to point that friggin' thing at me!

LION: Let me repeat: How much. Is your life. Worth to you? Because to me, it's worth absolutely nothing.

MARSHALL: You're no cop.

LION: Never said I was.

MARSHALL: I want that ring and wallet back, missy.

LION: Never going to happen. Now tell me who killed Archie Hughes.

MARSHALL: F█████ you.

LION: I'm not a cop, but I am working for the district attorney.
    And I have zero problem explaining to them that I found a
    shot-up corpse in possession of a dead man's ring and wallet.
    Who do you think they're going to believe? Oh, that's right,
    they'll have to believe me, because you won't be able to say a
    ███████ word.
MARSHALL: Man. This week keeps circling the drain.
LION: Tell me who killed Archie.
MARSHALL: I can't.
LION: What did I just say?
MARSHALL: No, no, no! I can't tell you because I don't know their
    names. But I can show you. It's right here on my phone.

CHAPTER 114

Transcript of encrypted phone conversation between Veena Lion and Cooper Lamb

VEENA LION: Where are you? What are you doing?

COOPER LAMB: I'm looking at vintage screenshots of high-priced Atlantic City call girls. How about you?

LION: I'm about to catch the Frankford El. Can you meet me at Thirtieth Street Station in twenty-five minutes?

LAMB: You know, I'm pretty wrapped up in this research at the moment.

LION: I'm sure you are.

LAMB: Our friend Maya Rain? She used to be one of Atlantic City's finest escorts. And, even better, she used to work for Roz Cline.

LION: Incredible.

LAMB: Also, I discovered that Mickey Bernstein moonlights for the Atlantic City Mob, which runs all of the escorts in town. So it's not a huge leap to assume that Mickey and Maya go way back.

LION: Nice work, Cooper. But I can do you one better.

LAMB: Ha! No, you can't.

LION: Yes, I can.

LAMB: Impossible. There's no way you can top this. I'm like one
    baby step away from figuring out this whole sordid story. I just
    have to sort out why the Mob wanted Archie dead a week
    before the championship game. I'm thinking it was some kind
    of—

LION: Cooper.

LAMB: What.

LION: I have a video clip on my phone showing Archie's killers
    leaving the scene of the crime.

LAMB: I'm sorry, you have what, now?

LION: I'm also wearing his Super Bowl ring on my middle finger.

LAMB: No, you're not.

LION: Yes, I am.

LAMB: No, what I mean is, you should absolutely *not* ride the
    Frankford El wearing Archie Hughes's Super Bowl ring. Some-
    one will knife you for it. Hell, *I'd* knife you for it.

LION: So you can sell it for crackhead prices?

LAMB: What?

LION: Never mind. Okay, okay, it's in my pocket now. Are you
    going to say it?

LAMB: Say what?

LION: Are you going to say, "Veena, how on earth did you manage
    to solve this case all by yourself?"

LAMB: No. I figure you'll tell me all about it when I pick you up
    from Thirtieth Street Station in twenty-four minutes.

LION: Perfect. Oh, and bring your gun. And leave Lupe at home.

CHAPTER 115

AN HOUR later, Cooper Lamb and Veena Lion knocked on the front door of the Hughes estate and were met by a monster.

"You two need to leave right now," Jimmy Tua said, practically growling the words. "Francine doesn't want to see you."

"She's my client," Cooper protested.

"Well, consider yourself fired. Goodbye."

Tua slammed the front door in their faces. Tried to, anyway. Cooper threw out his palm and stopped the door a few inches from closing. Tua pushed. Cooper held firm, but he knew he couldn't do this forever. Maybe not even for another few seconds.

Tua let up for a moment, but only to ask a couple of questions. "Are you insane? Or do you want to leave here with a broken arm?"

"Look, man, I know you mean well and you have the family's best interests at heart. But the future of this family depends on us speaking with Francine right now."

"Get the hell out of here."

"We're not leaving."

"*Now.*"

Cooper turned to Veena. *You want to give me a hand here?* is what he started to say, but all he got out was "You want to" before Jimmy Tua launched an atomic bomb against the side of Cooper's skull.

Actually, it was Jimmy's fist. But the effect was the same.

Cooper's conscious self lagged a few seconds behind his physical body, which was doing a clumsy tap dance down the Hugheses' walkway. He couldn't blame his legs. They were trying their best. But ultimately, their best wasn't good enough.

CHAPTER 116

EVENTS USUALLY happened in threes.

Veena firmly believed that. And since she had pointed her derringer at three different people in a twenty-hour period, she assumed she was done with gun incidents.

But Jimmy Tua had disproven that axiom when he knocked Cooper Lamb on his ass, forcing Veena to draw her weapon and point it at a living human being a fourth time.

Tua was not impressed with the gun. Not in the least. Where he'd grown up, people were always sticking guns in each other's faces. "You're not gonna shoot me."

A chunk of the wooden doorframe directly above Tua exploded. Splinters showered down on his head. The tight end flinched, then locked eyes with Veena. She knew she looked like a madwoman capable of pretty much anything. He hadn't seen that often where he'd grown up, especially not in a woman's eyes.

"That was me missing," Veena said. "Next time I won't."

Jimmy Tua seemed undecided about what to do next. Backing down wasn't in his DNA, but this crazy lady with the derringer seemed serious. He was saved by a voice calling out from inside the house, "Jimmy, it's okay."

Francine Pearl Hughes appeared behind the massive athlete. She reached up and touched his shoulders, encouraging him to look at her. Tua seemed reluctant to take his eyes off Veena—what if this lady opened fire on *both* of them? Francine was gently insistent. Tua turned to face her.

Cooper Lamb, meanwhile, had gotten to his feet, but he looked confused. Veena wondered if he knew what year it was. "You alive over there?" Veena asked.

"I'm just quietly applauding myself," Cooper said, "for not pursuing a career in the NFL."

Okay, Cooper was fine. Jimmy Tua, however, looked like he was on the verge of tears. This was a little boy in a big man's body, a boy who had tried his best but let down his friend. Francine stood on her tiptoes and wrapped her arms around him. Tua settled into the hug, relieved. Maybe he hadn't failed her and the children after all.

"I love you," she whispered. "So, so much." Her voice was barely audible, but Veena heard her.

Then, slightly louder, she said, "Let me talk to these good people now. I'll call you later, sweetheart."

Jimmy Tua nodded in agreement and left without another word and without looking either Veena or Cooper in the eye. Which was okay. If the rule of threes held up, they'd see Jimmy again soon.

CHAPTER 117

"IT'S NOT what you think," Francine said.

"Okay," said Cooper, following Francine up the hallway. "Tell me what you think I think."

"That Jimmy and me are a thing. I mean, I know how you private eyes like to collect salacious gossip."

Francine was slurring her words a little, possibly due to alcohol or a couple of Xanax or just plain exhaustion. Cooper watched her walk, preparing to catch her if he had to. Hopefully it wouldn't come to that. Cooper was sure he was wobbling a bit after that hurricane-force punch from the Eagles' star tight end.

"Well, that's not the case. We're not. For one thing, Jimmy is gay."

"Yes, we know," Veena said.

"We know pretty much everything," Cooper said.

If she had been slightly drunk, Francine Pearl Hughes sobered up instantly. "Come into the parlor."

CHAPTER 118

MAYA RAIN was sitting there, although the children weren't around. Maybe they were busy elsewhere in the house or out with friends. But Veena was pretty sure that Francine and Maya had sent them to their rooms the moment she and Cooper knocked on the door.

"I have something for you," Veena said. She reached into her pocket, pulled out Archie's Super Bowl ring, and held it out to Francine, who stared at it unbelievingly. She hesitated to take it, as if Veena were trying to hand her a cursed talisman.

"How on earth did you find—"

"That's what we're here to discuss," Veena said.

"Francine, we don't have to do this now," Maya said, rising from her chair. "In fact, I'm going to insist that we don't do this now. Let me call your attorney and have her arrange a proper meeting."

"Have a seat, Vanessa," Cooper said.

"I'm sorry, what did you say?" There was no anger in her voice. On the contrary, Maya seemed amused.

"I saw a bunch of your old escort ads, Vanessa. You were beautiful then, but I like your current look a lot more. What I'm wondering is, which name is real, Vanessa or Maya? Or is it something else entirely? Am I talking to a Wanda June?"

Maya smiled. "I still like you, Cooper. Even though you say the cruelest things sometimes."

Francine's confusion seemed genuine. "Will someone explain to me what's going on?"

"Happily," Veena said, giving Cooper a look that said *Please stop taunting the potential murder suspect.*

CHAPTER 119

"WE HAVE proof that both of you were at the scene of the murder," Veena explained. "I have a video clip on my phone that shows your car, Francine, and the figures of two women who look like you and Maya. It won't take much digital forensic work to positively match both of you to those women."

Maya smiled. "It was the guy in the hoodie, right? I thought he was snapping a photo of Archie's car."

Veena was puzzled. "So you admit you were there?"

Maya shrugged. "Go on."

"Obviously, one of you drove Archie there in his own car with the other following in Francine's burgundy Bentley, the only other car you had available on such short notice. Which means that Archie was shot and killed elsewhere, and his body was left in his car at Eakins Oval so that it would look like a carjacking gone wrong."

"No," Francine said quietly. "It was a message."

Cooper's jaw dropped. "I'm sorry—what did you say?"

"Archie and I met at the Museum of Art. I was performing on the Fourth of July, and he was one of the parade guests. We met backstage. He told me he'd been in love with me since he was a kid. I figured I ought to say goodbye to him in the same place I'd said hello."

Cooper couldn't believe what he was hearing. "Francine, you do realize you're admitting to killing your husband, right?"

"No, she's not," Maya said. "Also, at best, you have evidence of us leaving the scene of a crime. And I don't think you even have that. You two like to bluff."

"The murder weapon was buried right here! In the flower bed in back of your house!" Cooper said.

Francine shot Cooper and Maya cold, hard looks. "Keep your voices down. Please."

"Could have been a home invasion gone wrong," Maya continued. "Archie resists and is killed. The killers force us to drive with them to the art museum to dump his body. And then they get frightened and let us go."

Cooper shook his head. "So these alleged home invaders forgot to bring a gun and had to borrow yours, Vanessa? The very one you received from Mickey Bernstein? Who, by the way, should be a thousand miles away from this murder investigation."

"Stop it, I'm begging you!" Francine shout-whispered.

"The details don't matter," Veena said. "We just want the truth. That's *all* we've wanted since the beginning of this thing."

Francine lowered her head and shook it gently as if to the beat of the saddest, slowest ballad she knew. She was beyond weary. This entire conversation seemed to drain the life from her body. "I don't know what you want me to say," she said.

"Easy," Veena replied. "Just tell me which one of you shot and killed Archie."

CHAPTER 120

"*BAAAAA,* SAID the little lamb."

The noise was so out of place, it startled all four adults in the parlor. Cooper was the first to realize who it was and responded to the comment.

"*Baaaaa,* little one," he said. "Come on out from your hiding place."

Five-year-old Maddie crawled out from behind a sofa, and a moment later her older brother stepped into the room with a solemn look on his face. Cooper expected him to say something along the lines of *Sorry, Mom, I accidentally threw a football into the windshield of the Bentley.*

For the first time since Cooper had met Maya, she appeared horrified. "I told both of you to stay in your rooms," she said with a coldness in her voice that was as far away from Mary Poppins as you could get.

Francine, trembling with uncontrollable anger or fear or maybe both, said, "Both of you. Upstairs. *Now.*"

"No, Mom," said Archie Jr. "I have something to say." He looked at his sister. "Maddie, go upstairs. I have to talk to these people about something important."

Maddie saw the seriousness in her brother's eyes. Her lower

lip trembled. She didn't understand what was going on. Maddie looked over at Cooper for reassurance. Cooper felt himself slip into dad mode. He smiled, nodded. "It's okay, sweetie," he said softly. "Your mom will be up in just a moment."

Maddie wanted to do a lot of things in that moment. She wanted to *baaaaa* at the man with the funny name (and the cute dog). She wanted to run to her mother and jump into her arms. She wanted to understand why everyone was so angry and sad all the time.

But in the end she turned around and went up to her room. She had a stuffed lamb on her bed, a gift from Nanny Maya just a week ago—though the timing meant little to Maddie. She just loved the stuffed animal and hugged it tight.

CHAPTER 121

"I KILLED Dad," Archie Jr. said, his voice barely a whisper.

"Archie…" His mother began to protest, but she trailed off when she realized that all hope had evaporated. There was no way for him to take back what he'd said. No way to rewind any of this, although she would have given almost anything to do so.

"It's okay, Archie," Veena said. "You're in a safe place right now, and we're all here to help you. You don't have to be afraid."

The kid unconsciously balled his hands into fists as he worked up the nerve to continue. "My mom and Maya didn't want you two to know that, but I didn't want to lie and get them in any more trouble."

"We understand, buddy," Cooper said. "And by the way, what you're doing right now is incredibly brave."

"I don't feel brave."

"I know that's not how you feel," Veena said, "but your mother couldn't be prouder of you. Isn't that right, Mom?"

Archie Jr. looked over at his mother. Francine could only beam love at her child as she slowly nodded. "You can tell them the truth."

"I'm sorry, Mom."

"It's okay, baby," Francine said. "And they're right. You're the bravest person I've ever met."

"Can you tell us what happened?" Veena asked.

Archie Jr. relaxed his hands as if he'd just realized he'd been clenching them. "I shot Dad," he said. "I knew it was wrong, but...I had to do something. When Mom found out, she asked where I'd gotten a gun, and I'd found it in Ms. Maya's bag but I didn't want to get her in trouble, so I lied and said I found it near school."

"And then you buried it in the garden," Cooper said.

"Yeah. But the police found it anyway. Or Mr. Mauricio did, and he told the police. I swear I didn't mean to get Ms. Maya in trouble."

"You didn't, Archie," Maya said, forcing a smile as if that would hold back her tears. It failed.

"Why did you do that, honey?" Veena asked. "Why did you shoot your dad?"

Archie Jr. swallowed. "I *had* to."

Cooper nodded. "Tell us what your dad said."

"It's not what he said. It's what he did."

"What did he do?"

Archie Jr. didn't reply, but the way he looked at his mother confirmed it for Cooper. The boy had known *exactly* what was going on. Archie Jr. hadn't cared if his father hit him. But his father hitting his mother was too much. What kind of young man could let his mother be beat up, even if it was his own father doing the hitting?

"Dad always said blood is thicker than water," Archie Jr. continued. "Nothing was more important than Mom and me and Maddie. I think he forgot that. I was just trying to remind him."

"How?" Veena asked.

"I didn't mean it. I just wanted him to stop and listen to me. So I pointed Maya's gun at him so he would stop. I didn't want to..."

"It's okay," Cooper said. "It's not your fault."

"But it *is* my fault!" Archie Jr. yelled. "I should have known Dad wouldn't stop! He tried to take the gun, and I just wanted to pull it away from him, and I must have pulled too hard and..." The boy trailed off and stared off into space as if it were happening all over again.

Cooper fought hard to control the tightening in his chest. It felt like the onset of a heart attack, but he knew he was just trying to avoid crying in front of everyone. He glanced around the room and realized he didn't need to bother. All of them were sobbing.

CHAPTER 122

THE SUN had set by the time Cooper and Veena got on I-76 and headed back to Philly. It was rush hour but everyone was leaving the city, so they hit very little traffic. It seemed like someone had turned down the volume of the world. Philadelphia was cold and quiet.

"You going to tell that prick DA about this?"

"No," Veena said. "Not about little Archie, anyway. You telling Francine's lawyer?"

"Pretty sure she knows. Starting to think she hired me for window dressing. 'We got the best, Your Honor,' and so on."

"So we finally know the truth."

"Yeah, we do."

"We should be happy about this."

"We should."

"So why does the truth feel so horrible?"

Cooper drove in silence, mostly because he knew the answer to that question. A lot of people thought that life was a struggle between virtue and temptation, angels and devils, good and bad. But that wasn't the case. The truth was, life was often a choice between bad and worse. Neither of those options felt good, but human beings were compelled to choose, hoping everything would turn out okay despite all evidence to the contrary.

CHAPTER 123

9:09 p.m.

"ARE WE doing the right thing?"

"That's a loaded question," Cooper said. "So the only answer is to get loaded."

They were back at the bar in the Rittenhouse Hotel. Same low-key bartender, same flirtatious server. But they felt like they were sipping martinis in an alternative universe. Nothing about this world felt right, so they took comfort in each other's company. Which in itself felt strange. Could Cooper Lamb have imagined doing this with Veena, his former nemesis, two weeks ago?

"Seriously," she said. "There's no way Francine would ever be convicted. No jury in the world would punish a woman for protecting her own child."

"I don't think there would be a trial," Cooper said. "I imagine that even a hard-ass like Mostel would cut a deal to keep this family out of the courtroom."

"Even if I believed that, it's nothing but a waking nightmare for Francine and those kids."

"And the monster who beat them gets off the easiest. Death is too good for him."

"The greatest of all time."

"And, somehow, the worst."

They finished their initial round and considered ordering food but opted for another round instead. By the end of the third round, they were ready to hide away from this twisted world. For a little while, anyway.

"How about we go to your place this time?" Cooper asked with what he hoped was a knowing gleam in his eye.

"We can't."

"Why not?"

"We're already here."

"What do you mean?"

"I currently live here," Veena said. "At the Rittenhouse Hotel."

"What, is your apartment being remodeled or something?"

"No. I've decided to sell the place and forgo apartments altogether. Hang on, hear me out. I crunched the numbers and realized I was wasting a ton of money on a physical space I almost never occupy. Factor in the upkeep of that space, even if I hired help—which I would never do—and it's even more wasted time and money. So my plan is to hop from hotel to hotel. I'll stay until a place bores me, then move on. If I like a place enough, I'll go back to it."

Cooper looked as if he'd taken another punch from tight end Jimmy Tua. "Wow. So all this time, we could have been enjoying our drinks in the comfort of your room, which is just a short elevator ride away?"

Veena shook her head. "Nope, not in my sanctuary. Nobody goes inside except me. Oh, and housekeeping. That's another thing I decided."

"That is the most Veena Lion thing I've ever heard."

"Besides, I prefer your place."

"You mean you prefer Lupe."

"Mayyyybe..."

"And the kick-ass breakfast I make when I'm a little hungover or have escaped the clutches of death."

"Also very possible. So shall we head to your place?"

"Wait. Exactly when did you make this decision about your apartment? And did it have anything to do with hit men being after us?"

"Cooper, I don't *have* to go back to your place."

"Let me take care of the check."

CHAPTER 124

LUPE WAS over the moon when he saw—and smelled—Veena. He was not so pleased when Cooper and Veena slowly undressed each other on the way to his bedroom, stopping for frequent make-out breaks, or when Cooper nudged the door almost completely shut, which was his way of telling the pup, *No climbing into bed with us. For now.*

Something woke Cooper later that night, although he didn't know exactly how late it was—he'd muted his phone and turned it facedown on the nightstand right before they fell into his bed together so there would be no interruptions.

But there were, of course.

Tiny metallic sounds that Cooper wasn't meant to hear but heard anyway. Like...scraping. Was it some kind of animal? he wondered, still half asleep. He rolled over and saw that Veena was awake too.

"Did you hear that?"

"Yeah. I think it's an animal in the backyard. Probably a squirrel."

"I think the sound is coming from your front door. Also, I thought we settled this. That is not a backyard, it's a glorified al—"

"Shhh." Cooper realized the clicking sound was indeed coming from the vicinity of his foyer. There was also a low growl—Lupe had sensed something too.

"What is it?" Veena asked.

"I'm beginning to think you were right about moving to a hotel." *Watch your backs*, everyone had said. *You don't know who you're messing with.*

Without warning, the entire bedroom lit up. Cooper had a sudden realization and lunged for his phone on the nightstand.

CHAPTER 125

**TEXT MESSAGE FROM VICTOR SUAREZ
TO COOPER LAMB**

They're coming for you. Two of them!

CHAPTER 126

COOPER SHOUTED, "Get down!" and he and Veena hurled themselves from the bed in opposite directions. Both were very naked. Neither of them cared at that moment.

Cooper landed awkwardly and hard but was able to grab the shotgun under his bed. Veena landed lightly on her hands and feet, almost like a cat. Cooper racked the shotgun, partly to pump two shells into the chamber but also warn anyone who was thinking about entering this room.

Veena felt along the ground for her bag, only to realize that she'd dropped it somewhere in the hall. *Damn it!*

Cooper aimed his shotgun at the windows behind his bed just as the glass shattered. Lupe started barking like crazy. Cooper crouched down farther and tried to make sense of the shadowy form that was stepping through the broken glass.

Lupe's barking intensified as he ran down the hall—Veena could hear his claws scrabbling on the hardwood floor. The pup was headed to the front door to deal with the intruder. *No, Lupe!* Veena screamed in her mind and took off after him.

"Don't move!" Cooper shouted.

Veena cleared the doorway just as gunfire filled the room,

blasting apart Cooper's computer monitor and dresser mirror and, based on the sound of it, every other glass object he owned.

Screw this, Veena thought.

Cooper stood up and pulled the trigger of his shotgun. Whatever glass had remained in the window frame was obliterated, and it took the shadowy form along with it, the force blasting him back into the alley. The shooter collapsed on top of a folding chair with a loud, messy clatter.

Meanwhile, out in the hall, Veena did two incredibly complex things without really thinking about them. She managed to tackle Lupe midstride, sliding with him along the floor a few inches, which ripped some of the skin from her knees. She also located and scooped up her bag in the darkness.

The front door was nearly ripped from its hinges as a heavy boot forced it open. This was a second attacker; he must have heard the gunfire and decided the time for subtlety had passed.

That man rushed in with a revolver and looked down at Veena's naked body as she cradled a growling Lupe under one arm and clutched her bag with her other hand.

"What the . . . *Veena Lion*? What are you doing here?"

The second attacker was Mickey Bernstein.

Veena didn't reply. She dropped her arms, giving him a free show. Bernstein couldn't help himself—he gawked. Lupe took off like a supersonic jet, eyes focused on the intruder. Bernstein yelled and pointed his revolver down at the running dog. Veena lifted the derringer out of her bag and didn't even think twice about emptying it.

Bang-bang-bang-bang. Four shots, expertly grouped around the chest.

Bernstein tap-danced backward and collapsed in the doorway. Lupe screeched to a halt, knowing that his services were no longer required.

Farther inside the apartment, Cooper heard the shots, but he was too stunned by what he was looking at to react to them. He stood naked in the empty frame of his bedroom window, shotgun in hand, staring down at the wounded figure of . . .

Vanessa Harlowe.

Maya Rain.

Whoever she was claiming to be on any given day.

Her eyes found Cooper's, and despite bleeding to death, she worked up a smile that melted his heart a little. Blood streaked across her lips and perfect white teeth, and as he watched, her eyes started to dim.

But now he realized her true name, one he'd only heard spoken a few days ago:

The Quiet One.

Cooper Lamb knew he could never prove it in court or produce any evidence linking Maya Rain to that name and her many crimes. But locking eyes with her now, he could see that all of her masks had slipped away. He just *knew.*

Which begged the question: Why would the Hughes family have a professional killer caring for their children?

Maybe Archie's creditors wanted someone to keep an ultra-close eye on Archie. And maybe Archie and Francine knew and had no choice. But if Maya, aka the Quiet One, was that good at her job, she would have had little trouble infiltrating the household.

"I still like you, Cooper," she said now.

Cooper wanted to reply but hesitated. He knew the Quiet One was dying; when serving overseas, he'd seen the face of imminent death way too many times. Some people never looked more alive than they did right before dying.

Cooper didn't want the last words Maya ever heard to be something cheap or sarcastic. He wanted to tell her that somehow, impossibly, he still liked her too.

But by the time he'd formulated that thought, she was gone.

SUPER BOWL SUNDAY, FEBRUARY 6

CHAPTER 127

WHERE WAS the very last place Veena had ever thought she'd find herself?

There was no clear number one, but pretty high up on the list would be *Walking with Cooper Lamb and a police escort behind the scenes at the Super Bowl at SoFi Stadium in Los Angeles, California.*

Yet here she was, and despite her natural aversion to team sports in general (and football in particular), Veena found herself in a good mood, caught up in the spirit of the game. The halftime show had just ended, and Veena had listened to a scorching, for-the-ages performance by Francine Pearl Hughes. If she had been carrying demons for the past few years, she'd exorcised quite a few of them on the stage tonight. Forget Janet Jackson flashing the crowd; forget the dancing sharks. People would be talking about *this* halftime show forever.

Archie Jr. and Maddie watched from the sidelines, proud of their mom and, for the first time in a long while, excited for the future. They were going on tour with their mother, and the family had no plans to return to Philadelphia anytime soon.

As far as the public knew, rogue homicide cop Mickey Bernstein had been responsible for the murder of Archie Hughes. The reason? For now, the story went that the GOAT owed way too much money to the Mob, and Mickey was the Mob's combined hatchet man / fixer. Who better to investigate a murder than the person who'd committed it?

The Quiet One was not mentioned in any media report under that name or any other. But an FBI source quietly confirmed to Cooper and Veena that, yeah, Vanessa's/Maya's prints had been matched to a series of unsolved killings and were discovered on the security cameras near Eakins Oval too. Cooper almost pressed for more information, then thought better of it. Perhaps some truths weren't worth knowing.

"Admit it—you're having a good time," he said now as they rode the elevator up to the luxury boxes.

"Maybe," Veena said. "But I'm about to have an even better time."

They were joined by a small battalion of law enforcement officers from an array of departments: FBI, Treasury, LAPD. Also squeezed into the elevator were Ariel and Cooper Jr. There was no way their father would go to the Super Bowl in LA and *not* bring them along.

Ariel had warned her dad: "If you don't take us, I won't speak to you for the rest of your life. And when we're reincarnated, I won't speak to you in that life either." The point was taken.

But the kids were about to see an even more impressive show than the one they'd just seen.

Harold and Glenn Sable were completely outraged to learn that their beloved player had been murdered by the "crooked tools of organized crime." They promptly stopped talking to the press when it was revealed that one of those "crooked tools," Mickey Bernstein, was on their payroll too. But silence wasn't going to protect them, because the law was here to arrest the Sable men on gambling and fraud charges.

Thousands of people were here to see the Eagles try to climb their way back from an eleven-point deficit.

Veena and Cooper were here to watch the Harold and Glenn Halftime Show.

The kids were here to enjoy Glenn Sable's dessert table.

CHAPTER 128

THE GENERATIONAL differences were obvious. Longtime busi-nessman Harold Sable surrendered himself without a fight, knowing that he'd taken a shot and lost. *C'est la vie.*

Glenn, however, still believed in fairy-tale comebacks. He inched away from the officers of the law before breaking into a full run, hoping, presumably, to make it to the hallway and from there to a non-extradition country. But the fat man got about three feet before he was tackled to the carpet, which put an end to his NFL career.

Sports fans would be talking about the notorious Sables for decades to come. Their story would be held up as a cautionary tale for the ages.

Not that the Eagles players on the field knew about any of this. And if they had, they wouldn't have cared. They were here, at the Super Bowl, with the eyes of the planet on them, and even if the world around them started burning down, they would not be distracted. Also: the Birds were now behind by fourteen points.

"There's no way the Eagles can win," Veena said, elbowing Cooper in the ribs.

"Maybe not, but I feel like I've already won."

"How much money will I end up losing to Red?"

"But won't it be worth it, V.?"

"Not really."

"Come on, you'll be dining out on this story for years."

However, Lion and Lamb had spoken too soon, because in the fourth quarter, Terry Mortelite led a furious drive that stunned everyone and sent the game into overtime.

After the Birds won the toss (another piece of luck), Mortelite and McCoy pulled off five straight passes that led to Jimmy Tua scoring a two-yard touchdown, an epic upset that electrified Philadelphia and applied a bit of salve to the city's many wounds.

But that was the crazy-beautiful thing about this town. It was a place where anything could happen and often did.

Totally random things—like Veena Lion and Cooper Lamb leaving SoFi Stadium arm in arm after the game with a giggling Ariel and Cooper Jr. by their sides.

How crazy and beautiful is that?

ACKNOWLEDGMENTS

We would like to thank Matt DeLucia, Peter Katz, Robert Kulb, Shannon Morris-King, and Joseph Murray for their generous research assistance. And none of this would have been possible without the love and support of Meredith, Parker, and Evie.

We hope you enjoyed *Lion & Lamb*!

Get ready for *The No. 1 Lawyer* . . .

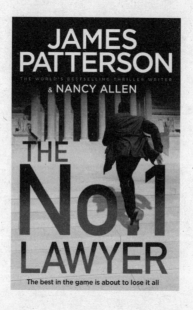

He's never lost a case. But can he outwit a killer?

Read on for an exclusive extract . . .

CHAPTER 1

IT WAS a Monday morning in Biloxi.

I had on my best suit, fresh out of the dry-cleaning bag. I wore my lucky tie, the one my wife, Carrie Ann, had given me two Christmases ago. I'd bought a new pair of cap-toe oxfords for the occasion because my old ones were worn down at the heel.

I didn't want to look shabby next to my client on this big day.

The capital murder trial *State of Mississippi v. Daniel Caro* was set to begin.

I took a deep breath to center myself, gave a final glance at the note card in my right hand, made eye contact with my audience.

"I'm Stafford Lee Penney, attorney for the defendant, Dr. Daniel Caro. Ladies and gentlemen of the jury, this is what the evidence will show."

I'm a second-generation Mississippi attorney. My father, Charles Jackson Penney, is also a trial lawyer in Biloxi, Mississippi. He has been known to proclaim — so often over the years that I've lost count — that a lawyer wins or loses his case in the opening statement.

The old man is half right. After fifteen years of practicing law, I know you can lose a jury with a weak opening. But the opening is too early to win the case. Witnesses will take the stand and evidence

3

will pour in; there are too many unknowns, too many battles to be fought.

Particularly in the Daniel Caro murder trial.

"We all heard the district attorney, Henry Gordon-James, outline the evidence he plans to bring before you," I said. "He went on and on about exhibits and experts, didn't he? Made all kinds of promises. But you need to think about what Mr. Gordon-James failed to mention. What word did he *not* say?"

I took a step forward. I wanted to move closer to the jury to ensure they'd listen to my key point.

"Ladies and gentlemen, that word is *circumstantial*. All the evidence in this case is purely circumstantial. The prosecution will not produce a single witness or a shred of evidence that directly ties my client to the crime he's been accused of committing."

I was warming to the speech. I could feel it. My blood was pumping; the words flowed easily.

"The criminal defendant in this case, Daniel Caro, is highly regarded in this community. He grew up in Biloxi, received his medical degree from Duke. His ob-gyn practice is a blessing to this town. For over a decade, he has delivered our babies and cared for our mothers and wives and daughters. Dr. Caro is an asset to this region. I've known him all my life. We played Little League baseball together. He's my client and my friend."

That last line contained a gross exaggeration. Caro and I weren't friends. In fact, I'd never particularly liked him. He wasn't my kind of cat. But the opening statement was my opportunity to humanize him before the evidence demonized him.

After I wrapped up my client's glowing bio, I took two steps to the right to signify a change of direction.

"The events that you'll hear about in this trial are tragic, undeniably horrific. They never should have happened anywhere, certainly not in Biloxi."

Careful, I thought. It was time to mention the murder victim, to speak her name. It was imperative that I proceed delicately.

"Aurora Gates's untimely death was a terrible loss. She was an exceptional woman: Valedictorian of her class at Biloxi High School. A promising law student at Ole Miss. Her future was bright. Someone took a gun and stole that future from her, cut her life short."

Time to switch it up and alter the tone.

"But the person who committed that vile act was not my client, the man who sits in the courtroom today."

I teased a few items after that, hinting at important evidentiary points I intended to score at trial without directly revealing the strategy. My father has another saying about the start of a jury trial: A defense attorney who shows his hand in the opening is a damn fool.

The old man's not wrong. We see eye to eye on that one.

CHAPTER 2

I GLANCED at the clock just before I wrapped it up. Good—not too short, not too long. I said thank you and smiled warmly but without flashing any teeth so the jury could see that I was not flamboyant or showy, that I respected the gravity of the situation.

I stood there waiting. When I didn't get a reaction, I said: "Well? What do you think?"

Mason grimaced. "Meh. Not your best effort, Stafford Lee."

I tossed the crumpled note card onto the conference-room table. I'd been gripping it too hard. "Really? That bad?"

The guttural noise Mason made in reply could have been interpreted as neutral, but he followed it up with "Pretty bad."

"No!" Jenny, seated next to Mason, leaned over and swatted the back of his head. "Are you trying to jinx him? It was great, Stafford Lee. Really good."

"I've heard better," Mason said under his breath.

"Mason, quit being so negative," Jenny snapped. "You always do that."

Jenny was right. Over the past fifteen years, we'd done the ritual of the trial run scores of times, and Mason did always do that.

I performed these run-throughs at my law office for an audience of two: Mason Burnett, a trial attorney with his own law office, and

Jenny Glaser, a licensed private investigator. They were my closest friends and both were excellent sounding boards. Helpful, even when it hurt.

Predictably, Mason skewered my weak spots, especially what he called my lackluster delivery. Without Jenny's supportive yin to balance Mason's criticizing yang, on the first day of any jury trial, I might have walked right past the courthouse, kept going until I reached the waters of the Gulf, and dived in, fully clothed.

Mason said, "All right, it wasn't a total flop. Remember the first time you did your opening for me, right after we graduated from Ole Miss? You essentially admitted your client's guilt in the first two minutes."

Jenny snickered. I didn't blame her; that misstep could have destroyed my legal career before it began. But on that long-ago occasion, Mason had pointed out my gaffe, and we fixed it. To the surprise of everyone in the courthouse, I went on to win the case even though it was a loser, almost as tough as the case I was handling now.

Since that first jury trial fifteen years ago, I had managed to win them all. Whether that was due to good luck or good tactics, I'd be hesitant to opine. Criminal defense lawyers are supposed to lose, so mine was a pretty unusual record.

If it ain't broke...

Leaning on a chairback, I asked, "Was there too much bio? Or not enough?"

Across the table, Jenny said, "The background on Daniel Caro was effective, the part about delivering babies and caring for mothers and daughters. People will respond to that."

"They'll like him until they hear the evidence." Mason put his feet up on the conference table.

He was pushing my buttons, but I kept going. "Did it sound genuine, the stuff I said about Caro being a great guy?" I worried that the jury might detect a note of insincerity.

"Yeah, that was all right," Mason conceded. "They'll buy it. Unless they know him very well. Or know you at all."

We were all Biloxi kids with a shared history going clear back to grade school. Mason's mom had been my Cub Scout leader. She'd been like a second mom to me after my own mother passed away from non-Hodgkin's lymphoma in her thirties. Jenny and I had had a brief romance in fifth grade—we went steady for almost forty-eight hours.

Jenny reached into a bright red attaché case and pulled out a stapled sheaf of papers. As she slid it across the varnished table, she said, "I did the background you wanted, ran more information down on the jurors and the alternate. No big surprises which ones might be defense-team-oriented and which lean toward the prosecution."

Even from a cursory glance, I could see it was stellar work. "Jenny, you're worth every damn cent I pay you."

Mason chuckled. "Paste that quote on a billboard for your PI business, Jenny, right smack next to a picture of Stafford Lee. His fan club will love it."

Jenny rolled her eyes. "Have you always been jealous of Stafford Lee, Mason? Even back when we were kids?"

"I'm not jealous of him." Mason made a show of peering down at my feet. "But I'm seriously impressed by those shoes."

I ignored the comment about my footwear and checked the clock again. I met Mason's eyes and said, "Any final suggestions?"

Mason the irreverent comic disappeared. He was shooting straight and serious when he said, "The jurors are going to need a tangible reason to root for the defendant, so give them something to sink their teeth into. Go ahead and call the murder victim a floozy."

I must have recoiled.

"Do it." He raised his voice. "Call her a homewrecker. Give her a black eye at the outset. They love that shit in Biloxi."

Not my style, trashing the victim of violent crime. But in this situation, it might give me a boost. God knew I was going to need one when the evidence started rolling in.

Jenny weighed in, playing her part in the ritual. "Mason, you can't try the case in opening. And attacking that young woman is a dangerous gambit. If Stafford Lee offends jurors on day one, he'll have trouble winning them back."

We could have gone more rounds, but the chiming from my phone ended the fight. I turned off the alarm and slid my phone into my pocket.

My parting question: "What are the odds of winning this one?"

"Of getting a not-guilty verdict?" Jenny asked. "I'd say fifty-fifty."

I swallowed down a groan. "Your odds, Mason?"

"Sixty-forty."

Better.

"Sixty percent that your client will go down," Mason added. "Just to be clear."

I'd preferred the fuzzy odds.

I picked up my briefcase and shot a wry grin at my two closest friends. "Thanks for the vote of confidence."

CHAPTER 3

THE HEAVINESS of my briefcase as I walked to the courthouse provided a physical reminder of the weight of the Caro case. My briefcase wasn't a slim nylon bag designed to carry a laptop and nothing else. Constructed of black leather and secured with nickel locks, it was more like a mobile filing cabinet. Mason thought I was crazy to haul the massive briefcase the blocks from my law office to the Biloxi Circuit Court.

Taking this solitary walk on the first day of trial was another of my long-standing rituals. Even when hurricanes threatened, I stubbornly adhered to it. Today, the September sun reflected off my sunglasses; the Gulf breeze blew balmy.

Big casinos lined the water's edge. People pointed to them and said, "We're the New South now, not the old fishing town famous only for shrimp and oysters and Jefferson Davis. It's twenty-first-century progress, these hotels rising up twenty-five stories, hotels that dominate local revenue. Biloxi has changed."

That's what people say, anyway. But we're still a small city with one public high school that serves a population hovering around fifty thousand.

The first couple of blocks cleared my head, and I girded myself for battle. I was acutely aware that I was in for the fight of my life against my opponent Henry Gordon-James, the district attorney for Harrison County. Harrison County has two county seats, Biloxi and Gulfport, and Gordon-James served in both communities. He was personally handling the trial, and he was a powerhouse in the courtroom.

A whole lot was riding on the outcome of this trial. First and foremost, my client's life was at stake. It was a death-penalty case.

Tensions around town were running high, and when the jury returned its verdict, Biloxi would likely be in an uproar. Whichever way the case went, there were many issues that would leave people fired up.

Issues like race.

The murder victim, Aurora Gates, was a person of color. The population of Biloxi was about 21 percent Black, but the defendants charged in local criminal cases were about 75 percent Black. This defendant, my client, was a white man. And the particulars of the accusations against him were extremely inflammatory.

For several blocks, I had the sidewalks to myself. I turned the corner, and the courthouse came into view. The Second Judicial District Courthouse is a flat-topped, two-story structure built in 1968 for function rather than architectural style or grace.

Even from a distance, I could see the gathered crowd of onlookers and the news vans circling the building. I switched the briefcase from my right hand to my left and picked up the pace.

A woman coming off the graveyard shift at one of the casinos, still dressed in her poker dealer's uniform, called out, "It's Stafford Lee Penney! Hey there, Stafford Lee!"

I paused to return her greeting. "Good morning to you, ma'am."

As the woman shouted, "Good luck," the crowd surged toward me. A guy from my high-school class pushed through to clap me on the shoulder excitedly, like he'd come to watch the state football championship. I smiled, said hello, and continued on my way.

Standing near the courthouse entrance was a former client of mine, a young woman I had represented on a minor traffic charge. I had gotten her a good deal on a plea bargain and charged a reasonable fee. I hoped she was there to support me.

I stepped up to her, extending my right hand. "Hey, it's Arnette, isn't that right? It's been a while. How are you doing?"

She stared at my outstretched hand without moving. Finally, she met my eye. "I went to school with Aurora Gates," she said.

I dropped my hand. Clearly, trying to get the man who was charged with her schoolmate's death acquitted made me a villain.

But it bothered me that my former client might misunderstand my motivation for taking on the Caro defense. Whether we like our clients or not, criminal defense lawyers sincerely believe in the Fifth Amendment right to due process for everyone. A person's entitled to a defense, and I was in the business of providing one—for a price.

Still, I wanted to show Arnette that I was not a heartless guy, not just another white good ol' boy.

"I'm sorry for your loss, Arnette. Ms. Gates was an exceptional young woman. What happened to her is a tragedy."

Her face was stony, her expression unforgiving. "Right. If you're so sorry, why are you trying to let her killer walk?"

She turned and left. I wanted to reach across the abyss, but this was not the time. I headed for the courthouse door.

Just before I entered the building, one of the locals who had come to witness the ruckus shouted, "You'll get him off, Stafford Lee!"

When the door shut behind me, his voice rang in my ears.

Two women, clerks from the recorder's office, grabbed me before I reached security. One of them, Liz Craig, was remarkably pretty. Mason had asked her out more times than any sensible man would have, but she invariably rebuffed him.

Breathless, Liz said, "You're famous, Stafford Lee. Did you see the cameras following you to the door? Do you think you're going to be on TV?"

"I don't know, Liz. I guess we'll have to tune in and see."

"I love watching you in court. When we take our break, Renee and I are going to come and sit in for a minute just to see you do your thing."

Her eyes were shining with admiration. A man would have had to be blind, senile, or both to miss it.

"That's a real boost for me, knowing I have your support." I gave the women a friendly smile. "Thank you, ladies, both of you. Now, I better get on upstairs."

Before I stepped through security, Liz tugged on my sleeve and whispered, "Good luck, Stafford Lee."

Walking up the stairs to the second floor, I was glad that Mason had not witnessed the exchange. He frequently claimed that I had a flock of lawyer groupies. Unfortunately, he'd been known to joke about that in the presence of my wife. Carrie Ann didn't think it was funny.

In fact, it was one of the reasons she'd kicked me out of the house five weeks ago.

CHAPTER 4

I PEERED through the glass panel into the courtroom. It was too early for the press or the public to be admitted, but my client was already inside, seated on the front bench of the spectator section, his wife next to him.

I called out a greeting and hurried down the center aisle to the defense table. I set down the briefcase, shook out my left hand to get the blood flowing, and reached out to Caro with my right. "Daniel, join me at the counsel table as soon as you're ready." I smiled warmly at his wife. "Iris, how are you holding up? I know this is a difficult day for you."

I liked Iris. Caro's wife and I had gone on a couple of dates in college, when she was the reigning belle of Ole Miss. I'd stepped aside when Mason fell for her; he'd even escorted her to a sorority formal. All of this predated her romance with Caro and my marriage to Carrie Ann by many years. Ancient history, but I'd always had a soft spot for Iris.

Iris began to say something, but her husband cut her off. "Where the hell have you been? I've been waiting here for twenty minutes. Do you know how much I'm paying you?"

I certainly did know, down to the penny. Like a lot of defense attorneys, I charged my clients on a sliding scale, based in part on their ability to pay. Daniel Caro's lucrative medical practice netted him almost half a million a year, and that annual income put him in the top 1 percent in the state of Mississippi.

Caro's income was one of the few things I liked about him—it enabled him to pay his attorney fees in advance and in full—but the money wouldn't necessarily endear him to everyone. I made a mental note to check Jenny's background information on the jurors' household incomes. One in five people in my community lived in poverty.

Iris Caro eyed her husband warily as she scooted down the bench, creating distance between them. Obviously, she didn't like to be too close when his temper flared. Daniel got up and came over to the counsel table.

Caro's father claimed the family had roots in Sicily, and my angry client did resemble Michael Corleone. His hair, longish and slicked back, added to the *Godfather* aura. We had to work on that. In front of a jury, it wouldn't be a good look. "Daniel, you need to calm down."

"Calm down? Really?"

Two people took their seats in the back row, and Caro dropped his voice to a whisper. "There are people here today who are out for my blood." The newcomers were too far away to hear him, but the deputy standing near the judge's bench wasn't. She was serving as bailiff, and she was listening.

I could not deny that Caro was right, so I didn't try. Nonetheless, I had to reassure him. "Daniel, thanks to trained personnel from the sheriff's department, the courtroom is the safest place a person can be." I turned to the deputy. "Isn't that right, Charlene?"

She nodded. "We are on top of it, Stafford Lee."

Caro grabbed my sleeve. "That little girl is supposed to protect me? That's the best you've got?"

I looked down at the hand clutching my suit jacket. When he released it, I said, "Charlene is extremely competent. And she won't be alone. They're doubling up on officers for the trial. You've got nothing to worry about."

His eyelid twitched. "Nothing to worry about? I stand to lose everything. It's preposterous that you ever let this matter reach the trial stage. I didn't do anything wrong."

That wasn't entirely accurate, but I wasn't going to argue about it, not in front of his wife.

He continued. "You should know that I heard threats when we arrived. Actual threats from people milling around out there."

I was running out of patience—and time. I was due in chambers to meet the judge and the DA, so I made a statement certain to shut him up: "If you really feel unsafe, you should talk to your father. Maybe he'll provide a security detail for your protection."

Caro blanched. He rejoined his wife on the bench and said something into her ear; her face crumpled, and she raked her fingers through her carefully styled ash-blond hair.

It was no surprise that Caro backed off when I mentioned his Mob-connected father. I picked up my briefcase, recalling my client's embarrassment that his medical education at Duke had been paid for with money from Hiram Caro's casinos. Daniel distanced himself from his roots. If he could have, he'd have rewritten history. But that's hard to do in Biloxi, where roots are deep and memories are long. Everyone knew that the seed money for old man Caro's casino complex had come from underground gambling in the 1970s and 1980s. Before casinos were legal in Mississippi, Caro ran slots and card games in the back room of the Black Orchid, his seamy striptease joint. The rest of the Dixie Mafia was taken down in 1985, but my father kept Caro's father out of prison.

And here we were, the next generation, with a Penney again defending a Caro in court.

Things never really change in Biloxi.

CHAPTER 5

SPEAK OF the devil and he shall appear.

On my way to chambers, I ran smack into my old man. He was at the top of the courthouse stairs, leaning on the railing for balance.

"Hey, Dad. How you doing?" Without waiting for a reply, I veered to the left, giving him a wide berth. But he followed me.

"Hold up, Stafford Lee. I've come all the way up here to wish you good luck."

I didn't believe that, not for a minute. He had come to offer me unsolicited and unwanted advice. And the truth was, I didn't have time to fool with him. Over my shoulder, I said, "Dad, Judge Walker is waiting on me. And you always told me never to keep a judge waiting."

"Horseshit. I never said that. And Tyrone Walker isn't a stickler for timeliness, never was." Running a hand through his mane of white hair, he tried to keep up with me. He wore that bulldog look he got when he was determined to say his piece.

I paused at the door to the clerk's office. "Later, Dad. Thanks for checking in."

Something must have made him change his mind. He waved a hand, releasing me. "Go on, then."

I did go, speeding past the judge's clerk, Megan Dunn. The young woman glanced up at me with the serene expression she always wore, regardless of the circumstances. "Judge is waiting on you, Stafford Lee."

"Thanks, Megan."

When I stepped into chambers, Judge Tyrone Walker was perched behind his desk. Across from him sat the district attorney of Harrison County, Henry Gordon-James, somberly dressed in charcoal gray. Though the DA was about my age, his grave demeanor made him seem older. We weren't close, but I respected his talent and his maturity. He was the first Black man to serve as the district attorney of Harrison County.

As soon as the door shut behind me, I picked up the uneasy vibe; the tension in the room was so thick, the air seemed to vibrate with it.

I nodded at them. "Morning, Judge, Henry."

The judge pointed to a seat. "Join us, Stafford Lee. Henry has been wondering whether you'd be here. But I assured him you wouldn't bail on us."

Gordon-James's eyes briefly met mine. "I don't believe I suggested that Penney would be a no-show. I did, however, mention that he had failed to appear on time."

I was late by three or four minutes. But my old man was right; Walker's nose wasn't out of joint about that. The DA, however, was less forgiving.

The judge announced, almost gleefully, "We are going to have the battle of the gladiators in the Second Judicial Circuit today. Did you see the crowd out there? TV cameras, the whole nine yards. Good thing that jury is sequestered."

I nodded in acknowledgment. Henry Gordon-James did not react.

The judge didn't seem to notice the DA's lack of enthusiasm. "In this trial, we've got the hottest district attorney in Mississippi duking it out with the best defense attorney in the state. Henry, you're still undefeated, right? No acquittals on your personal trial record?"

"That's correct."

The judge chuckled, shaking his head. "Somebody's record is going to take a hit this time. Stafford Lee has never lost a case before a jury either. I expect y'all both got a copy of the *Bar Association Journal*."

The judge held up the publication. My photograph was on the cover above the words *The #1 Lawyer for Southern Mississippi.*

He tossed the magazine onto his desk. "I wouldn't be surprised if people all over this town were laying bets on the outcome."

I caught the distaste that flashed across the prosecutor's features. "Surely people aren't making wagers on a case involving a young woman's grisly death," he said. "People wouldn't do that, not even in Biloxi."

A timer dinged, and the judge pulled a tea bag from a steaming cup. He squeezed the bag, discarded it, pulled out a penknife, and, using his desk as a cutting board, sliced a lemon. I could smell the citrus as it sprayed into the air.

Walker sipped his tea, his eyes crinkling at me over the mug he held. "Stafford Lee, is your daddy retiring soon?"

I was surprised by the change of topic. "He's slowing down these days. I'd say he's semiretired."

The judge snorted. "Well, that explains why the ERs and funeral parlors haven't seen much of Charlie." To the DA, Judge Walker said, "In his day, Charlie Penney had a deal with all the undertakers in town. He handed out business cards at every funeral. And he was notorious for jawboning injured people being carried into the hospital on stretchers." He gave us a sly wink. "You know what they called him."

Gordon-James avoided my eye and said shortly, "An ambulance chaser."

19

The judge nodded, chuckling.

What Walker had said about my dad was true. But there's a thing called family loyalty, and it chafed me to hear my father belittled, even if he deserved it. I had to exercise profound control to keep my fists from clenching and my jaw shut. This was no day to pick a fight with Judge Walker. Judges wield tremendous power over the outcome of a case. A trial lawyer is absolutely obligated to remain silent in these situations. The judge holds all the cards.

Maybe my discomfort showed. The judge took a swallow of the tea and set the mug on a coaster on his desk. "Stafford Lee, don't get your hackles up. I'm not putting you in the same class with Charlie, no, sir. You've got star quality. Charisma. You don't need to chase down widows and orphans." With a nod to the prosecutor, he added, "Henry's got it too—the magic. I say with total honesty that Henry here is the best DA in Mississippi."

"A lot of people in Harrison County were shocked when I was elected to this office," the DA said, his voice cool. "Others called it progress. But you know what they say: Progress in Mississippi is one step forward, one step back."

The judge leaned forward, interested. "Who said that? Faulkner?"

The DA's face looked chiseled from granite. "I'm not talking about literature; I'm talking about the Caro case." His gaze slid to me. "I'm determined to see justice done in this trial."

I said, my voice ringing with all the sincerity I could pump into it, "We are all interested in justice here."

"I'm getting justice for the victim, for Aurora Gates," the prosecutor said, his voice sharp as a razor. "It's personal for me. This shit keeps happening, and I'm sick of it. My people are dying."

After a moment of silence, he repeated, "It's personal."

Also By James Patterson

ALEX CROSS NOVELS

Along Came a Spider • Kiss the Girls • Jack and Jill • Cat and Mouse • Pop Goes the Weasel • Roses are Red • Violets are Blue • Four Blind Mice • The Big Bad Wolf • London Bridges • Mary, Mary • Cross • Double Cross • Cross Country • Alex Cross's Trial (*with Richard DiLallo*) • I, Alex Cross • Cross Fire • Kill Alex Cross • Merry Christmas, Alex Cross • Alex Cross, Run • Cross My Heart • Hope to Die • Cross Justice • Cross the Line • The People vs. Alex Cross • Target: Alex Cross • Criss Cross • Deadly Cross • Fear No Evil • Triple Cross • Alex Cross Must Die

THE WOMEN'S MURDER CLUB SERIES

1st to Die (*with Andrew Gross*) • 2nd Chance (*with Andrew Gross*) • 3rd Degree (*with Andrew Gross*) • 4th of July (*with Maxine Paetro*) • The 5th Horseman (*with Maxine Paetro*) • The 6th Target (*with Maxine Paetro*) • 7th Heaven (*with Maxine Paetro*) • 8th Confession (*with Maxine Paetro*) • 9th Judgement (*with Maxine Paetro*) • 10th Anniversary (*with Maxine Paetro*) • 11th Hour (*with Maxine Paetro*) • 12th of Never (*with Maxine Paetro*) • Unlucky 13 (*with Maxine Paetro*) • 14th Deadly Sin (*with Maxine Paetro*) • 15th Affair (*with Maxine Paetro*) • 16th Seduction (*with Maxine Paetro*) • 17th Suspect (*with Maxine Paetro*) • 18th Abduction (*with Maxine Paetro*) • 19th Christmas (*with Maxine Paetro*) • 20th Victim (*with Maxine Paetro*) • 21st Birthday (*with Maxine Paetro*) • 22 Seconds (*with Maxine Paetro*) • 23rd Midnight (*with Maxine Paetro*) • The 24th Hour (*with Maxine Paetro*)

DETECTIVE MICHAEL BENNETT SERIES

Step on a Crack (*with Michael Ledwidge*) • Run for Your Life (*with Michael Ledwidge*) • Worst Case (*with Michael Ledwidge*) • Tick Tock (*with Michael Ledwidge*) • I, Michael Bennett (*with Michael Ledwidge*) • Gone (*with Michael Ledwidge*) • Burn (*with Michael Ledwidge*) • Alert (*with Michael Ledwidge*) • Bullseye (*with Michael Ledwidge*) • Haunted (*with James O. Born*) • Ambush (*with James O. Born*) • Blindside (*with James O. Born*) • The Russian (*with James O. Born*) • Shattered (*with James O. Born*) • Obsessed (*with James O. Born*) • Crosshairs (*with James O. Born*)

PRIVATE NOVELS

Private (*with Maxine Paetro*) • Private London (*with Mark Pearson*) • Private Games (*with Mark Sullivan*) • Private: No. 1 Suspect (*with Maxine Paetro*) • Private Berlin (*with Mark Sullivan*) • Private Down Under (*with Michael White*) • Private L.A. (*with Mark Sullivan*) • Private India (*with Ashwin Sanghi*) • Private Vegas (*with Maxine Paetro*) • Private Sydney (*with Kathryn Fox*) • Private Paris (*with Mark Sullivan*) • The Games (*with Mark Sullivan*) • Private Delhi (*with Ashwin Sanghi*) • Private Princess (*with Rees Jones*) • Private Moscow (*with Adam Hamdy*) • Private Rogue (*with Adam Hamdy*) • Private Beijing (*with Adam Hamdy*) • Private Rome (*with Adam Hamdy*)

NYPD RED SERIES

NYPD Red (*with Marshall Karp*) • NYPD Red 2 (*with Marshall Karp*) • NYPD Red 3 (*with Marshall Karp*) • NYPD Red 4 (*with Marshall Karp*) • NYPD Red 5 (*with Marshall Karp*) • NYPD Red 6 (*with Marshall Karp*)

DETECTIVE HARRIET BLUE SERIES

Never Never (*with Candice Fox*) • Fifty Fifty (*with Candice Fox*) • Liar Liar (*with Candice Fox*) • Hush Hush (*with Candice Fox*)

INSTINCT SERIES

Instinct (*with Howard Roughan, previously published as* Murder Games) • Killer Instinct (*with Howard Roughan*) • Steal (*with Howard Roughan*)

THE BLACK BOOK SERIES

The Black Book (*with David Ellis*) • The Red Book (*with David Ellis*) • Escape (*with David Ellis*)

STAND-ALONE THRILLERS

The Thomas Berryman Number • Hide and Seek • Black Market • The Midnight Club • Sail (*with Howard Roughan*) • Swimsuit (*with Maxine Paetro*) • Don't Blink (*with Howard Roughan*) • Postcard Killers (*with Liza Marklund*) • Toys (*with Neil McMahon*) • Now You See Her (*with Michael Ledwidge*) • Kill Me If You Can (*with Marshall*

Karp) • Guilty Wives (*with David Ellis*) • Zoo (*with Michael Ledwidge*) • Second Honeymoon (*with Howard Roughan*) • Mistress (*with David Ellis*) • Invisible (*with David Ellis*) • Truth or Die (*with Howard Roughan*) • Murder House (*with David Ellis*) • The Store (*with Richard DiLallo*) • Texas Ranger (*with Andrew Bourelle*) • The President is Missing (*with Bill Clinton*) • Revenge (*with Andrew Holmes*) • Juror No. 3 (*with Nancy Allen*) • The First Lady (*with Brendan DuBois*) • The Chef (*with Max DiLallo*) • Out of Sight (*with Brendan DuBois*) • Unsolved (*with David Ellis*) • The Inn (*with Candice Fox*) • Lost (*with James O. Born*) • Texas Outlaw (*with Andrew Bourelle*) • The Summer House (*with Brendan DuBois*) • 1st Case (*with Chris Tebbetts*) • Cajun Justice (*with Tucker Axum*)• The Midwife Murders (*with Richard DiLallo*) • The Coast-to-Coast Murders (*with J.D. Barker*) • Three Women Disappear (*with Shan Serafin*) • The President's Daughter (*with Bill Clinton*) • The Shadow (*with Brian Sitts*) • The Noise (*with J.D. Barker*) • 2 Sisters Detective Agency (*with Candice Fox*) • Jailhouse Lawyer (*with Nancy Allen*) • The Horsewoman (*with Mike Lupica*) • Run Rose Run (*with Dolly Parton*) • Death of the Black Widow (*with J.D. Barker*) • The Ninth Month (*with Richard DiLallo*) • The Girl in the Castle (*with Emily Raymond*) • Blowback (*with Brendan DuBois*) • The Twelve Topsy-Turvy, Very Messy Days of Christmas (*with Tad Safran*) • The Perfect Assassin (*with Brian Sitts*) • House of Wolves (*with Mike Lupica*) • Countdown (*with Brendan DuBois*) • Cross Down (*with Brendan DuBois*) • Circle of Death (*with Brian Sitts*) • Lion & Lamb (with *Duane Swierczynski*) • 12 Months to Live (*with Mike Lupica*) • Holmes, Margaret and Poe (*with Brian Sitts*) • The No. 1 Lawyer (*with Nancy Allen*)

NON-FICTION

Torn Apart (*with Hal and Cory Friedman*) • The Murder of King Tut (*with Martin Dugard*) • All-American Murder (*with Alex Abramovich and Mike Harvkey*) • The Kennedy Curse (*with Cynthia Fagen*) • The Last Days of John Lennon (*with Casey Sherman and Dave Wedge*) • Walk in My Combat Boots (*with Matt Eversmann and Chris Mooney*) • ER Nurses (*with Matt Eversmann*) • James Patterson by James Patterson: The Stories of My Life • Diana, William and Harry (*with Chris Mooney*) • American Cops (*with Matt Eversmann*) • What Really Happens in Vegas (*with Mark Seal*) • The Secret Lives of Booksellers and Librarians (*with Matt Eversmann*)

MURDER IS FOREVER TRUE CRIME

Murder, Interrupted (*with Alex Abramovich and Christopher Charles*) • Home Sweet Murder (*with Andrew Bourelle and Scott Slaven*) • Murder Beyond the Grave (*with Andrew Bourelle and Christopher Charles*) • Murder Thy Neighbour (*with Andrew Bourelle and Max DiLallo*) • Murder of Innocence (*with Max DiLallo and Andrew Bourelle*) • Till Murder Do Us Part (*with Andrew Bourelle and Max DiLallo*)

COLLECTIONS

Triple Threat (*with Max DiLallo and Andrew Bourelle*) • Kill or Be Killed (*with Maxine Paetro, Rees Jones, Shan Serafin and Emily Raymond*) • The Moores are Missing (*with Loren D. Estleman, Sam Hawken and Ed Chatterton*) • The Family Lawyer (*with Robert Rotstein, Christopher Charles and Rachel Howzell Hall*) • Murder in Paradise (*with Doug Allyn, Connor Hyde and Duane Swierczynski*) • The House Next Door (*with Susan DiLallo, Max DiLallo and Brendan DuBois*) • 13-Minute Murder (*with Shan Serafin, Christopher Farnsworth and Scott Slaven*) • The River Murders (*with James O. Born*) • The Palm Beach Murders (*with James O. Born, Duane Swierczynski and Tim Arnold*) • Paris Detective • 3 Days to Live • 23 ½ Lies (*with Maxine Paetro*)

For more information about James Patterson's novels,
visit www.penguin.co.uk.